THE PARLIAMENT HOUSE

TAYLOR SIMONDS

The Parliament House Press Edition, June 2019

Copyright ©2019 by Taylor Simonds

COLLATERAL DAMAGE

All rights reserved. Published in the United States by The Parliament House, a division of Machovi Productions Inc., Florida.

This is a work of fiction. Names, characters, places, and incidents are either the product of the author's imagination or are used fictitiously. Any resemblance to actual persons, living or dead, events, or locales is entirely coincidental.

ISBN: 978-0578457321

Except for the use of any review, the reproduction or utilization of this work, in whole or in part, in any form by any electronic, mechanical, or other means now known or hereafter invented, are forbideen without the written permission of the publisher.

Cover & Interior Design by
Shayne Leighton | Parliament House Book Design
Illustrations & Cover Art by
Loremae Albano
Cover Emboss Design by @noverantale

Edited by
Celeste DeQuincey
and
Erica Farner

Published by The Parliament House
www.parliamenthousepress.com

Printed in the United States of America.

DEAR READER,

Okay, I know this book is about a girl who is over the whole superhero "thing," but here's a confession—I as a human am pretty much the exact opposite. I see every Marvel movie at least three times in theaters; I will personally finance Spider-Man remakes until I die; one of my favorite shows is Miraculous Ladybug. You get the picture.

Is it because superpowers are inherently fun to hear stories about? Maybe, but I don't think that's the real reason so many people flock to premieres wearing elaborate costumes and crying into their popcorn buckets and hugging their Peter Parker plushes to death (Is that last one just me? Can we tell I like Spider-Man?). It's not just the superpowers—it's the humans that wield them, and the way these narratives examine how difficult it can be to balance godlike abilities with everyday human problems. I don't care so much about the superhero personas—I care about the humans who wear them, who are just Trying Their Best. I care a *lot*, probably more than should be directed at fictional characters.

So yeah, even though this is a book about the background extras who typically have a Very Bad TimeTM with the inevitable shenanigans and destruction superpowered battles tend to cause, don't worry—this is not an angry, critical, I Hate Superheroes book. This is just a book that takes the stories we all love and flips them to a new angle—one that, honestly, most of us would probably get stuck in if superheroes actually existed. I mean, we can't *all* be Iron Man. Most people have to be the café barista in constant danger of being crushed by a falling skyscraper.

So to all the people who have spent a lifetime watching superhero stories unfold from the sidelines, whether by reading them on comic book pages or watching them on film—this one's for us. Safety helmets on, everybody; it's about to get messy.

—Taylor Simonds

ONE

ARNOLD IS DEAD.

It's not my fault. Let's get that clear. These kinds of things usually aren't, but that doesn't change the unavoidable fact that he's super, super dead.

I wish I could say Arnold's dead-ness is unexpected, but the truth is, I'm impressed he even survived this long.

My last car only made it six months.

To be fair, he's not technically dead yet, but he's definitely going to be in a few minutes. Maybe it's fatalistic to write this off as an inevitability, but I've lived in Lunar City long enough to know when it's someone's—or something's, in this case—final day.

In this case, it's the police scanner duct-taped to my dashboard that sets off the feeling of impending doom—but even before it starts blaring, I can already tell something's wrong. The desperate hope that maybe the hordes of people running

✖ COLLATERAL DAMAGE ✖

hysterically down the street toward my car are participating in some kind of 5K only lasts a few moments before, with a pavement-rattling eruption, the tidal wave of dark smoke starts rolling in behind them. This, as you'd imagine, shuts my original theory down pretty quickly.

As if the stampeding herd isn't enough of an indicator, the police scanner suddenly lets out a static-laced crackle that quickly gives way to a garbled, warped version of the authoritative shouting I've come to expect from it. I prod the finicky device until the muffled noise turns into something that sounds like "two casualties," "East Seventh Avenue," and "SuperVariants have engaged," and that's enough for me.

"Absolutely not," I mutter, yanking the steering wheel to the left and dodging across the traffic down a side road. "Not today."

This turns out to be one of my worse ideas, because the side road is already occupied by one of the Supers.

SuperVariant Three, if we're being specific.

I would accuse the Lunar City Police Department of misinformation (East Seventh, right? Did the scanner not just say he was on East Seventh?), but I'm not really supposed to have a scanner, so there's no one to complain to.

My tires screech as I hit the brakes, just feet away from the standstill traffic blocking the road, the owners having abandoned their cars in favor of running. And there, about six cars ahead of me, boots firmly planted on the hood like it's some kind of pedestal, is SuperVariant Three. The morning sun glistens off the gray leather supersuit he's wearing like it's a second skin, his famously perfect blue-black hair positioned in its trademark coil over his forehead.

"Everybody out of the streets!" he's ordering, a gloved hand cupped around his chiseled jaw. "Get to someplace safe! You need to—"

A piercing scream grabs both of our attention. It's impossible to tell who it came from, but it's clearly someone out of the cluster on the sidewalk—one of the dozen or so heads gaping upward in terror at a massive billboard groaning on its hinges, a light breeze away from crashing down to the street below.

"Oh, *no*," I whisper, and then Three and I both move at the same time.

I'm not worried about the people underneath the billboard. I'm worried about *me*. Because I've seen Three in action before, and I know his MO.

In the few seconds that it takes me to lunge for my backpack—an unwieldy black monstrosity jangling with a color-coded assortment of safety gear all firmly labeled *please return to Meg Sawyer*—and smash a thumb into the release on my seatbelt, the billboard has wrenched free with a fantastic howl. I can see Three flying toward it in a gray blur.

Get out of the way, get out of the way, get out of the way—

I tumble out of the car and lunge for the sidewalk just as Three reaches the falling metal. There's a weird moment of optimism where I wonder if maybe today, he'll be different; maybe today, he'll just catch it and gently put it down on the ground like a normal, rational human. No show of power, no flashy stunts.

But then he raises his fist and decks the absolute hell out of it.

I have just enough time to snatch the closest thing I can grab off my backpack—which turns out to be a safety helmet, thank god, and not something completely useless for the situation, like a Band-Aid or hand sanitizer—and jam it on my head before the billboard's trajectory is walloped away from the paralyzed citizens and toward the small army of abandoned cars lining the road.

I'll give Three this: the guy's got a future career in bowling if he ever wants it.

There's something weirdly satisfying about watching the ripple of cars get smashed to pieces. It's like when you line up a chain of dominos and push one over. The *not*-satisfying thing is the knowledge that the billboard on its own would never have been able to cause this much damage, but I guess you can turn anything into a missile if you super-punch it hard enough.

The rippling of the first few cars is the only thing I see, however, because that's when I dive behind the closest tree, cover my organs with my backpack, and clamp my eyes and mouth shut against the impending cloud of dust and debris. The last thing I need today is to get impaled by flying shrapnel.

The next few moments are underscored by a soundtrack I know very well—the sound of metal screeching as it wrenches apart, glass shattering, steel pounding into the sidewalk. When the noise gets replaced by silence, followed by the clamor of breathless, relieved sobs of gratitude that can only mean the people on the other side of the street have suddenly realized they're not dead, I know it's safe enough to open my eyes and peer around the corner.

As expected, SuperVariant Three is not looking in horror at the destruction he's just caused to eight different vehicles (including my poor, useless Arnold, which is now a blackened, charred mess with a sliced-off roof and an eruption of smoke pouring out of the engine). No, he's floating above the awestruck crowd, beaming down at them. I can't make out any of what they're all saying to him—probably something along the lines of "I love you" or "sign my face" or "let me name my children after you"—but his proud, confident voice carries.

"Not a problem," he's saying. "Just doing my duty."

My mouth falls open. Not a *problem*? *I* have a problem. I have several problems. I'm about to step off the sidewalk to march over and tell him so, but then there's a near-intangible blur of orange light accompanied by a gust of wind that rips past me so quickly, my helmet clatters to the ground and my choppy red hair blows over my eyes. "Watch it!" I yell, shaking my bangs back into place.

"Hey, *Three*!" The blur zig-zags through the maze of destroyed cars and slams to a stop near Three and his fawning fans, coming into focus as a tall figure with a sleek wave of black hair, coated in a dull orange neoprene bodysuit. SuperVariant Four. Take a guess what his thing is.

"Quit flirting; One needs backup." Four stands still long enough to get the words out before he readjusts his opaque goggles and runs up the side of a building, disappearing in another orange flash over the top.

"I do *not!*" an unseen voice screams in outrage, and then, oh, what a surprise, another Super. A deep purple blotch in the distance that I recognize immediately as SuperVariant One, asymmetrical cape trailing behind her, rockets out from over the building Four has just disappeared behind. I vaguely wonder where SuperVariant Two is in all this. If *I* had invisibility powers, I probably wouldn't show up to these shenanigans at all. No one would even know.

SuperVariant One executes a sharp swivel in midair that makes her thick, dark braid snap like a whip, and yells, "I can handle this!" She makes a claw shape with her hands, reaches toward the ground, and scoops upward. In response, a car parked at the end of the street rises languidly into the air. She uncurls her right hand into a flat palm and presses it forward, sending the car catapulting over her head and toward some unseen enemy.

"Oh, *no*," I moan, and instinctively try to shield Arnold behind my body, even though he's pretty much a lost cause as a vehicle at this point. "It never works!" I yell up at her. "Throw something else!"

She doesn't even look my way. Before I can say anything else, her left hand is thrown out in that claw shape again, and Arnold is hurtling through the air to join the other car. The thing that's been antagonizing the Supers has come into view from behind the building, and I can see the polished gleam of an eight-story-tall robot, with some human operating it from inside its transparent head. A *robot*. Not for the first time, I feel myself filled with irritation rather than terror at the threat of the day. I mean, come on, guys. How did someone build a giant robot in this city without anyone noticing? If someone's getting eight hundred tons of metal delivered to their house, that needs to be a red flag.

The robot doesn't even turn its head as its right arm swings up and blocks my car with the earsplitting clang of metal on metal, sending it careening back toward the pavement in a shower of sparks.

I shield my head with my arm as my car crashes and rolls, coming to a smoking stop a few yards away from me, then look back up dejectedly. The Supers are already gone, leading the robot farther down the street.

"You're fine, right Arnold?" I yell at my car.

It erupts into flames.

Okay. I'll just walk to work.

I reach around for the metal rod clipped magnetically to the side of my backpack and press a button. It instantly lengthens and expands into a titanium umbrella, riddled with minor dents and scratches. A bowling ball-size crater dips into the left side, giving the whole umbrella an uneven, sagging look. A burn mark from who knows what (I want to say maybe lasers) is just below that. It's been through a lot, but it still works, I think. I mean, I'm not dead yet.

I raise it above my head and start walking.

TWO

IT WASN'T ALWAYS LIKE THIS, you know.

That's the weird part. I remember the "before." I was just a kid, but I remember it.

There was definitely crime. I'd never been to another city long enough to know whether there was significantly more than anywhere else, but the local government seemed to think so. Every news report contained the words "time of crisis" or "state of emergency," with the images all dark and grainy. People used to call it "Lawless City" instead of "Lunar City" as a joke, which I never thought was all that creative, but it stuck anyway.

I guess there was kind of a lot, though. Bunch of gangs. Bank robberies. Organized crime syndicates. Normal action-movie stuff.

The police were in over their heads—or so they told us. There was just too much for them to handle alone. I feel like maybe it would have been easier for them to do their jobs if half of them weren't also part of the crime syndicates themselves, but what do I know?

I'm obviously not a professional member of law enforcement, but I still think a more obvious solution would have been to just fire the corrupt ones and hire better police officers. I mean, clearly they did that too, later, but now we'll never know whether that would have been enough to stop the crime on its own. Oh, no. They just had to pick the sci-fi route.

I don't know whose idea it was, exactly, to start turning random citizens into genetically enhanced superhumans, but I would like to meet them someday. I've got some bills I'd like to send them.

They called it the Genetically Enhanced SuperVariant Program. Which is, you know, just the absolute dumbest mouthful of a pretentious title in existence, so mostly everyone just calls the Genetically Enhanced SuperVariants, "Supers."

It sounds fun, right? Flashy. Cool. Like a comic book come to life.

And when they first arrived, that's exactly how it played out. Like a comic book.

Building on fire, blah, blah, blah.

Freaky man in a mask flying in from out of nowhere and saving everyone, yada, yada, yada.

Heroic and clichéd things were said, photos were taken, and the original SuperVariant was introduced to the city. Everyone lost their minds. Twelve years later, they're still losing them, especially now that there are four heroes instead of just one. That's three more signed-poster options.

Okay, I'll give credit where it's due. The organized crime syndicates did dissipate after the Supers showed up. Most of the petty criminals got scared into hiding. The police are less corrupt (although again, I'm pretty sure that's just because of the staff changes). Fine. Bring out the confetti cannons. But all it really did was leave a gaping hole of potential disaster that was filled by weirdos with homemade genetic enhancements trying to take over the city, wielding bizarre weapons with physics-defying abilities and building nonsense like the cartoonishly large robot currently ransacking the street behind me. See? The crime isn't really gone. It's just weirder, and more theatrical.

Great job, Lunar City.

Do I sound cynical? I don't mean to be. It can just get a little trying when I have to leave my apartment every day wondering if I'm going to be the kind of background extra who runs away screaming from the wreckage or the kind who dies trapped under it.

THREE

A MASSIVE *BOOM* RESOUNDS above me, and I shift my umbrella marginally to the right, enjoying the sound of chunks of brick and shrapnel clanging off the steel instead of my skull. One piece ricochets against my heel, glancing off the thick rubber encasing it. I peer down, turning my ankle to get a better look. The new scuffmark blends in nicely with the dozens of others coating my boots.

I take the risk of peering out from underneath my umbrella by a millimeter and squint upward. SuperVariant Three is floating in midair four stories up in all his gray glory, one fist closed around the neck of a man cloaked in deep crimson and black, grinding him into the side of the building. It looks like they got the driver out of the robot. That explains the raining bricks.

Even from the slight distance, I can make out the man's sharp chin, wild mass of dark, tangled hair, and manic sneer.

✖ COLLATERAL DAMAGE ✖

"Wonderful grip today," he howls gleefully. "Has someone been exercising?"

I groan inwardly as I recognize his crackling voice—it's a particularly notorious city antagonist, a recurring creep called "Doctor Defect." His sinister yellow-green eyes, skin riddled with unhealed scars and burn marks from every one of his past failed schemes, and seemingly endless arsenal of homemade weapons gave me nightmares when I was little, but now his presence is too constant to inspire any new fear. Any normal person who had been thrown through walls, off bridges, and into prison as many times as Doctor Defect has would have given up and died by now, but he just keeps coming back for more. He's been around swearing vengeance against the Supers for pretty much as long as they've existed. It's getting real old.

Despite the imminent danger from the ash and smoke and falling debris, there are still way too many people milling around on the sidewalks and blocking traffic in the street. A few police officers in Hi-Viz vests are trying to herd everyone away from the action, but it's not going great. I discreetly fumble around inside my backpack until I find my lanyard of fake IDs, all of which claim that I'm in my twenties and competent instead of seventeen and one step up from homeless, and detach a press pass from the metal ring. I flash the pass at one of the neon-vested officers as I squeeze through the crowd.

The people resisting the police officers' desperate attempts to clear the street are pointing up to where Three and Doctor Defect are going at it with exaggerated expressions of shock and terror plastered on their faces, clearly hoping to be noticed in the background footage of the local news coverage. I elbow past the camera crew and their perky brunette reporter, who have set up shop practically inside the doorframe of The Pure Bean—the coffee shop that I work at.

"Bringing you *live* coverage of the *thrilling* battle between the fearless SuperVariant Three and the villainous Doctor Defect—"

I stick my face into the frame. "And now, bringing you *live* coverage of the *thrilling* Meg Sawyer, as she prepares to serve mediocre coffee to cranky citizens."

The guy holding the boom mic glares at me and gives me a *stop talking, this is live* kind of face. I roll my eyes and push against the heavy, shatter-proof door of the café until it yields, putting me face to face with my short, brown-haired, pink-cheeked, very annoyed-looking manager. She's wielding a mop like a staff.

"Thanks for showing up today," she quips.

"Really, Carly?" I trudge past her and shrug my backpack off, leaving it leaning against the wall. "It's too early for this."

Carly trails behind me, pushing the mop over the mud I've tracked in. "If by 'too early,' you mean nearly a half-hour late, then yeah, you're right. What's wrong with your clothes? You don't think you're going to serve customers like that, do you?"

I look down at my jeans, which are spattered with dirt and grime. My green THE PURE BEAN T-shirt has a gash in the sleeve. I don't even have to look at my face in a mirror to know that it's covered in a fine layer of dirt. "Carly," I explain calmly. "Which do you think is more likely: that I'm experimenting with the heavy grunge look, or that I almost got crushed by a falling billboard this morning?"

She wrinkles her nose and begins to retreat back behind the front counter. "I saw the news," she says as she starts dumping coffee beans into the espresso machine. "Next time, text me if you're going to be late. Go change."

"Into *what*?" In response, an extra-large "Coffee or Death" T-shirt from our merch wall collides with my face.

"What did I say about throwing things? What have I told you about my hand-eye coordination?" I complain as I scoop the shirt off the ground, but I head for the bathroom to change. The lights start flickering as I replace my ripped shirt with the fresh one, and by the time I'm back to the front of the café, they're snapping on and off like we're in a horror movie about ghosts while the ceiling tiles rattle in merry accompaniment.

They're on the roof, aren't they? I'm about to say, when suddenly, the entire building jolts like an airplane going through turbulence. The light fixtures swing dangerously, and the few that are on sputter off. Carly lunges for the mugs behind the counter before they swing off their iron hooks and shatter.

Yeah. I think they're on the roof.

I look at my watch. It's been twenty-eight minutes since SuperVariant Three and Doctor Defect destroyed my car. Aren't they burned out by now?

"Hey!" I shout, grabbing a broom and pounding the ceiling with the handle. "Knock it off up there! Go work out your issues somewhere else!"

In response, the pounding of fists and aggravated grunting noises move abruptly somewhere off to the right, and I suddenly see Three fall outside our front window and collide impressively with the pavement, leaving the concrete poking up around him in jagged chunks. Doctor Defect makes a cat-like leap to join him, gnashing his crooked teeth into a triumphant grin as he whips something sharp and metallic out of his belt and raises it above his head, but barely has time to register his victory before Three has back-flipped to his feet, grabbed him by the throat, and smashed his head into our window.

I flinch instinctively, but the bulletproof glass holds up without so much as a crack. I'll have to remember to leave a good review on the supplier's website.

"Maniacs!" Carly yells through the glass as they shoot off down the street, fists still flying. She cups her hands around her mouth like she's winding up to shout something even more aggressive, but whatever it is gets swallowed by a loud, explosive *honk* from somewhere outside.

We both peer out to the street, where a rusted orange pickup truck is idling. I mean, it used to be a pickup truck. I don't know if you can still logically call it that when a good third of the truck bed is missing, the remaining part ending with a giant, rusted bite mark. Long story.

Honk, honk, honk, honk, hooooooonk.

The truck is diagonal from the café, decidedly stuck in the traffic of the dozens of people milling about in the street, recording the action with their phones. About four feet separates it from the parallel parking spot it's clearly aiming for.

I grin and wrench the front door open, ignoring Carly's shrieks that I'm going to let in rubble, or worse, bugs. "Hey, Oliver!" I yell through the hail of shrapnel still falling onto the street, "Nice weather today, huh?"

Oliver Lee sticks his head out the window, which has been devoid of glass for several months, and rakes his fingers through his glossy black bangs. "Can I just leave it here, then?" he yells back, gesturing in apparent frustration with the other hand to the mess in front of him. "Can I just leave my car in the middle of the street, since that's what everyone else seems to be doing?"

I snicker, dash to grab my umbrella from where I've left it leaning against the wall, and shake it back open outside the door, nearly impaling one of the camera crew guys. "Watch it, kid," he grunts, scowling.

I ignore him and beeline for the street, holding my umbrella out in front of me like a shield. "*Yaaaaaaah!*" I yell, and a dozen people leap out of the way of impalement. "That's it!" I shout, shooing the rest with my free hand while still stabbing through the more congested part of the road with my umbrella. It's a little disconcerting to note that they're more afraid of a crazy teenager with an umbrella than the threat of being crushed by falling debris. "Go to work, everybody! You can watch it on the internet later! Hey, you—" I stride over to the window of the car directly in front of Oliver's truck and bang on the glass. The woman inside jumps, startled, and rolls down the window.

"Hi. Yeah. Are we having fun?" I smile amiably and lean on the door. I look up to my left, where SuperVariant Three and

Doctor Defect are grappling twenty yards in the air, muscles rippling. "Ah." I nod sympathetically at the driver. "I get it. He's just *sooooo* amazing, right?"

She blushes and starts to gush, "Oh, I just—"

I cup my hands around my mouth. "*No one cares. You're blocking traffic, woman.*"

She jumps again and gestures to the sky. "But I—"

"No."

"But—"

"No."

"He—"

"*Drive.*"

Finally giving up, the woman jerks her car away, skirting a giant chunk of building as it breaks off and rolls right through the area that had been full to capacity with citizens just moments before.

"Okay, that's everyone," I mutter, surveying the cleared street. One of the police officers who'd been trying to achieve the exact same goal a few minutes before gapes at me, his whistle hanging uselessly from its cord. "You're welcome!" I shout toward him, then jump out of the way and give Oliver a thumbs-up.

"You're all set!"

He returns the gesture, then whips into the parking spot, smashing into both the car parked in front of him and the one parked behind while trying to straighten out.

The driver behind Oliver's truck, who's idly watching a video on his phone in the front seat, looks up with an unfocused, lazy blink for a moment when his car jolts, then shrugs and turns back to his video. The addition of another dent to the dozens already littering his vehicle is clearly not worth getting out of the car for.

Oliver turns his engine off with a loud, pained sputter, then hops down from the front seat and attempts to force his hair into a baseball cap emblazoned with a pizza slice logo. A few clumps stick out haphazardly from the back and sides.

"Well, good *morning*," I gush with false cheer as another chunk of roof dislodges itself and falls to the pavement behind me.

He cracks a smile and relocates his sunglasses to the brim of his hat, resting a skinny elbow on top of my head as he squints up at the building behind me. "I win, I think."

"Huh?" I turn around and stare at the strip of storefronts bordering the sidewalk. The windows on The Pure Bean are all intact, but the roof is in shambles, with so many shingles missing that the entire look is vaguely that of a checkerboard designed by a child. A cloud of smoke is rising in a dim patch out of the corner, and a couple of tree branches litter the ground in front of the café. Next door, the only visible issue with the pizza place Oliver delivers for is that the sign above the doorframe is missing an indeterminate number of letters, leaving only a flashing "-o's Pizza." Unfortunately, the sign's been broken for a while, so the damage doesn't count. I don't even remember what the name was before, to be honest.

I slump. "Okay, yes, mine did get more damage today, but in our defense, that is because Three decided our roof was suitable for combat."

"Doesn't matter." Oliver smirks. "Pay up."

"Yeah, yeah, get inside." I shove his arm. "Before you're late. Or get crushed by a falling building."

"When am I ever late?" he grumbles, but he follows me back onto the sidewalk and into our respective restaurants.

I lean my umbrella back against the wall, grab a bottle of surface cleaner so Carly will think I'm doing something productive, and position myself behind the register at the pastry counter. I turn to my right. "What do you want today?"

Oliver blinks back at me through the four-foot hole in the wall connecting our restaurants and taps his chin. "Double-fudge brownie?"

"Double-fudge brownie," I say, grabbing one out of its case

and handing it through the wall.

I honestly have no idea how the hole happened, because I was off that day, but all I know is that Carly insists that it came from Oliver's side of the building, while his manager insists that it came from ours. Consequentially, both refuse to be the one to pay to get it fixed. Which is fine with me, because now I get to hang out with Oliver whenever we're both working, which is often.

"This tastes like cardboard," Oliver says, making a face, but still cramming another bite in his mouth before he's finished chewing the piece he was already working on.

"It's gluten-free. We're gluten-free now."

"*Why?*"

"Because I had started thinking that living here couldn't get any worse, and the universe wanted to prove me wrong."

"It can always be worse." He shoves the rest in his mouth, then leans on his elbows against the counter, directing a perturbed glance out through the window on his side of the restaurant. "Wheh yur ca?"

"There's no way you could possibly expect me to understand whatever you just said." I notice Carly looking my way and absentmindedly move a dry paper towel in a circle to make it look like I'm cleaning. "Digest. Try again."

He pretends to swallow theatrically. "I said, where's your car?"

"Billboard fell on it," I sigh. "Then someone threw it at a giant robot."

"*Again?*"

I nod sadly.

"Well..." His face turns serious, a strong indicator that whatever he's about to say is decidedly not. "It's a good thing you have such great insurance."

I roll my eyes. Even if I *could* afford insurance—which he knows I can't—it wouldn't have applied to Arnold. After all, you can't get car insurance for a car that isn't legally yours.

I didn't steal it, for the record. The local car dealership fell into a sinkhole. So really, I *saved* it.

"I can give you rides when we're both working," Oliver continues, but then the corner of his mouth curves up slyly, "or you can always fly here on your broom."

I lunge for another brownie to throw at him and he ducks out of sight, laughing.

"I hope you're paying for all that food you're throwing away!" Carly yells from somewhere in the back room.

"How does she do that?" I mutter, pulling five dollars out of my pocket and cramming it in the tip jar.

Oliver reemerges. "Don't the tips go to you?"

"Shh."

"You little felon." He shakes his head and starts striding toward the wide television screen mounted on his wall, but pauses mid-reach to press the power button and cocks his head in my direction. "Wait, place your bets: recap footage or expert interview?"

"Recap footage," I predict. "No question."

The TV emits a few staticky sputters, then clicks to life. The confident voice of a local news anchor echoes throughout both restaurants, narrating a close-up montage of the SuperVariants battling Doctor Defect, framed by smoke and crumbling bricks and screaming citizens.

"Bam. Recap footage." I smirk.

Oliver shakes his head. "Every time. You're so good at this game."

"Once again," the anchor interrupts us, "the dangerous criminal who wreaked havoc upon the western side of Lunar City at approximately 11:18 a.m. this morning has been apprehended by SuperVariant Three. The identity of the suspect has been confirmed as the notorious Doctor Defect—"

"Him *again*?" Oliver complains. "This is the second time this month. They really need to build a better jail."

"But it's just so interesting. I mean, he always gets defeated, but he just keeps coming back. What's his story? What's his *motivation*? Why does he dedicate himself to a life as a human punching bag?"

"You know, I actually thought you were serious for half a second, there." Oliver raises an eyebrow as the circular take-out-order interface on the counter starts to beep.

"Wow. I'm disappointed. Eight years of friendship, and you still don't know my sense of humor?" I respond over the tinny chirping. "When have you ever known me to care about what goes on in this town apart from whether it results in our imminent death?"

"*Everything* could result in our imminent death." Oliver slaps the takeout screen to confirm the order's been received and starts heading for the kitchen, shouting for whoever's back there cooking, "Hey, do we have any pepperonis ready to go?"

"That's the kind of paranoia that keeps us alive," I call approvingly after his retreating back. I turn around in time to see Carly finally reappear, now clutching a broom and a store-bought black wreath interwoven with plastic skulls and spiders. "Did you call the roof tiling company yet?" she demands.

"No. You didn't ask me to." I stare at the wreath. "What the heck is *that*?"

She reaches behind me and hangs it above one of the coffeemakers. "It's festive. If people are excited about Halloween, they'll buy more pumpkin spice."

"It's the middle of September!" I shriek.

"Call the roof tiling company, please." With a grunt of effort, she rolls a large boulder into place to prop the front door open and starts sweeping broken shingles into a pile.

I dial the number and immediately get sent to an automated recording that starts monotonously explaining that the entire city also needs new roofs and I'm gonna have to wait.

The kitchen door swings open and Oliver stumbles out, barely visible behind a teetering stack of ten pizza boxes. "Later," he calls, his voice muffled. "Don't die while I'm gone."

"Later. I—hey, *hey*! Safety helmet!" I tuck the phone under one ear, half-listening to the irritable screeching of the secretary I've finally gotten through to—something about a long waitlist and low priority and four to twelve weeks—then reach under the counter and grab my spare. Oliver clambers over and sticks his head through the wall, and I balance the safety helmet on top of his hat, straps dangling. "Don't die."

"Not today." There's a cacophony of clanging from the restaurant's front door as he tries to maneuver himself through the archway without using his hands, followed by a loud slam.

"The roofing people say four to twelve weeks!" I yell to Carly.

"Oh, I don't think so. Gimme that," she shouts back. I throw her the receiver and she snatches it, dragging the extra-long extension cord behind her as she stalks back outside. I hear the words "most loyal customer" and "unacceptable" being delivered with loud, even fury. She's so engaged with berating the terrified secretary, she almost bowls over the customer trying to get into the café: a thin, short girl with silver-dyed hair growing out dark brown at the roots, a face streaked with dirt, and dark, deeply-sunken eyes.

She looks a little young for coffee—thirteen, fourteen maybe—so I'm hoping maybe she just went in the wrong door. After all, there's no way anyone is voluntarily coming in here for stale pastries.

"Pizza's next door," I offer, hoping she'll leave so I can continue to not work.

She doesn't move. She just stands a few feet inside the doorway looking lost, which is when I notice that her arms are shaking slightly, held out from her body like she's scared to touch herself. I wonder briefly if she's new to town, if her family made the mistake of moving here, drawn by the comic-book appeal of *real life superhumans*, and the harsh reality of her first crisis has just extinguished the fantasy.

"Can I—" I have to strain forward to listen to her, her voice is so quiet and cracked. "Can I just have a cup of water?"

Carly's head pops around the open door frame, because apparently she's starting to develop a skill for being summoned at the mere *thought* of me giving away something for free. She gives me a firm shake of her head—*no, get rid of her*—which I ignore. Normally, I'd welcome an excuse to not deal with a customer, but come on. It's *water*. And this girl is like, a baby. I'm lazy, not evil.

I turn to fill a plastic cup from the tap next to espresso machine, feeling the girl's hollow eyes staring at the back of my head. If she's as new to town as the post-traumatic shock on her face indicates, I guess I should give her some pointers. *Collect safety equipment like it's a hobby. Don't get attached to people. Run first, ask questions later. Just move somewhere else.* That sort of thing.

I turn around to start telling her that, but my desire to help her is quickly replaced with dull irritation. It ought to have been complete outrage, but I've gotten pretty used to disappointment when it comes to other people.

She's holding the tip jar.

No, she's *stealing* the tip jar.

It's Saturday, and Carly won't let me empty it until the end of the week—something about customers being more likely to contribute to it if they see how many other people have already done so—so it's stuffed. There has to be almost twenty dollars in there; grocery money for a week or two at least. More if I commit to a ramen-exclusive diet, as I often do.

I can't believe I fell for such a dumb trap, can't believe I was actually trying to be nice to this kid. She doesn't even say anything, just stands there with her dirt-streaked hand covering the ugly drawing of a shark proclaiming *Feed the Starving Predator* taped to the jar. Her brown eyes are wide and at least have the decency to look guilty, but I don't feel bad for her. Like, I'm sorry that she's having a bad enough day that she needs to rob us, but in case no one noticed, I am too.

"Seriously?" I yank the jar out of her hand, making her flinch. "Today is *not* the day to—" And then I cut my own sentence off, because there's a yellow band around her right wrist that I hadn't noticed before, and that changes things a little.

She's not new to town after all. She's a Shelter for the Misplaced kid.

The band doesn't tell me what her situation is. She could be an orphan, or homeless, or both, or something else entirely.

Mine, before I made my first good fake ID and tricked the facility into thinking my sixteenth birthday was my eighteenth and ran away, was for both.

What the band does tell me is that something very, very bad has happened to her as a result of one of the daily crises, and now she lives in a tent in a warehouse with all the other kids who had very, very bad things happen to them and their families.

I nod at the girl's hand. "That place still suck?"

She looks confused for half a second until she realizes where I'm looking and tugs the sleeve of her jacket down over the band—a reflexive gesture I've always found particularly useless. I've got enough of a grasp on object permanence to remember what the band looks like and what it symbolizes without having it in front of me, after all.

Her eyes shift back and forth, but right when I think she's going to run for it rather than answer the question, she mutters, "Yeah."

A pang of pity stabs inside me. Sometimes, caught up in the joy that comes from constantly complaining about my life, I forget that it could be worse. At least I have somewhere to live, and a job that lets me take home food, and Oliver. At least I've never been so desperate that I have to steal seventeen dollars' worth of quarters from a mediocre café.

"Here," I say before I can change my mind, and I push the jar back toward her. "Just take it."

Her eyes widen. "No, it was a mistake. I didn't mean to—"

"It's fine." I need her to get out of the store before the part of my brain that's already battling me with *You idiot, do you know how many noodles we could buy with that* takes over. "Oh wait, no." I pull the jar back, and disappointment flickers across her face, but all I do is pull the wad of bills out in a messy clump. I stuff them in her hands, then wave the jar, jangling the few coins left inside. "Gotta keep this. Worked hard on the artwork, you know."

The subtle attempt at a joke—the shark is stick-figure quality at best—manages to relax her a fraction. She swallows, opens her mouth, looks from me to the money and back, and—

And she's gone, racing out the door.

I sigh and replace the jar on its grimy ring next to the register. "You're welcome," I mutter.

"The roof repairman will be here tomorrow," Carly announces triumphantly, rounding the corner. Her eyes go straight to the counter, narrowed with suspicion, because she misses nothing. "Where's the tip money?" she demands.

"I…" I can't decide whether she'll be more mad at me if I tell her I gave it away or if I tell her it was stolen. It doesn't matter, though; she makes the decision for me.

"You let us get robbed, didn't you?" Carly accuses me, her face a familiar mask of exasperation. "That kid asked you for water and then stole the money. Meg, you have *got* to start paying attention. If I'm gonna let you be here instead of at school—"

Let me? "You don't have to 'let me' anything," I shoot back defensively. I know I should be focusing on explaining what really happened, but her comment is infuriating. "And I don't *have* to be at school. I got my GED. It's not like I'm some loser dropout."

"Then you have to be a better employee," she finishes, her hazel eyes doing their very best to pierce right through me. "That means being here on time. Actually cleaning, instead of pretending to. Not letting us get *robbed*."

I was late because a billboard almost fell on me. This café is the cleanest six hundred square feet of space in the city; you're just the world's most intense germophobe. We weren't robbed; I was just trying to do something nice for once. All things that I want to say, but don't. It wouldn't matter. Carly's selective hearing only extends to about two words when it comes to me.

"I'm sorry," I say. I can't let her stay mad at me. I need this job. I need Carly continuing to be the only person in the city willing to employee a seventeen-year-old with full-time hours. I need the leftover food that I get to take home at the end of the day. I need the luxury of working right next to Oliver, so we can keep an eye on each other. "I'll do better."

"Maybe one day I'll believe you," she says, but her tone is, miraculously, softer. "If you really want to do better, turn in the damage reports when you leave, okay? You know reimbursement takes forever if they don't get done the day of."

"Okay," I reply. I realize with a sense of vague irony that I'm fairly certain Carly snapped at me about my work ethic the exact same way last month too, right down to the order to file damage reports afterward. My life is a giant, inescapable circle.

Still, if I'd known that was going to be my last day before things went from predictably bad to cataclysmic, I might have tried to enjoy it a little more.

FOUR

FOR THE REST OF THE DAY, people come in like zombies and leave like slightly more energized zombies in a steady stream. There's a lull at two p.m., when the citywide cleanup crew rattles down the street, vacuuming up debris and replacing broken traffic lights and knocked-over signs. People around here usually try to avoid loud, aggressive noises, and the cleanup crew could win an award for their loudness and aggressiveness. I spend a good twenty minutes alone watching a giant white vehicle shaped like a large egg inching down the road, sucking broken building chunks into its ultra-powered vacuum with a noise like a jet engine. Carly uses the lull to flit around the outside of the café, taking photos of everything broken for the damage report.

The monotony doesn't break until later in the afternoon, when Oliver's TV gets turned back on. The perky news reporter from earlier has returned, accompanied by a banner on the bottom of the screen announcing that there have been three confirmed casualties since this morning.

"Viewers will be relieved to hear that known criminal Doctor Defect, who was responsible for the events of this morning, has been returned to custody by SuperVariant Three. Representing the Genetic Enhancement Program, we are pleased to welcome Dr. Aiden Crenshaw—"

The screen splits in half to make room for a thin, enthusiastic face and a polished crop of salt-and-pepper hair—Dr. Aiden Crenshaw, the creator of the SuperVariant serum and director of the entire program. He flashes a wide smile at the camera, adjusts his frameless triangular glasses, and smooths the front of his button-down absentmindedly. "Yes," he says before the anchor can even ask him a question, "Three—SuperVariant Three, that is—he did do a remarkable job today, didn't he?" He beams like a proud father. "You know, it's unfortunate that we have to live in a world where people like Doctor Defect exist, but villainy has never stood a chance against the forces of compassion, righteousness, and courage. As long as the SuperVariants are around to uphold these forces, fear and evil will never triumph."

"What a nice sentiment, Dr. Crenshaw," the news anchor responds with a plastic smile. "Now, I'm sure we're all curious, what revisions will be made for the next version of Three?" Her voice takes on a twinge of subtle adoration. "It seems impossible to improve—"

The next version. I shudder involuntarily. I'm not looking forward to it.

Oh, yeah. I forgot to mention. This is a rotating gig.

Well, you can't expect the same person to hold the mantle forever, can you?

Here's the thing. Not that I've ever experienced it personally, but I guess it's pretty hard to be a superhero. In addition to destroying citizens' cars, there's a lot of responsibility there, and I guess the city government is pretty attentive to the emotional security of its employees. They probably just don't want to have to deal with the therapy costs of turning a bunch of citizens into the angst-filled emotional wrecks they would no doubt become if they had to spend more than a couple of years making sure every action they took was completely selfless and responsible and dutiful.

So every two years, they get replaced. Their weird powers get transferred to someone else, and they go back to being normal citizens. Not all at once, of course. Two in the spring, two in the fall. SuperVariants One and Two were replaced back in March, so it's only a matter of time before SuperVariant Three hands his tights off to someone else. Anyway, the idea is that this way, nobody has to be a SuperVariant long enough to become overwhelmed by the responsibilities it comes with. And by spacing the replacements out, the new kids get time to get through their angsty, confused, dramatic period while the old two cover their backs. What would we do if we got all four new people at once, and they *all* had to go through the "oh-crap-I-have-powers" thing together? Nothing would ever get done.

Still, no one's ever been quite as beloved as this particular SuperVariant Three. People are going to go into collective depression no matter who replaces him. I'd better find my earplugs.

I stop focusing on the words of the reporter, instead squinting at the accompanying footage of Doctor Defect, who isn't even fighting the cluster of police officers escorting him back into the prison. He wiggles his fingers at the camera, the movement of the rest of his hands hindered by tight steel manacles. "See you all soon," he sings, his voice dry and raspy as a chain-smoker's. His eyes crinkle up in a smile, and he winks as he disappears through the doors.

"What a creep," I observe. "Why does it always have to be him? Why can't someone cool try to take over the city for once? Like aliens, or evil twins."

"What, that woman with the ice ray last month wasn't cool

enough for you?" Oliver demands, looking up from the dollar bill he's attempting to fold into a plane. He's been in and out all day. Distraught people love their pizza. "And don't joke about evil twins. Remember last week? Those girls that kept coming in saying I got their order wrong and I had to make a new one?"

"Those weren't evil twins, those were normal twins," I remind him. "And scamming you to get free pizza isn't evil; it's brilliant, and I wish I'd thought of it."

"I already give you free pizza."

"It's true, it's the only reason we're friends," I agree.

"A-*hem*." I hear a pointed cough and turn to see Carly's face a foot away from mine.

I flinch. "Yeah?"

"Oh, nothing." Her eyes are narrowed. "Just that your shift is over in twelve minutes and you haven't asked to leave early yet. Just wanted to make sure you haven't been possessed or mind-controlled."

"If I had been possessed or mind-controlled, I probably wouldn't be able to tell you," I say, checking my watch. She's right; it's 4:48 p.m., a full eighteen minutes past the start of my can-I-go-now window.

"Can I go now?" I ask, then instantly become suspicious. "Or is this a test? I thought you were upset with me. I thought you wanted me to be a better employee."

"I do. But it's slow. Just be here on time tomorrow." She empties the remains of the tip jar into her palm and starts counting out pennies into two sad piles.

"Really?" I grab my backpack and umbrella before she can change her mind. "Oliver!"

"What?" He looks up from his dollar-bill origami.

"You gotta leave early, too; I need a ride home."

"I can't leave early. I'm the only one working."

I stick my head through the wall, craning to view the rest of his restaurant. "Where'd everybody else go?"

Oliver shrugs. "Artie and Daniel said something about going to check on a bridge collapse?" he says, referring to the two brothers who usually make the pizzas. "Or maybe the fridge collapsed. I don't know. I wasn't paying attention."

"Well, you can't deliver pizzas if there's no one here to cook them, now, can you?"

He hesitates, then throws off his apron. "Your motivations are selfish, but I can't argue with your logic."

"Hey!" Carly sticks out an arm as I try to maneuver around the counter, and shoves a manila envelope in my face. "Damage reports. Turned in today, got it?"

I stuff the envelope in my backpack, wedging it in around my safety helmet. "I get overtime for this, right?"

She doesn't respond, so I'm assuming not. I tramp out the front door and plant myself next to the passenger side of Oliver's truck, then pull on the handle absentmindedly, planning on tugging on the locked door until Oliver comes out. Instead, the entire door comes off its hinge.

"Oliver!" I shout as he strides across the sidewalk. "Check it out! I've developed super strength!"

"Ha, ha," he says drily, then shakes his head. "This truck is falling apart."

"Understatement." I've put the door down by this point, letting it rest against the dirty side of the truck. The thing is heavy. I wipe the grime off on my pants. "What happened this time? Is it a fun story? Will I laugh?"

Oliver comes around behind me and, grunting slightly, lifts the door and throws it into the truck bed. "What always happens. Somebody aimed for a Super and missed."

"Ah." I jump into the gaping hole of the truck's side and buckle my seat belt, tucking my backpack between my legs. I open my umbrella sideways, so the circle of steel forms a makeshift shield in case anything hits us from the side on the way home. The city seems to have calmed down a bunch since this morning, but you never know. "Well, now you have a Jeep."

"I always wanted a Jeep. Look out, coming through." Oliver climbs around my umbrella and makes a point of stepping on as much of my legs and feet as he can as he clambers into the driver's seat.

"Ow—Oliver—why—can you *not*—"

"The driver's door is facing the street. There are cars. I'm being *safe*."

"You're being something."

"Statistically speaking, I usually am." With a dramatic sigh of expelled effort, he settles into the faded, crinkled leather. "Shall we go drown the pain of life in discounted cake mix and bad movies?"

"You know me so well," I say, stretching an arm out to ruffle his hair, and with a grin and a bone-jarring jolt, Oliver whips us out of the parking spot.

FIVE

"SO, SCALE OF ONE TO TEN, catastrophic work day or tolerable work day? I barely saw you," I ask Oliver with my mouth half full of double-chocolate cake mix. I'm curled up in a blue beanbag chair, ratty and faded with the stuffing leaking out the bottom, scraping a mixing bowl clean with a plastic fork while its former contents bake in an ancient aluminum pan. The beanbag chair shares a dismal amount of floor space with its purple twin, a striped gray rug artfully positioned to hide several burn marks on the carpet (my fault this time, not the Supers'), and two small white coffee tables pushed together to form one less-small coffee table, occupied by a dingy laptop that probably existed along with the dinosaurs. The rest of the floor is caught in the middle of a turf war between half-empty pizza boxes and plastic movie cases from the dollar bin of the Super Savers grocery store. If you're wondering how a seventeen-year-old who works at a café can afford to live in a quality inner-city one-bedroom apartment complex by herself, the answer is simple: this particular unit used to be a two-bedroom apartment. The second bedroom sort of exploded.

I honestly don't know the whole story.

But the good news is that apartments charge you next to nothing for a unit that has an entire outer wall missing, and the better news is that Oliver and I patched most of the missing wall with a bunch of wood we found on the curb, then covered the whole thing with a giant blue tarp, so now me and all the bugs and rodents that manage to slip through the cracks are living almost rent-free (emphasis on the rodents; I'm pretty sure there's a colony of rats living somewhere in my ceiling). But as long as I don't accidentally sleepwalk through the tarp and plummet down seven stories to my death, everything's great.

"How much raw egg is in this?" Oliver asks, examining the empty cake mix box and ignoring my question. "Are you going to get salmonella and die?"

"Nothing else has killed me yet. Cake would never betray me like that," I retort. "And my day was a solid six out of ten."

"Is ten worst or is one worst? You presented your ranking system weird."

"One is worst. One is obviously worst."

"And you give it a six?" He starts tearing the box into neat cardboard strips, like he's planning on setting out an offering for the ceiling rats. Whatever keeps them from eating me, I guess. "Your car exploded."

"Yeah, but I wasn't in it. Still, a six isn't ideal. I think I need a new job."

"You say that every day."

I cram another bite of cake mix in my mouth. "Okay, yes, but this time I mean it. Aren't I better than serving mediocre coffee to tired corporate robots and screechy youths?"

"'Youths?' How old are you?" Oliver flashes me a wry, mischievous smile. "You know, I heard there's a Super replacement coming up."

I lift my fork like I'm going to throw it at him and he ducks, laughing. "How dare you."

"Just a joke, Meg!" he calls from behind the sink.

"First of all"—I stab the fork toward him accusingly—"even if I wanted to get paid to smash things, which you are fully aware I do not, you know they would literally not pick me if I was the last living person in town." I lower my fork. "Second, how do you even know there's one coming up? Since when have they ever told us ahead of time? Did I miss some kind of announcement?"

Oliver reemerges. "Simple logic. It's been over two years since the last Three was replaced. It has to be any day now."

Part of me hopes he's wrong, even though Oliver has always been uncannily good at predicting when replacements are about to happen. It's not like they can announce it or anything, or space them at exactly two years apart. Can you imagine? It'd be like putting up a giant sign saying, "The city's understaffed, come attack us."

Beep. Beep. Beep. Beep.

I shriek and dive under my beanbag chair. "Emergency alarm! Everybody panic!"

"Calm down, you lunatic." I hear Oliver kick the oven door in the top right corner—the only way to get it to open. It tips over with a thunk. "It's just the cake timer."

I poke my head out from under the beanbag. "We need to move."

Oliver laughs. "Hey, when you have more than thirty dollars in your bank account, let me know."

I salute him with the fork. "Touché."

He opens his mouth, but whatever he's about to say in response is interrupted by a different voice—high and furious and decidedly female.

"You're seriously still not getting this? How reckless can you possibly—"

The voice is muffled, but high-pitched enough to cut

through the wall. I look at Oliver. "Did you hear that?"

"Hmph?" He looks back at me with puffy cheeks, his mouth full of cake.

I scramble the rest of the way out from under the chair and put my finger to my lips, cocking my head to the side. We both listen in silence for a few moments. Then—

"I can't believe you actually left work to yell at me about this. This is my duty—"

"Your duty? Are you really going to just keep throwing that word around? You're so irresponsible!"

"Juniper—"

"Oh, no," I groan, trying to cover my head with the beanbag chair again. "They're back."

Oliver is already carrying the pan over with an oven mitt. He sets it down on the floor between the two beanbag chairs and plops himself into the one I'm not trying to wear as a hat. "You know, I've always found it a bit entertaining."

"Well, that's because you don't live next door to them," I argue, reaching over to grab a fistful of cake and wincing as it burns my fingers. "You get to take a break from it sometimes."

"Shh!" he whispers. "We're gonna miss it."

"We need to get you a hobby," I mutter, but begrudgingly join him in staring at the dilapidated, utterly blank wall separating my apartment and my next-door neighbor's.

Despite living next to her for almost a year, I've only seen Juniper Jensen once—when she almost stepped on me the time I got locked out of my apartment and fell asleep in the hall—so all I know about her is that she's a couple of years older than me but clearly has a much better paying job (her unit isn't missing a wall, so she has to be paying at least three times as much as me), and she's dating a guy named Sam who always visits after dark, speaks exclusively in sentences that involve words like "responsibility" or "duty," and apparently has a job that poses a constant threat on his life.

At first, I thought maybe he worked at a daycare, but then

I caught on.

I bet if I had an ounce more interest, I could easily put effort into figuring out which of the city's probably hundreds of Sams is moonlighting as SuperVariant Three. But I've never seen his face, so figuring it out based on voice alone seems like a lot of work for something that ultimately doesn't matter to me much.

The shouting continues.

"You're not even listening to me. If you were, you wouldn't be doing this—"

"Doing what, Juniper? My job? Which, by the way, is going to be over soon! So why does this even matter?"

"That's exactly the problem, Sam! How could you take lead on that crisis today? Why would you put another target on your back this close to the end of your term?"

"I didn't—"

"Do you think Doctor Defect is going to just leave you alone after you get replaced? This was the fifth time you put him away this year! He's always had a vendetta against the Supers, but you keep making it personal. You should have let one of the other Supers handle it. What if he finds out your secret identity? What if he—?"

"He's not going to find out my secret identity." Three's exasperation is practically burning through the wall. "You're the only person who knows it."

"Well, not counting us," I whisper.

"Are you really willing to risk your life on that bet?" Juniper snaps. "What if he does find out somehow? What if the next time he escapes, he comes for you just for the satisfaction of beating you, knowing you won't be able to protect yourself?"

I can hear Three's grin in his voice. "You'll protect me, I expect."

His comment is met with only a stony silence. Then—"You should have let someone else take lead. You're supposed to be a team. You're supposed to operate as a team. But you just can't help yourself, can you? You just have to have all the glory."

Three begins to raise his voice. "You think this is about glory?"

"Yes, I do think this is about glory," Juniper replies defiantly. "And if you act like this now—" Her voice suddenly cracks, sacrificing some of the edge for a much rawer emotion. "What are you going to be like when you're not a Super anymore? What are you going to do, become a vigilante? Keep running around the city looking for danger?"

"And what would be so wrong with that?" Three shouts.

"What's wrong is you're going to get yourself killed!"

"Not if I'm careful. I can train, I can learn how to fight without my super strength, I can keep—"

"Oh, grow up, Sam! You don't get a free pass to do whatever you want for the rest of your life just because you were once a Super. I wish—" There's a tense silence that permeates the apartment wall. And then, Juniper, her voice quiet and tired, finishes, "I wish you'd never been chosen."

Yikes. I mean, same, but it's still a little harsh.

Juniper seems to think so, too. "I'm sorry," she says before the words have hung in the air for more than a second. "You know that all I meant was…" She trails off, unable to find an excuse. When Three offers no response except for dumbfounded, hurt silence, she clears her throat. "I have to get back to work."

"Yeah?" Three finally finds his voice, and it's low and furious. "Well, so do I." There's a noise like a window being flung open, and then the tarp covering my missing wall rustles noisily as something whooshes past it. A second later, I hear Juniper's front door slam closed.

Oliver lets out a soft whistle. "Well, there goes the entertainment."

"Oh, no." I fake concern. "Now we'll never know how it ends."

"Sure we will—you heard him. I was right. He's being replaced soon. It's gonna end with him not being a Super anymore."

"Yeah," I observe. "You know, people are going to lose their minds when they don't have him around to obsess over anymore. I can't even remember the last Super that people loved this much."

"It was—" Oliver screws his face up and snaps his fingers as the memory comes back. "Four. Back when we were freshmen. He was cool."

"No way. The one with the catchphrase? Nobody thought he was cool." I yawn and roll half my face into the beanbag chair.

"Well, hopefully the next one doesn't like battling on your roof quite as much."

"Yeah." The phrase "battling on your roof" clicks something in my mind, and I leap off the beanbag. Oh, no. "Oh, crap," I mutter, lunging for my backpack. "Crap, crap, crap."

"Now what?" Oliver doesn't even look fazed by my unanticipated freak-out. I guess I should relax more. I snatch the manila folder out of my bag. "Damage reports! Unfiled damage reports! Carly's going to have a cow."

"So, what?" He yawns. "Do it tomorrow."

"I can't do it tomorrow! Damage reports have to be turned into city hall the day the damage occurs, or you live in wait-listed purgatory forever. You know this." I grab clumps of my hair with both hands and pull. "If we don't get reimbursed for the roof repairs because I didn't turn this in, it's so coming out of my paycheck. What time does city hall close? Is there a mailbox? Can I just leave it in their mailbox?"

"Dude, calm down." Oliver tries to take the envelope from me. "I'll just drop it off on my way home."

"No way, I can't make you do that. It's completely the wrong direction from you." I pull it back from him.

"Come on, it's no big deal." He manages to snatch it from me and holds it above his head.

"Oh, really?" I fold my arms, not letting him have the satisfaction of watching me jump up and down trying to get it back. "You've never even turned in a damage report. Do you even know which department this is going to?"

"Um," he looks down and guesses, "Citizen Reimbursement?"

He's right, but I don't want him to know that. "Nope."

"Fine." He drops the envelope, and I catch it before it hits the floor. "Let me give you a ride."

"What did I just say? It's the wrong direction. I'm not gonna make you waste your gas money just because I messed up." I already have my safety helmet on.

"So what, you're gonna bike halfway across town? By yourself? At eleven o'clock at night?"

"Yes." I click the straps on my helmet closed.

He rolls his eyes, watching me nearly topple over as I coerce Arnold Jr.—my grungy blue emergency back-up bike—off the wall it's rigged up to. "You're gonna die."

"Hey!" I manage to get the bike straightened up. "What if I do, and those are your last words to me?"

"Then I'll get to tell everyone at your funeral that I told you so."

"Wo-ow." I make a face at him, kicking the front door open. "Okay. Thanks. Are you going home now, or are you staying here and eating the rest of my food?"

"Oh, I'm definitely staying here and eating the rest of your food." He flops back onto the floor.

I force the handlebars through the doorway. "Lock the door after. See you tomorrow, weirdo."

"Yep. Don't die."

I grin. "Not today."

SIX

SO, I DON'T DIE. That's the good news. It's always nice to prove people wrong, even Oliver.

I make it all the way to city hall without hitting even a minor crisis. No robberies, no ice rays or heat rays or death rays, not even a jaywalker. I pull up in front of the magnificent marble building just after eleven, pause, and cut down the side of it to stash my bike in back. I don't have a lock, and it would be just like the universe to let me lose my car *and* have someone steal my bike in the same day.

The bad news, as I realize once I've sprinted back to the side of the building facing the street and tugged on the front door, is that city hall is closed.

This really shouldn't have been a surprise. It's almost midnight. Government officials have to sleep too, I guess. I dig around in my backpack until I find a pen.

"*To Department of Citizen Reimbursement,*" I scribble on top, holding the cap between my teeth. "*Technically it's still today even though it's like eleven o'clock at night, so please accept this late, and don't tell my boss or she will literally kill me, thank you.*" I run out of space to sign my name, recap the pen, and slide the envelope under the door. There. If Carly asks whether I gave the paperwork to city hall, I won't be lying.

As I turn around, I realize that the remnants of late-night traffic have died away, and the streets are virtually empty. It makes me uncomfortable. I always feel like I'm less likely to be murdered if there are more potential witnesses around. I jump down the grand staircase steps leading to the entrance of city hall two at a time, then run around the corner as fast I can, hoping nothing weird is lurking in the shadows.

My heartbeat is pounding with exertion as I duck back around the dumpster I've stashed my bike behind and start trying to swipe the rusted kickstand up. Why did I turn down a ride from Oliver? That was stupid.

As I'm lifting my leg off the ground to mount the bike and drag myself back home, the night silence is punctured by an impossibly loud whirring noise, like an electric drill, over my head. Before I even have time to look up to see what it is, everything around me is shaken by a giant *wham.*

My shriek is masked by the insanely loud reverberation of the metal dumpster, which shakes like a drum in response to whatever giant thing has crashed into it.

I swivel my backpack around so the bulletproof side is covering my front and extend my umbrella out like a sword. I don't have enough space to expand it into its shield, but it's still pretty heavy, and I could totally club somebody with it if I need to.

I crouch next to the dumpster, legs quivering. The rattling has stopped and the silence has returned; whatever fell into the dumpster hasn't moved.

My heart starts thumping again. Should I look? Should I just keep waiting here for whatever it is to jump out and attack me?

I'll just peek. It might not even be anything.

I peek.

I peek really, really slowly, just in case, with just the top of my eyeballs sticking over the edge, then lift my chin a fraction more when the angle isn't good enough for me to actually see what's inside the dumpster.

I almost don't see it, because the force from the fall was strong enough to bury it below a couple layers of trash, but then I realize what I'm looking at.

A foot clad in black leather is sticking out from underneath the garbage. A few feet farther up, an arm covered in thick, dark-gray fabric is visibly askew. The only other part of the person's body that I can see is his stomach, also coated in gray everywhere except for the five-inch-long gash ripping through both fabric and skin and gushing blood absolutely everywhere.

"Oh my *god*," I mutter, rehooking my umbrella to the side of my backpack and using my bike seat as a step-stool to boost me awkwardly over the rim of the dumpster. I let myself drop into the heap of trash, almost losing my balance in my attempt to not land on any body parts.

"Uh, okay. Don't panic," I say to both of us. "Sir? Please don't be dead. Your bones are probably all broken, but we can fix that." I begin pushing trash off him, starting with his torso and working outward, like I'm excavating a dinosaur fossil. What *happened*? Did he fall out of a helicopter? That would explain the whirring. Wow, he is *real* lucky this dumpster was here.

"Don't be dead. I'll call somebody, you'll be fine—" I keep moving trash aside, but look up at the sky, squinting through the fog, trying to figure out what attacked this guy. And, more importantly, whether it's coming back.

"It's, uh, it'll be okay—" I push away the trash bag flattening his face and cut my own sentence off short in shock.

I'm actually mad at myself for not recognizing that gray fabric immediately. How many times had I seen it before?

His blue-black hair is disheveled; his right arm is sprawled at an impossible angle; the gash in his stomach is even more grotesque now that I know it belongs to someone who is supposed to be invincible.

I know that one of the side-effects of being a Super is self-healing, though, so I'm really hoping Three's kicks in soon. Otherwise, Juniper is gonna feel *real* guilty.

I've never actually seen a Super this close before. With his eyes closed like that, he looks almost mortal. And young, really young. He can't be more than twenty or twenty-one. Man, he's having a day, isn't he? First a fight with his girlfriend, and now this.

It *almost* makes me forgive him for totaling my car, but not completely.

If he's a Super, he's definitely the only person who could survive falling out of the sky like that, though. I poke him in the cheek, right below his mask. "Uh, so are you dead, or what?"

His eyes snap open.

"Ahhhh!" I yell and scramble backward, throwing my backpack in front of my face like a shield.

I sit there for a few moments, waiting for something to happen, but he doesn't move. I peek out from over the top of my backpack. Three's eyes are still open, staring blandly up at the foggy sky. I inch a little closer, frowning. "Uh…so…you're okay then, right?"

He takes so long to respond that, at first, I think maybe he didn't hear me, but then he says, "Fine. Just need a few minutes."

"Oh, yeah, sure, okay," I say sardonically. "I'll just give you a few minutes to bleed to death. Do you want me to call an ambulance, or is it okay if I run away before I get blamed for your murder?"

"I'm not going to bleed to death," he mumbles, still staring up at the sky instead of me. "It just takes a few minutes to heal. Look."

I look down at the gash in his side. It looks smaller than it did a minute ago. The blood isn't even seeping out of it anymore. It's weird; I've never seen super-powered healing work up close before. I know that a lesser version of the formula used to give the Supers their invincibility is available to heal citizens who get injured in citywide catastrophes, but no one I know can afford it.

I sit down on my knees, still keeping my backpack on in front of me, and nod at the gash. "What did you do to yourself, anyway?"

"Stupid," he says, moving his shoulders in a halfhearted semblance of a shrug. "Helicopter. Propeller malfunction."

I shrug too, like catching a dying helicopter midair and fixing its propeller with your bare hands is the most normal thing ever. "So, did you fix it?"

He squints down his chin at me, still lying prone, but finally making eye contact. "*Obviously.*"

"You don't have to be *rude.*" I flare up. "It's not like you really look like you have things under control right now, you know."

He visibly sinks into his shoulders a bit. "Sorry. Just tired."

So, even Supers get cranky when they're tired. Weird. I can't believe this. I could have been at home finishing off a cake with Oliver, and instead I'm sitting in the garbage talking to a Super.

I don't realize that I muttered the last few words out loud until Three responds, cracking a smile. "Pretty cool, isn't it? Must be pretty exciting, getting to talk to me."

My minimal sympathy at his injuries vanishes. Arrogant, much? And why would I want to talk to him? These guys are moving targets. And right now, he's not even moving at all. I don't want to wait around for his inevitable chaos to find him and destroy me in the process.

But it's not like I can say that. Three probably isn't used to talking to citizens who aren't gushing adoration toward him. The shock might kill him.

✖ COLLATERAL DAMAGE ✖

I try my hand at subtlety instead. "So, it looks like you're stitching yourself up pretty nicely, huh? Think you might be able to move soon?"

"Probably," he says dismissively. "But to be honest, it's kind of nice to just lie here and not have to do anything for once."

I forget about trying to be subtle.

"You're kidding, right?" I snap. "You know you have basically unlimited power to do whatever you want without consequences, don't you? But sure, poor you, congratulations on getting to take a *nap* for once without launching a billboard through my car."

His deep brown eyes flicker with recognition. "You were there this morning? I destroyed your car?" He sounds almost apologetic.

"You actually remember? Incredible." I don't mean to sound so scathing, but it comes out that way anyway. It *is* incredible. I'd assumed it would be difficult for a Super to keep track of all the things they accidentally wreck.

"Look, I didn't mean—" He winces and adjusts himself so he's sitting up, propping his hands behind him. The movement brings his face into the light cast by the overhang illuminating the back exit of the building. His smooth, evenly-tanned skin looks almost fused to the dark-gray mask surrounding his eyes.

"For what it's worth, I'm sorry," he says with transparent sincerity. "I promise, the last thing I'm trying to do is make life harder for anyone."

Well, it ain't working is the response that instantly rises to my tongue, but I swallow it. He's apologizing. He's actually apologizing. It doesn't fix what he's done; nothing could. But it does make me hate him a little less.

Three continues, "Maybe the next guy—or girl, I guess—will be better at this."

I let out a snort of laughter before I can stop myself. I have years of experience testifying that the "next one" is rarely less destructive, but I don't say that. "I guess we'll find out," I say instead.

We sit there in awkward silence for a few moments. I don't know what to say next. All I can focus on is how, up close, he doesn't seem quite so immortally unapproachable. He just looks like a guy in a costume. Even the illusion of his famously perfect blue-black hair is shattered: from this close, I can see the fibrous strands close enough to recognize how plasticky they actually are. It's a wig.

I wonder how much of his appearance is real and how much is a façade gifted to him along with the rest of his genetic alterations. Was his jawline that sharp before, or is that a superhero thing?

"You're staring at me," Three says, but smugly, like he's used to having people stare at him and never gets tired of it.

"What?" I snap out of it. "Deflate your ego, Super. I'm staring at your wig."

The confidence immediately seeps from his face, and he brings one hand up to the sleek curl over his forehead defensively. "It's not a wig! It came with the powers!"

That doesn't make it not a wig, I want to say, but I don't want to make him feel worse. He did just fall out of the sky. "So…" I hunt for a new topic and settle on one that I'm actually interested in. "How much longer do you have to be a Super?"

He looks down at the silver band around his wrist, which flashes the time. "About seven or eight hours, I'd guess."

So, Oliver was right. I feel an unwanted jolt of panic go through me, and wonder why the news that it's Three's last day startles me so much. It's not like it'll affect *me*. Maybe I'd been getting used to him after all. I guess change is always terrifying, no matter the form.

"Oh," I reply. "Happy retirement?"

"Thanks." He doesn't look happy, but he manages a wry, teasing chuckle. "It's supposed to be a secret. Don't take over the city or anything."

Yeah, sure. A teenage barista, taking over the city with an

umbrella. That'd work well. "Pass," I say. "I'll let whichever loser inherits your costume handle city takeovers."

"What's that supposed to mean?" Three crosses his arms over his knees and narrows his eyes. "What's your problem with the Supers? You know, everyone else thinks we're wonderful."

"By 'everyone else,' I'm assuming you mean people with better protective gear, homes away from prime crisis locations, and a weird obsession with muscles," I snap. "I don't have any of those things, so my 'problem' is that all I want to do is save enough money to move someplace safer, and you guys constantly get in the way of that."

"Why would you want to move?" Three sounds puzzled. "This city's great."

I glare at him. "Maybe for someone who has powers. For me... not so much." He looks at me expectantly, and I realize that was a pretty vague response. I exhale through my nose in a stifled show of irritation. "You have to remember what it was like before you were a Super, don't you? Don't you remember not being able to leave your house without being loaded down with safety equipment? Didn't you ever lose someone you cared about in a crisis?"

His eyes widen. "Did you?"

This was such a mistake. I shouldn't have started this conversation. I fold my arms into my chest, to keep them warm as much as to shut everything else out. I suddenly wish I were wearing something other than a pair of koala-print boxer shorts and an "I survived my trip to the Midtown Aquarium" T-shirt. "Forget it."

"No." He sits all the way up and crosses his legs, inching a few centimeters closer to me. "Tell me. Your mom? Your dad?"

I look down. I don't owe him anything. I don't have to answer. But, "Both," I mutter.

He nods. "Me too."

When I look back up at him, he's still staring at me. "What?"

I demand. He'd better not be expecting a life story.

"What happened?" he asks, as predicted.

I scowl. "Why should I tell you? Why do you even care?"

"Was it a Super's fault?" I'm startled by his expression, by the stiffness in his jaw and the tension in his eyes. He's actually terrified that the answer will be yes. It's impossible to tell, though. In battles, no one really knows who directly causes the collateral damage. It could have been the Supers, or the villains, or both. All I know is that my mom was gone when I was nine, and my dad followed her just a couple of years ago, when I was fifteen.

When they were both gone, I lasted less than a month in the Shelter for the Misplaced, and then I snapped. The fake ID that got me out was just the first of a string of forgeries: the one that cleared me to rent an apartment, the one that let me drive a car without ever passing a test, the one that let me take the GED without a guardian's permission. The worst part—the part that makes my stomach twist and my brain try to push its own thoughts down into submission whenever the feeling comes up—is that when I lost my dad, I didn't feel broken or destroyed. I didn't lock myself in my room and cry for weeks. I just felt numb.

I guess I'd just spent too much of my life with the inherent knowledge that nothing was safe. Anything could disappear, at any time.

"No," I say, even though I don't know if that's the truth. Whether it was a Super or not, it wasn't this Three. He wasn't part of this yet. It would be pointless to hurt him just for the sake of hurting him. "It wasn't."

There are a few moments of silence. I'm just about to start climbing out of the dumpster, when, "Bank robbery," he says, and I freeze mid-climb.

"What?"

"They were taken hostage, and…well." He looks up at the sky. "The Supers didn't get to them on time. And then they were gone."

I sit back down, partially because my knees are howling at me for forcing them to do a squat.

"You're right," he says. "I'd forgotten what it was like before I was... before I was like this. My parents were reporters—kind of famous ones, actually. They broke the story about the original SuperVariant, so moving wasn't an option. And when they died..." He swallows hard, and I wonder if he's talked to anyone else about this. Probably Juniper, but that had to have been a while ago. And I know from experience that talking about losing people doesn't get easier over time. You think that having experienced the pain already will dull it, but it doesn't. It just means you know what to expect.

"You don't have to talk about this," I cut him off. "You just met me. You don't owe me anything." Besides, I can already guess how this ends. He lost his parents, but then he got offered the chance to be a Super. He probably wanted to help—to do better than the ones that came before him. To try to make sure no one else lost their family the way he did.

I don't know what to say. I suddenly realize how dumb this must look. A girl in koala-print boxers, sitting in a dumpster, talking to a muscly superhero about their dead families. So dumb, but so bizarrely comfortable as well. I try to remember the last time I talked—really talked—to someone who wasn't Oliver. And Sam's not allowed to tell anyone about his secret life as a Super, so apart from Juniper (who clearly found out somehow), he probably doesn't have anyone, either.

I feel a twinge somewhere in my chest cavity. What is this? Heartburn? Oh, no. It's *sympathy*. I feel sorry for him. I try to subdue it, but my mouth, acting independently of my brain, blurts out, "I'm sorry, Sam."

His head jerks up. "What did you just call me?"

Dammit. I hold my hands up. "Your girlfriend lives next door to me. Don't worry; I'm not going to tell anyone."

His face doesn't look less tense, but his shoulders loosen a bit and he slouches back into his seat. "It's not like it matters anymore at this point," he sighs. "You know, everything is falling apart. I'm losing my powers. Juniper's mad at me. Maybe I should just move away, too."

I let out a disbelieving snort before I can stop myself, and his eyes flick to mine, a scowl cutting through his layer of sorrow. "*What?*"

"You, that's what." I swing my backpack back over my shoulders and tighten both straps with a yank. "*Maybe I should just move away too.* See, *you* actually could. You could just decide right now to move, and be gone tomorrow. And I…" *I'll be stuck here forever. And even if I do manage to get out, my life will never look like yours.*

"You what?" When I look back at him, confusion is wrinkling the skin around his mask. "I don't get it. If you hate it so much here, why *don't* you just move now? Why wait?"

I choke back a snort of laughter. "Sam, I work at a coffee shop. I have no family. My apartment is missing a *wall*. If I lived anywhere else, the only house I could afford would be a cardboard box." I play with the handle of my umbrella. "It doesn't matter. I have a system. I know how to protect myself. I'm not dead yet."

"Yeah, a system based on luck." His eyebrows knit together in worry. Why is he *worried* about me? I just met him. Oh, this must be that compassion thing that probably landed him a job as a Super in the first place. Suddenly, his face lights up, and he looks at me with near-manic intensity. "Let me help you."

I look down at myself. I'm definitely not injured. I don't need to be rescued. "With what?"

"Moving."

That's a nice gesture, but all my possessions would probably fit in my backpack. He must see my confusion, because he elaborates, "Let me give you the money you need to move."

… *what?*

I can feel my eyes bug out. "Excuse?"

"You heard me," he says eagerly. "I'll give you the money you need to go someplace safer."

I can feel my jaw drop to the floor. There's no way he just said that. I must have misheard. Or hallucinated. "Don't mess around with me, Sam. I'm very tired. I don't have time for emotional roller coasters today."

"I'm not messing with you," he insists, and I can't ignore the sincerity in his voice. I can't let him do this. Right? It doesn't matter that my brain is already racing a million miles per hour, drawing visions of towns with Population: 3,000 and absolutely no Supers or powers or catastrophe. This is a joke. This isn't happening. "I can't let you do that." I stand up and crawl over the side of the dumpster, like walking away from him will erase his offer.

"Yes, you can." There's a familiar *whoosh* sound, and then he's standing in front of me. "The thing is, my parents actually left me a lot of money. I haven't really used any of it, because I haven't needed to. Actually, I guess I should have been doing more with it. Donating it, and stuff. I don't know. I thought working as a Super counted as doing enough to help people, but…" He frowns, looking guilty. "Anyway, helping you won't make a dent."

I start laughing. I can't help myself. "You're insane."

"I am not."

"Okay, then why?" I demand, still trying to keep myself from going into shock. A hysterical grin is plastered to my face. He has to be joking. There's no way he isn't joking. "Why would you do that? You just met me. You don't owe me anything."

"It sounds like this city owes you a lot." His dark eyes bore into mine. "As its representative, it's time you were reimbursed. Please, I want to help you. I ruined your car, and who knows what else. The last thing I wanted to do was make things harder for people, but it seems like your entire life has been one giant catastrophe. Whether that was directly my fault or not, I want to make up for it. Please. It's the least I can do."

I raise an eyebrow. "That's the stupidest thing I've ever heard. If that were the case, you'd have to give money to everyone else in this city." I fold my arms across my chest. "I'm not the only person whose car you've ruined, you know. Tell me the truth."

His eyes twitch. Maybe this was a mistake. Why did I fight so hard against this? I should have just taken the money. But then, "I don't know who I am if I'm not a Super, okay?" he blurts.

I lower my arms back down to my sides. "What?"

"I haven't been ordinary in two years." He clenches his fists. "I don't know what ordinary me is like anymore. I took this job because I wanted to help people. I always knew I wanted to be a Super, but I never planned for what I would do after." His eyes bore into me with so much intensity that I involuntarily take a step back, half-concerned they're going to start shooting out lasers or something. "I need to prove that I can still be a good person after today, even without the powers. I need to prove that I'll still be able to help people."

So there it is. For the first time, I realize why he must have been picked to be a Super in the first place. Does it come from a place of true compassion, or does he just have a desperate need to be liked?

You know what, actually? I don't care.

"Do you seriously understand what you're saying?" I ask slowly, just to make final sure. "You would really just, just *gift* me an entirely new life? Just like that? No strings or anything?"

"No strings or anything." He holds out a gloved hand. "You can trust me."

There are very few people that I trust completely apart from Oliver, but at this point, I have nothing to lose.

A life without catastrophe. Somewhere else. Somewhere *safe.* This can't be happening. But then again, nothing good has ever happened to me around the Supers.

Karma, I suddenly realize. *Is this karma?* I've never believed in it before, but maybe by giving that kid at the café my tip money, the universe is rewarding me. It's the only thing that makes this make any sense.

It's good enough for me.

The dam of paranoia and bewilderment I'd built around myself comes tumbling down, giving way to an unstoppable torrent of giddy, disbelieving elation. I take his hand.

"Okay," he says, grinning as he shakes it. I wince at his grip. "I'll come by tomorrow. I'd do it now, but—"

"No, no, I get it." I pull my hand back and try to discreetly shake the feeling back into it. "You've only got a few hours as a Super left. You want to go jump off some buildings and stop some criminals, right?"

Three laughs. "Right. Ten o'clock okay?"

"Yeah, sure, that's fine," I respond. I'm practically in a daze. Something in the back of my head tells me that I have work tomorrow, but I tell it to shut up. I'm obviously calling in sick.

Three gives my hand a parting squeeze that I barely register with both of his own. "I'm sorry again, for everything that's happened to you. I hope this helps."

"Yeah..." I suddenly realize what I need to be saying as he's prepping to take off into the sky again. "Three—Sam, wait!"

He looks back at me. "Yes?"

"I just—" I ball up my hand and tap it awkwardly against my leg. "Thank you. You didn't have to do this. But thank you."

He smiles like he depends on those two words for survival. "You're welcome," he says, tipping his head forward into a jaunty sort of bow, and in a flash, he's gone.

I look up at the dark speck disappearing into the clouds, unable to fight the irrational fear that as soon as I can't see him anymore, the promise he's made me will vanish with him. I try to remember that breathing exercise from the one yoga class I went to before I gave up. It was supposed to help with panicking.

It's happening. This is happening. *Inhale. Exhale.*

A new life, somewhere else. Somewhere safe. *Inhale. Exhale.*

I'm leaving. I'm getting out. I'm leaving tomorrow. *Inhale. Ex—*

I grab my bike. As I speed home, even the pain in my legs feels like a reminder that something better is finally coming.

SEVEN

IT'S NOT HARD TO PACK ALL MY STUFF. I figured out a while ago that the less stuff you own, the less stuff you can have destroyed.

Clothes. Toothbrush. Some photos. That's mostly it.

What am I forgetting? I'm forgetting something. *Oh.*

"Call Oliver!" I shout into my phone, then put it on speaker, prop it against a pillow, and listen to it ring as I leap around the corners of my room, checking for anything important I might have left behind.

"Oliver Lee, leave a message." Voicemail. "Oliver!" I practically sing, diving onto my mattress so my face is a couple of inches from the screen. "Call me back! Just—call me right now, okay?" I go to press the End Call button, then pause and lean back toward the phone. "It's an emergency!"

Okay. I press the red circle and survey my room. That should be everything.

I'm not worried about whether Oliver will come with me.

We've been talking about getting out for forever, once we got enough money. I'll go over there tomorrow and help him pack. We'll have to figure out which direction to go in, too. Someplace tiny and cute and barely on a map.

I can go to college.

I can live in an apartment with all four walls.

I can get to not fear for my life every second of the day.

My blood pressure is so jacked up, it feels like every molecule in my body is trying to run a marathon. I let myself collapse backward onto the mattress, bouncing a few times in a puff of ever-present dirt.

Goodbye, room. I think blissfully, listening to the scratchy sound of tiny rat feet scrabbling around above me. *You shan't be missed.*

I really don't think I'll be able to fall asleep, but I'm constantly underestimating myself.

I dream that I'm sitting on a porch in front of a tiny wooden house, with nothing in view for a mile in any direction. I look to my left, and Oliver is sitting on one of those old-timey rocking chairs, chewing on a brownie. He looks over at me. "Do you hear that?"

I cock my head and glance around. "I don't hear anything."

He grins. "Exactly."

And then I wake up and the world's on fire.

MY FIRST THOUGHT WHEN I regain consciousness is *barbecue*? But then I open my eyes and see the flames.

"Oh, come *on*," I shriek, and leap out of bed, kicking my backpack away from the fire licking the edge of the wall. So far, the flames are only confined to two walls, having seeped in through the partially open door, but the smoke is already flooding my room. I quickly grab a sweatshirt out of my backpack, force it over my head, and yank the drawstrings so that only my eyes stick out through the opening, shielding my mouth.

"Decided to go out with a bang, did we?" I cough into my sweatshirt as I pull on my boots, then snatch up my backpack and umbrella and jam my safety helmet on my head without fastening the straps. "So long, apartment! So long, Lunar City!" I war cry over the scratchy, crackling sound of crumbling wood and kick open the door.

I immediately start coughing again. Oh man, the kicking-down-the-door thing was a mistake. The whole living room is on fire. The tarp protecting the missing wall is almost disintegrated, replaced with a column of writhing orange flame that's offering glimpses of the early morning light outside. Gray smoke curls around the room. There's no indication as to where the fire started, but my money is on one of the neighbor's kitchens. This building is like eighty thousand years old. The stoves all suck, and the smoke alarms don't work. As if to prove my point, a thick tendril of smoke twists around my own alarm on the ceiling. Nothing sounds. *Useless piece of junk.*

I spot my bike propped up against the wall where I left it last night and run for it, snatching it up in one fluid motion and sprinting for the door. It'll get me to Oliver's place faster. I use my sweatshirt sleeve to turn the handle and burst into the hallway, immediately almost getting bowled over by a neighbor from down the hall. "Out of the way!" he bellows, carrying a scowling cat out in front of him like a battering ram.

The rest of the hallway is in a similar state of chaos. Everyone stampedes in their pajamas toward one of the two stairwells, clutching bulky armfuls of possessions and screaming their heads off. It's like the world's worst slumber party.

I pick the south stairwell, in the opposite direction of the frantic man with the cat, and stumble down the steps. The bike wheels bang off the walls as I round each tight corner.

On the fourth floor, I start to notice that the smoke is getting thinner, and the air more breathable. I know that smoke rises, but it doesn't feel like that's what this is. I chance opening a stairwell door into the hallway, just to peek. Nothing. No flames.

Weird.

I keep running, until I finally topple out onto the street and set the bike down. I expect all the evacuees from my floor to be milling around in their pajama pants, waiting for the fire department to get here, but there's still a fair amount of running and screaming going on throughout the street itself. I pick out one person standing on the sidewalk, wide-eyed, mouth gaping, and follow the direction of his pointing finger with my eyes.

I immediately have to shield them from the glare. Less than a block away, a luminous red whirlwind of a man is summoning fire like he's conducting an orchestra. Crimson light bursts from his palms with each flick of his wrist, transforming into flames that devour trees, street lamps, storefronts. Heat singes my skin; even the air feels hungry. My fingers twitch toward my umbrella despite the distance. *What the heck is he aiming for*?

The answer suddenly becomes clear when another figure materializes just to the left of the last fireball, which whizzes past his ear and disintegrates against a sandwich shop's fireproof door. SuperVariant Four skids to a stop in a perfect superhero side lunge, one arm braced on the ground. He whips his head up. "Missed me!" he taunts.

Of course. Silly me.

I glance up at my building. The isolation of the fire to only one part of it makes sense now. It looks like the flames are containing themselves from the seventh floor upward, but that could change if the fire department doesn't get here soon. I don't want to stick around in case the whole apartment decides to crumble all the way down onto the street.

I throw one leg over my bike, but as I'm lifting the other onto the pedal, something slams into the concrete in the center of the street next to me, creating a ripple that cracks the surrounding pavement in a wide arc and causes the entire ground to quake spectacularly. The bike topples out from underneath me and I crash to the ground in a tangle of legs and wheels.

"Ow," I groan, rubbing the scrape the gravel leaves on my arm, and squint up sideways at the new arrival—someone tall and fierce, draped in a knee-length cape crackling with its own energy. She straightens and dusts some nonexistent dirt off a deep purple sleeve. "Sorry I'm late."

There's an eruption of cheers from the people on the sidewalk around me, who all crowd in front of my bike to get a closer look. I crane my neck to see through their legs.

There's a slight blur, and then a pair of dark orange boots appear next to SuperVariant One's purple ones. "What took you so long?" I hear Four say irritably.

"Don't tell me you can't manage Doctor Defect for five minutes without me."

Seriously? Doctor Defect? Again? I roll to my knees to get a better look at the flamethrower. Yep, there's that infamous, pointy-jawed, scar-streaked face and that maniacal expression. One day in prison. This has to be a record. "Give up!" he screams as he launches a flaming chunk of payment toward the two Supers.

"Well, since you asked so nicely." Four's masked face appears in my view for half a second as he ducks from the attack, which freezes in midair just a few feet from One's outstretched hand. She brings the other hand up, then shoots the fiery ball of cement straight up into the sky, where it explodes like an extra-destructive firework. Ash rains down on everyone. The whole street cheers. I get a stray piece of it in my eye.

"I don't know how he got out again," Four yells, and I mentally agree with him. Who is guarding this prison? Toddlers? "And I don't know what the fireballs are made of or where he's storing them. I can't get close enough without catching fire. You've got this, right?" I hear Four say, my eyes squeezed shut, trying to rub the ash out.

"Obviously," replies One. "But—hey, where are you going?"

His response is a disembodied echo in the wind; he's already speeding away. "There's people still in there!"

I squeeze my non-ashy eye open and catch a glimpse of a streak of orange dashing up the side of my apartment building before it mingles with the orange of the enflamed seventh story, disappearing. I wonder vaguely whether Sam has made it out yet, and how much he must hate not being able to be a part of this except as a useless victim like the rest of us.

I scramble up off the sidewalk, righting my bike. My safety helmet's fallen off, and I manage to jam it back on my head just in time to avoid a wave of flying chunks of road—the result of One telekinetically lifting Doctor Defect fifty feet in the air and slamming him back down, shattering even more of the street. "What are you waiting around for?" She turns her head toward me and the rest of the crowd on the sidewalk without pointing her hands away from Doctor Defect. "Get out of here! *Run!*"

Everyone's favorite trigger words. The crowd doesn't need to be asked twice, turning and sprinting with a vigor to rival the kinds of people who put marathon participation stickers on their cars.

I perform the regular mental check—helmet, umbrella, backpack—and hop back on my bike. I give myself exactly two seconds to pause, looking up at the apartment building that has been my home for the last year. The pyre it has been turned into seems like an appropriate send-off. "Bye, house," I eulogize, then kick off, joining the throng of citizens stampeding away down the street without a second look back.

EIGHT

I GET TIRED OF TRYING NOT to run over people with my bike after less than two blocks, and swerve off down a side alley to get away from the crowd. Besides, it's always best to stay away from large groups of people in times of crisis. I've noticed that most self-appointed "bad guys" tend to go for quantity, not quality, when they aim at citizens.

Something explodes down the street behind me, sending a wave of heat washing over my back and light streaming down the near-pitch-black street. The early-morning natural light is being blocked by all the buildings, and I'm now too far away from the main road for any street lamps. I pedal faster, turning left at the next intersection of back alleyways so I can coast down the slight incline. I've never been down this street before; I hope I'm still going the right way to get to Oliver's. It's weird that he hasn't called me back yet. He's not going to have very much time to pack, at this rate. But boy, is he gonna lose it when he finds out we're finally moving.

I awkwardly unzip my backpack behind me with one hand while still trying to steer the bike with the other, and fumble around for my phone. I almost tip the bike again trying to untangle it from my key lanyard, but when I finally get it out and check the screen, one eye still navigating the alley in front of me, there's nothing. No missed calls.

"Call Oliver!" I repeat into the mic until the little robot registers the command. There's a ten-second dial tone, then nothing. I glare at the screen, infuriated. *Why isn't he answering*? I reach around to shove the phone back in through the open zipper.

The inevitable finally happens. I'd been tempting fate too much by trying to multitask while operating a sort-of vehicle, and by the time I shift my attention from my backpack to the street in front of me and see the van, it's too late. I swerve my handlebars to the left, but the angle is too sharp, and all it does is jerk the tire ninety degrees. The last thing I see is a pair of screaming headlights as the bike screeches to a halt, throwing me over the handlebars.

"OW..."

Well, I'm capable of vocally responding to pain, so I guess I'm not dead. I crack my eyelids open, afraid that I'm going to see my legs all twisted up like a pretzel and my intestines spilling onto the sidewalk. Instead, I see a confusing mass of shapes. When my eyes finally adjust to the darkness, I realize that I'm staring up at the buildings lining the street, which I'm sprawled on the ground beneath.

The skin on my arms stings like it's been peeled with a cheese grater, and my bones feel weighted and stiff, as though they want nothing more than to drag me right into the pavement. But I can breathe. Nothing feels broken. I'm not dead. Thank god, I was wearing my safety helmet and backpack, which seem to have cushioned the most vital parts of my body.

With a groan of effort and an immense amount of protests from my limbs, I manage to shakily push myself back up to my feet, staggering as the street tilts around me. When the ringing in my head steadies, I realize that one of the formless shapes in my field of vision is the car that almost hit me, its left front wheel buried in the brick of the building next to us. It's a boxy gray monster of a van, like those industrial-strength ones they use for transporting money. It must have hit the brakes and swerved to the left, which I'm assuming is the only reason I'm not dead. But the headlights are still on and the car is still running, which makes me concerned for the driver.

My legs are still shaky and unreliable, but I stumble up onto the step attached under the van's door and try to peer through the side window. When the tinted glass is too dark, I reach behind me and grapple around all the objects clipped to my backpack until I find the one that feels like a flashlight and yank it off, shining it through the front windshield.

A surge of cold terror sears my veins instantly. The driver is motionless, his head tilted back into his nondescript cap, a trickle of blood running in a thin river from his forehead over his closed eye and down his neck, where a pool of crimson is blossoming into the top of his starched white shirt.

Oh my God.

Oh my *God*.

Crap. Crap, crap, crap, crap.

"Hey!" I whisper-shout, tapping on the glass. "Come on, buddy. Don't be dead. Please don't be dead."

Crash.

The noise from the back of the car erupts into the early morning quiet like a shotgun blast, the shock of it propelling me off the step and back onto the pavement. I stumble to regain my footing, my stomach curdling as I wait for the follow-up noise that would indicate a non-dead person is back there.

Silence.

I unclip my umbrella from my backpack with my other hand and expand it into a shield, then take cautious steps around the side of the van until I'm close enough to peer around the rear, my back pressed to the gas valve behind the passenger-side door.

The left back door of the van hangs slightly off its hinge, giving way to three or four inches of impenetrable darkness within. Something seeps out of the cracks at the bottom of the doorframe, slowly dripping onto the pavement. My stomach clenches for an instant—*blood*—but shining the flashlight beam in its direction reveals that the liquid is a pale, luminous blue, not red.

I inch closer and pull at the warped metal shell, straining until there's a space big enough for me to crawl through, then press the button that collapses my umbrella enough to fit it through the opening and clamber inside.

It's a mess. Large black crates that were probably neatly stacked at one point are in utter disarray all over the floor. One of them is cracked open, all of its contents spilling out. I lean down to get a closer look. A bundle of silky gray fabric, a fancy-looking watch, a bunch of papers. Two or three small vials of blue liquid, one of which is completely shattered, clearly causing the leakage by the door. A human foot.

I leap back, nearly dropping my flashlight.

What the—

My blood pressure picks up speed again, then doubles further as I lean in closer and realize that it's not a detached foot, thank god, but is instead connected to the lower half of a leg riddled with a strange crisscross pattern of blue lines. Some kind of tattoo? The lines look too luminous to be made of ink. I'm glad that the foot is connected to something, but if that something is a dead body, I am so done.

I try to move the boxes trapping the rest of the foot's body, struggling to shift the thick metal while still holding my umbrella and flashlight. After I get all the boxes cleared away, the entire body is still covered with a massive, seven-foot-long sheet of solid steel. I groan and shrug out of my backpack, dumping it in a pile along with my umbrella and flashlight. Plunged back into darkness, I put all of my minimal muscle into pulling the thick sheet over. "Come on," I mutter. "Please don't be dead."

I get a good grip on one end of the steel and grunt with effort until the heavy thing flips, leaping backward at the last second to avoid being crushed. The earsplitting crash it makes when it collides with the van floor seems to reverberate through my bones, and I wince as I fumble for my flashlight and turn it back on.

I cringe in horror immediately as the light returns. The foot—and the body connected to it—are strapped to the sheet of steel itself, like a patient in an ambulance. Or a corpse on a gurney, I guess.

I feel my cheeks turn red as I realize the guy is basically naked, apart from a nearly pointless strip of white material. But the worst part isn't the nudity—because hey, nice abs, I guess—it's the blue crisscross pattern that I'd noticed before. It's definitely not a tattoo. It's his *veins*.

I feel like gagging. The horrific, neon-blue veins are practically bulging out of his body, turning his skin into a pulsing network of thin, eerie tendrils. They cover every inch of him, from his ankles up his body to his neck, where they reach like tiny, grotesque hands up toward his—

My heart drops down into the pit of my stomach. The flashlight falls from my hand, and I hear a crack as it hits the floor. I cover my mouth with both hands to stop myself from screaming.

The face is swollen, putrid as a rotting watermelon, with unseeing eyes staring horrifically out of a face striped with those bulging blue veins. It's the eyes that do it. I might not have recognized him otherwise. You can change anything about a person's face, but you can always recognize someone by their eyes. And I sure recognize this person.

"Sam?" I whisper.

NINE

IT'S HIM. I'M CERTAIN OF IT. I feel sick.

How did this *happen*? Who could have done this to him? The Supers are invincible. Their immune systems are practically made of steel. I once saw SuperVariant One get shot in the head, *literally* in the head, and get back up after about ten minutes.

This doesn't make any sense. I can't think. I can barely breathe between the shock and the smell of rotting flesh. What does hyperventilation feel like? I've never experienced it, but this feels pretty darn close. The flashlight is doing nothing, pointed at a box, but the image of Sam's bulbous, empty eyes and his smooth skin riddled with pulsing, grotesque blue veins will be seared into my retinas forever.

He didn't deserve this. *Nobody* would deserve this. This poor guy—

And poor me, too, an awful, selfish part of me whispers deep down. I hate myself for even thinking it, considering the situation, but I can't help it. Sam is gone now, and with him went my best chance to be able to get out of this city.

Before I can get my panic under control, I hear a muffled voice through the wall of the storage trunk.

"Came out of nowhere. Yeah, I don't know what happened. Route compromised... send backup. 10–4. No. No. Yeah, boss, I'll go check."

I have no idea what any of that means, but "I'll go check" can only be referring to the contents of this van. And I may only have a minimal grasp of what's going on, but I know enough to guess that I probably *don't* want to be found back here by the owner of that voice.

In a flash, I scoop up everything in the vicinity of my flashlight, hoping that my umbrella and backpack end up in the pile.

A quick peek out through the eight-inch crack left by the open back door fortunately offers no view of an armored madman coming to attack me yet, so I shimmy back out and drop to the ground as lightly as possible. As soon as my feet hit the pavement, I hear the driver-seat door slam, rocking the entire van.

Well, at least the driver's not dead. The relief from that observation quickly vanishes as I hear heavy boots start to round the corner to the back of the van. Still carrying all my stuff awkwardly in my arms, I maneuver one hand free and use it to lift my sweatshirt hood over my head, just in case, and try to bolt for my bike as fast as I can without creating any more noise.

Heart pounding—*please don't see me, please don't see me*—I carefully pull it back upright, begging the rusty metal frame not to give me away.

And then, as I'm about to swing my leg over and speed away, the handlebar squeaks.

It sounds like just about the loudest noise in the entire world.

Before I can react, a face appears from behind the van.

The driver is so streaked with his own blood, he looks like

a zombie, or the survivor of a movie about them. Even from this distance, I can see his pale eyes narrow in the glow of the headlights.

Well. I can abandon all hope of a subtle getaway.

"Hey—" he shouts and reaches for his hip, then looks down in apparent confusion. Whatever he was reaching for—hopefully a gun that he's misplaced—isn't there. I don't wait for him to find a different weapon. I practically throw myself over my bike and windmill the pedals as fast as my legs will let me. If I make it out of this alive, this is definitely going to count as my cardio for, like, ever. Already, my heart feels like it's going to explode.

He can't outrun me on foot, I tell myself, panting. I can't even steer in a straight line. The bike zigzags out of control over the street. *His car is busted, he can't outrun me on foot—*

Something whistles past me.

A trash receptacle a few feet away from me glows silver for less than a second, and then it warps into itself, each half of the thick plastic contorting in an opposite direction, until it's just a smooth, twisted coil.

I turn back around, confusion and terror warring for control inside me, and see that the driver has his fist pointed at me, with a silver, spherical something attached to the top of a cuff on his wrist. The sphere emits a faintly pulsing light—enough to illuminate the driver's thin mouth and bleeding cheek—and then the light focuses into a narrow silver beam, aiming straight for me.

I've never seen anything like it before. The supervillains' usual homemade tech is never this sleek, this effortless. They're always big and clunky and ultimately ineffective, like that stupid robot from earlier. I've never seen the person holding it before, either.

A surge of energy streaks past my nose, striking someone's back door. The metal twists off its hinges, folding itself into a pretzel before clattering to the ground.

I suddenly have a vision of the beam hitting me, of my body twisting inside out until my organs wrap around my limbs.

Without wasting another moment analyzing the weapon or its owner, I finally get enough control over my handlebars to whip the bike around the corner and into a smaller side alley, pedaling for my life.

EVERYTHING HURTS. My hands are shaking so badly, I almost veer into buildings twice. Under any other circumstance, I would have already stopped to take a break, but my brain still has enough sense to try to keep everything together, and is insisting that I have to *keep moving, just keep moving, don't look back, keep moving.*

Every crank of my squeaky pedals sounds like a chant: *dead, dead, dead, dead.*

Dead, like Sam's grotesque, warped body in the back of that van.

Dead, like I'm definitely going to be if the person who did that finds out who I am or what I saw.

Never in my life have I wished that I'd just stayed in bed so much.

I'm not even going to try to puzzle piece together any of it yet—not the vials or the blue veins or the man in the van or *anything*. I'm gonna need a lot more coffee first. And a lot more certainty that I've put enough distance between myself and that terrifying piece of tech.

Without even realizing which direction I've been heading in, I suddenly find myself right back where I started, at the smoldering remains of my former apartment building. I skid to a stop, putting one leg down to prop myself up, and survey the damage.

The flames are gone, but the building is still smoking fantastically from the seventh floor upward. Some of the squad from the fire department are on giant ladders, half-heartedly poking hoses into the ashy clouds. The rest are on the ground, trying to calm down all the people begging them to go back in and save their stuff.

"—and *I'm* telling *you* that that's im*possible*—"

I instinctively turn toward the familiar voice. A few feet away from me, a tall girl with about three feet of pale blonde hair cascading down her back is berating a firefighter, who has his hands up and looks as though he's on the verge of quitting his job. The girl stands out as the only person in the area not in pajamas; she looks like she's coming either to or from work, wearing a dove-gray dress under a pale pink sweater. She taps one of her shoes on the ground impatiently as she snaps at the firefighter, and the noise triggers my memory. *Juniper?*

Oh, *no*.

I'm gonna have to tell her. *Somebody* has to tell her.

I hope she's not a shoot-the-messenger type.

I wheel my bike slightly closer, waiting for a chance to interrupt her, but can't help eavesdropping.

"Ma'am," says the fireman, in a voice teetering precariously between forced calm and despair. "I told you, there was nothing we could do. We were just too late. I'm—I'm very sorry."

"*Bull*shit." Juniper hisses. "There is *no* way he died in there. I don't care what you think. It wasn't him."

"Hon, it was a *very* powerful fire. Your—boyfriend, was it?—he probably just didn't wake up in time. Believe me, I've known plenty of strong, healthy men who have—"

Juniper cuts him off, looking like she's considering ripping his tongue out of his throat. I mentally give props to the guy for not disintegrating into ash from the ice in her gray-eyed stare. "I don't believe you. Let me see him."

"Miss, I can't—"

"That's supposed to be him, isn't it?" She thrusts a finger at a black body bag a few yards behind the fireman that I hadn't paid attention to before. "Let me *see* him."

"But I can't just—"

Exhaling in frustration, Juniper shoulders the officer aside and makes it to the bag in a matter of seconds. "Miss, you cannot—" shouts a nearby chief, but before he can reach her, she's snatched the zipper and yanked it open.

Nobody has been paying any attention to me next to Juniper's fury, so it's not hard for me to sneak up and peer into the bag with her. We both look down in silence, her in shock and me in confusion.

The face inside definitely looks like Sam, sort of, but it's practically melted from the burns. I have to stop myself from gagging for the second time this morning. The hair and skin tone are exactly the same, but most of his face looks like it's been coated in charred plastic. It's almost worse than the blue-veined Sam from an hour ago. I look away.

The chief who had shouted at Juniper materializes, leaning down and zipping Sam's face back into darkness. "That's enough, miss," he says curtly, then nods at the firefighter. "Get her out of here, please."

He nods back and takes Juniper's elbow, leading her back to the sidewalk. Still essentially invisible, I follow. She's stopped fighting, letting herself be led away by the arm while her other hand covers her lower face. Only her eyes peek out, wide and disbelieving.

"I tried to tell you," the man whispers apologetically. "I'm—I'm really sorry, miss." With an awkward pat on her shoulder, he retreats back into the fray of displaced tenants.

I stand a few feet away from her, zoning out at her shoulders, which are shaking with silent tears.

This doesn't make any sense. I know what I saw this morning. *That* was the real Sam. Who would go to the trouble of killing him and then disguising a burn victim as his body? He was dead either way, so what was the point?

Probably feeling me watching her, Juniper's head suddenly

snaps up in my direction. *Oh god, I must look so creepy.* Her gray eyes narrow.

She surreptitiously brushes underneath her eyes with her fingertips, but only manages to streak the tears in a pitiful stripe across either side of her face. "What are you looking at?" she tries to snap, but the edge in her voice is gone.

I swallow. "I—Hi, I'm Meg. I live next door to you."

She stares back at me, motionless. Her red-rimmed eyes seem to say, *And?*

"I—" Wow, there's no non-terrible way to start this conversation. I just blurt it out. "I don't think that was your boyfriend."

Her eyes narrow again. "*What?* How would you know?"

"I, um." I glance around, suddenly paranoid. "I sort of—I think I found his body this morning. In the back of a van. Something really weird is going on here; I think—"

Juniper clenches her fists, and first I think she's going to hit me, but then I realize that she's trying to stop herself from shaking. "What do you mean, you found his body?" Her teeth are gritted so tightly, the freckles on her nose look like they're going to pop off her face.

I swallow hard a second time, then give the fastest highlights reel I can about everything that happened this morning, especially the blue veins and the murderous driver. "And then he tried to shoot me with this insane weapon, and now I'm here," I finish, feeling extremely uncomfortable. "That's all I know, I swear. Listen, don't you think that's weird? I mean why would—"

I'm about to tell her about my suspicions about the body double Sam, but she cuts me off.

"I don't believe this," she whispers.

I've never been good at comforting people. I try to pat her on the shoulder. "I know. I'm so sorry, Juniper. He didn't deserve to—"

She swats my hand away. "No, I don't believe *you*. *Either* of you." She glares in the direction of the man from before, then turns her eyes back on me. I take an involuntary step back.

"He *isn't* dead. That's not him. It's impossible." She draws herself up to her full height, and I'm terrified to find that when she's not bent over crying, she's at least six inches taller than me. She could totally step on me, and I would die. She continues, "I don't know what's going on here, what kind of *joke* is being pulled, but I'm going to find out."

And without another word, she pivots and stalks away.

I stare after her retreating back in silent disbelief and fury. Her boyfriend is *dead,* and she can't pull her nose out of the air for two seconds to *listen* to me?

Okay. That's fine. I don't need her. I'll just call the police myself, and—

Before I can finish my thought, something slams into me with enough force to knock me over like a bowling pin.

I stagger backward, all the air forced out of my body, but I don't have enough balance to prevent myself from falling to the ground. My attacker goes down with me, pinning me down. My breathing stops—partly from terror, partly from the weight on my lungs.

They found me.

TEN

MY PARALYSIS ONLY LASTS a couple of seconds, and then my brain starts working again. I can't believe they found me so quickly. Why did I dye my hair such a loud shade of red? The original goal was to make it easier for Oliver to find me in a crowd if we got separated during a crisis, but now that's clearly working against me. I should have just invested in a tour guide flag.

I start screaming with my eyes shut, lashing out with every limb. No way am I letting them take me and do to me whatever they did to Sam. And why isn't anyone paying attention to what's happening? Did all the firemen swarming the area go on break at once?

It's not until my fist makes a sharp connection with something hard, something that flinches back and snaps, "Meg, *stop*!" that I quit moving and look at my attacker. Familiar dark eyes flashing with shock meet mine.

"*Oliver*?"

"Who did you *think* it was?" he demands, climbing off my legs and massaging his jaw. "What was that about? Have you lost your *mind*?"

"*Me*?" I wipe the dirt on my hands on my boxer shorts and look at him incredulously, still shaking. "I thought I was being attacked! Who *does* that? What's wrong with you?"

"What's wrong with *me*? You're the one who—" He spikes both hands through his bangs, pushing them off his forehead. "Do you know how it felt to wake up this morning and hear on the news that your *building* was on fire?"

He throws his arms wide, and at first I think that it's just for emphasis, but then he lunges forward on his knees and wraps his arms around my neck so tightly, my vision blurs.

"Oliver—" I gasp over his shoulder. "Choking. Not breathing."

"I can't believe I missed all your calls," he mumbles somewhere over my head. "And I got here as soon as I could, but you weren't anywhere. I thought you must have gotten trapped under something and..." he trails off meaningfully and shakes his head, the movement ruffling my hair. "God, the last thing I said to you was *don't die*. Like it was a joke. Like it was nothing. I can't—" He tightens his hold. "I lost everybody else. I *will not* lose you too."

Nausea and guilt flood me like they've been bottled and injected right into my veins. *Don't die.* It is a joke—our joke, to make the chaos seem less real. I'd become too casual about it. I'd forgotten what it felt like to *really* fear that something was going to happen to him. He's my constant; he's been my constant since grade school, when I lost my mom.

And I really could have died. In three separate ways this morning, by my count. Really died. Not a joke; a consequence. And if what happened to Sam is any point of reference, I wouldn't just have died; I would have vanished, another unimportant casualty in an everlasting, city-wide struggle between so-called good and evil. Oliver would never have known what happened to me.

This must be what the SuperVariants feel like all the time, I suddenly realize. *This is why they can't tell their families what their job is. The worry would eat them all alive.*

And I know in that moment that I can't tell him what I saw. What happened to me. Any of it.

I'll just tell the police as soon as Oliver is at work, and they'll handle it. They'll find Sam, and the truth about his murder. And then this will all be over.

"Don't worry, I just ran away," I tell him. It's not a lie, technically. "I should have left a message telling you I was okay. But I just ran away from the fire. That's all that happened." *Okay, that part is a lie.*

He pulls back and exhales with no sign of mistrust. "Next time," he says, relief etched in his face. "*Text* me that like a *normal person.*"

"I know. You're right. I'm sorry." I stare at the wreckage of the apartment building, my brain whirring at a million miles a second, processing the short but crucial list of things I really, really need to do. *Get off the street. Call the police. Don't let Oliver find out.*

"Okay." The voice comes from above me now, and I turn and realize that Oliver's back on his feet, reaching out a hand to help me up. "Let's go."

Does he think I'm going to work today? "Where?" I ask cautiously.

He rolls his eyes. "My apartment, genius. You're obviously staying with me."

The offer wipes out the rest of the buzzing in my head, replacing my anxious planning with genuine surprise. There's a reason we don't live together already, and it has nothing to with us not wanting to be roommates. See, Oliver lost his parents too, just like me. They died in a fire at their office building two years ago, when he was sixteen. I don't know how Oliver managed to evade being put in the Shelter for the Misplaced, but he still lives in the apartment they used to share. No one has even been in his parents' room since they died. And he keeps the rest of the apartment a museum-quality level of pristine, exactly the way it was the last morning they left for work, which is why we always hang out at my apartment even though it's at least ten times crappier than his. I know that letting someone, even me, in there is hard for him. "Are you sure?" I ask. "You don't have to do that."

He lets out an incredulous snort. "Are you serious? You think I'm going to—what, let my best friend sleep on the street? Or back at the Shelter? Come on, Meg. I hope you know me better than that."

Warmth tingles through me, cutting through the mountain of panic that's been stacking up since I woke up this morning. "You," I say, taking his hand and letting him help me up, "are the only good thing in this entire city."

"Yeah, I know." He lets his face relax, then walks over to my bike and props one foot up on the peg jutting out the back wheel. "Now come on, give me a ride back. I don't know *why* I thought running here would be faster than taking my truck."

ELEVEN

IT TAKES FOREVER TO GET OLIVER out of his apartment once we're there. He makes sure I'm going to be okay on the couch for at least ten minutes (since I refuse to take his parents' room), and then I have to explain to him that he has to go to work without me (since I'm pretty sure you get a free pass when your house burns down), and then he has to search for his spare key in case I want to leave, and by the end of it all, I just want to yell, *Oliver, I love you, but you're preventing me from reporting a murder.*

As soon as I'm sure Oliver isn't going to come running back up the stairs, complaining about how he's forgotten his keys or something, I leap off his couch, lunge for my backpack, and tip it upside down, letting everything spill out in a disorganized clump. I poke at the mess, sifting through it for my phone and shoving aside all my other unnecessary possessions—clothing, photos, tiny vial of blue liquid.

Huh?

✖ COLLATERAL DAMAGE ✖

I pluck out the bottle and examine it. It's one of the vials from the overturned box in the van. *How did that get in there?*

Oh. Before, when I heard the driver coming, and grabbed everything I could carry, it must have gotten scooped up with everything else in the dark.

I pull it closer to my face so I can read the label. I don't know what I was expecting—definitely not, like, nutritional information—but the only thing on it is a large, handwritten *3.5 final backup* label, which isn't even a little helpful. I peel it off to get a better look at the vial's contents.

The bottle is only about two inches tall, has the circumference of a dime, and is filled about three-quarters of the way with that blue liquid, which sort of looks like the syrup they put in blue raspberry slushes.

I uncork the top and sniff, realizing in retrospect that that was probably a terrible idea, since it could be toxic and I could die. It doesn't smell toxic, but it also doesn't smell like blue raspberry slush syrup.

I'm so transfixed on this bottle that I almost don't notice that my pile of clothes is wriggling. Almost, until the wriggling gives way to the second thing I definitely did not put in my backpack: something small and black and furry with a long, fleshy tail.

I lunge for it before it can take another step on Oliver's pristine carpet. "You little stowaway," I mutter, clutching it between my fists, nestled in with the bottle. It's the smallest rat I've ever seen, but has too much hair to be a baby. It has to be the runt. "I *knew* you guys were in the roof. You're gonna have to restart your colony somewhere else, because I—."

It bites me.

"*Ow!*" I screech and drop it, forgetting that I'm still holding the open vial, which tumbles out of my hands onto the floor along with the rodent. Most of the liquid lands on the rat itself, but the rest seeps into the spotless carpet around my knees. Oliver's going to *kill* me.

"Stay," I order the rat, which seems to be momentarily paralyzed from being drenched, and run for a paper towel.

In seconds, I'm back, an entire roll clutched under my arm, but before I can do anything with it, something gray and rough-looking begins to spread out of nowhere over the rat's tail, expanding over it like a second skin.

No, not like skin. Like *armor*.

I freeze. *I'm crazy. I'm hallucinating. I haven't had coffee yet today, and now my brain has shut down.*

The rat flicks its tail against the carpet with a sound like a tiny whip, and neat strands of nylon peel away in a perfect line.

Okay. Bye. I'm out. I did not sign up for this.

I want to run screaming out the door, but it's like watching a train crash. I can't look away.

The small rat pads around in a circle, armored whip-tail curling around it, then looks up at me and lets out a high squeak, which gives me a better look at its teeth. I can't remember what rat teeth are supposed to look like, but I don't think 'bright white, perfectly even' is the correct description. It's difficult to tell, but I could swear his matted fur is sleeker and shinier now too; his eyes bigger and less beady. It would be almost cute if the entire situation wasn't so, you know, terrifying.

And then it starts to scamper away, beelining for the space under the couch.

"Oh my god, this isn't happening," I shriek, lunging for it and missing. This has very quickly become the worst day of my life, in a very long string of worst days. "Demon rat" tops the list of weird, bar-none. I lunge for the back of the couch, turning it over to form a barricade that the rat can't fit under, then dance around frantically, looking for a better weapon. How am I supposed to get rid of it? I can't. What am I going to tell Oliver—that I accidentally mutated a rat and now it just lives here? I might as well just burn this apartment down, too, and be done.

My eyes land on the kitchen. I can fix this. All I have to do is trap it long enough to bring it outside. Then somebody else can deal with it.

I bolt for an empty pasta sauce jar sticking out of the top of the trash can, then pivot back toward the living room. The rat has started trying to climb up the bottom of the overturned couch, so it's easy to spot. I smash the mouth of the jar onto the fabric around it, scoop it inside, and slam on the lid, panting like I've defeated a much bigger enemy.

What. Is happening. Today?

What is that blue stuff? It's clearly responsible for whatever just happened to this animal. I can't believe I just had it lying around in my *backpack.*

I'm suddenly distracted from examining the near-emptied bottle by a faint, tiny *clink-clink-clink.*

I look down.

This freaking rat is literally trying to *gnaw through the glass.* Already, there's a tiny hole in the side of the jar. I don't even want to think about how sharp that makes his teeth.

"Nope, absolutely not," I say, holding the jar out at arm's length and dashing back to the kitchen to tear a corner off one of the empty pizza boxes stacked neatly on the floor. I unscrew the lid, toss in the scrap of cardboard like I'm leaving a sacrifice to appease an angry god, and slam it closed.

The rat, thank god, accepts the offering. Soon the only sound in the room is of him ripping into the cardboard with savage glee.

I grab my umbrella and phone with my free hand. Okay, forget setting this loose outside. This is going to the police. I'll just go report everything to them in person. *They* can figure out how to destroy it. I'll take it to the LCPD station, and then—

I wrench the door open and have my third or fourth heart-stopping moment of the day.

"Aahhh!" I yell, leaping away from the face that is suddenly inches from mine, with its fist raised like it was about to knock. The door almost slams shut in her face, but I manage to stop it in time with my foot as I realize who it is.

"*Juniper?*"

"Let's pretend I do believe you," she says without preamble, as though no time has passed between now and the conversation we had at my apartment this morning.

"How did you even *find* this *apartment*?"

"And I'm not saying I do, completely," she continues, like I've said nothing. "But Sam *has* disappeared, and right now, you're the only lead I have about what happened to him and how to find him." She suddenly looks down, narrowing her eyes suspiciously at the jar I'm still clutching. "What is *that*?"

I shove it behind my back. "Nothing!"

She's so much taller than me that all she has to do is reach over my shoulder to grab my wrist and pull it around to my front. *Yikes,* her grip is strong. She must have picked some things up from her Super boyfriend.

Her gray eyes widen as she takes in the animal's dagger-like teeth and steely tail. "How—?" she whispers, looking up at me in confusion. "How did you do that?"

Not, "Why do you have a mutant rat in a jar?" or "*Ew,* get that mutant rat in a jar away from me."

"*Me*?" I say, baffled. "I didn't do this! It was the—" I gesture behind me wordlessly toward the mess on the carpet.

Juniper peers around me, then swishes past like a cool breeze, her long hair rippling behind her. She kneels down and picks up the vial between two delicate fingers, making the remaining two centimeters of liquid inside swirl around like a tiny whirlpool. Her head snaps back toward me. "Where did you find this?" Her voice is like death. Really icy death. But that doesn't distract me from the fact that she's asking the wrong questions for someone who claimed to know nothing about the situation.

"It was in the van!" I snap back, exasperated. "I picked it up by accident when I ran away from the crazy people who murdered your *boyfriend*. Okay?" I try to throw my hands up in the air for emphasis, but it's hard when I'm still holding a phone and an umbrella and a demon-rat jar. "If it can create mutant rodents, maybe it had something to do with what happened to Sam."

She shakes her head, straightening up. "This isn't what killed Sam."

"How would *you* know?"

She fixes her piercing stare on me and lifts an eyebrow. "Because I created it."

TWELVE

I HAVE A LOT OF QUESTIONS. My brain knows that I have a lot of questions, and my mouth is waiting expectantly for my brain to figure out how to put these questions into coherent sentences so that I can vocalize these questions at Juniper, but the only word my brain is able to submit is the word *what*, over and over again.

"What?" I say dumbly.

She rattles the vial again, restarting the tiny whirlpool. "This is a Genetically Enhanced SuperVariant Program serum. I helped formulate this myself."

"What?" I wish I could think of literally anything else to say, but it's like my brain has lost its ability to access the "vocabulary" portion of my memory.

She cocks her head at me like she's annoyed that I'm not catching on fast enough. "I'm a biogenetic engineering assistant at the LCPD."

"Uh, what?" *Oh my god, come up with a new word.*

She exhales with near-tangible exasperation. "I help develop the formulas for the new strands of genetic enhancements when Supers are replaced. What, did you think they just kept the exact same level of power, the same strengths and weaknesses? We are *constantly* pushing the boundaries. We have to make them stronger. More resilient. More powerful." She looks very impressed with herself. I wonder if she wants me to applaud.

I finally find my ability to speak again. "So, does your department encourage dating its test subjects, or—?"

She flushes. "That's—we—I—that is *none* of your business!"

"You are *so* very correct," I agree. "*None* of this is any of my business. So maybe you should—"

She cuts me off in a way that indicates that she hasn't listened to a single word that just came out of my mouth. "So, this was in a van, this morning. Before dawn. With Sam."

"Well yeah, that one, plus, like, a few more."

Her head snaps back up. "You didn't say that before."

"I—"

"Tell me everything. *Everything* that was in that van. Don't leave out a detail."

This is all getting very intense.

"A couple of vials—Sam, all blue and veiny, just like I said…" She flinches, but I keep going. ". . . some papers. I didn't read them, so don't ask me about that. Some gray fabric…oh. Now that I'm thinking about it, that was probably the suit, right?"

She ignores me, waiting expectantly for me to go on.

I mimic her impatient look, shrugging my shoulders. "That was it, honestly."

"Did you take his pulse?" she asks sharply. "Check his vitals?"

I frown. "No. Why would I—"

"In other words," she interrupts me, the ghost of a desperate smile stretching across her face, "He might still be alive."

I swallow. I know what I saw, but I guess if anyone was going to survive turning into a blue-veined skin sack, it'd be one of the Supers. I'm also worried that if I take away her last shred of hope with my pessimism, she'll really lose it.

"And the driver?" she presses me further. "What can you remember about him, the person who abducted Sam?"

'Abducted.' I note the word choice. Not *'killed.'* The image of the driver's menacing face as it glowed in the light of the death-sphere resurfaces. "Pale eyes. Bloody face. Scary."

She pushes her curtain of hair behind her right shoulder and slumps back onto her calves, making an expression like she's trying to solve a very difficult crossword. "This doesn't make any sense," she mutters, then directs her piercing gaze at me again. "And the street name, any identifiable surroundings for where you found this truck?"

I try to turn my laugh into a cough, because I know this is serious. "Juniper, I promise you that I do *not* think to look at street signs when I'm running away from—" I freeze.

Her neck snaps up so quickly I swear I can hear the crack. "What? What is it?"

"I was running away from my apartment building, because Doctor Defect set it on fire." I frown. "A fire that a Super's body was planted in, while the real one was taken away. You don't think—"

"Impossible," Juniper interrupts me. "Defect couldn't have been behind this. He's been attacking the Supers for years. He never actually wins. He's a *joke*."

My frown deepens as I remember something else. "That driver wasn't working alone, though. I heard him talking; he was reporting to someone else. And you should have seen his tech, it was insane. What if Doctor Defect was just a diversion this time? What if"—my throat suddenly feels dry and papery—"what if he's working with a partner? Someone new, and more intelligent?"

Juniper's still staring at the bottle in her hand, the gears in her brain visibly churning. "If what you're saying is true," she says, "and someone dangerous got a hold of this, I don't even want to think about what could happen. They could use it to give themselves SuperVariant powers, or reverse-engineer it to create even more and build an entire army of villainous Supers."

"Someone could do that?" I suddenly realize that I've been pacing back and forth so much that I'm creating a track in Oliver's carpet, and I stop, shooting a frantic look at Juniper. "Make their own serum?"

"Of course they could," she snaps at me, which is rude, because *I'm* not the one who stole the SuperVariant serum. "It's just never happened before." She stares at the bottle clutched in her hand so intently that it looks like she's trying to shoot a laser through it with her eyeballs, but then—"We're going to the police," she finally announces, leaping to her feet.

"Wait, we? As in, including me?" I squawk. I know that I myself was just about to head to the police a few minutes ago, but everything about Juniper is freaking me out enough to not agree with any idea she suggests. This is suddenly starting to feel like a situation much bigger than my span of control, and I'd like to go back to the version of my life where I just hide from stuff like this. "I'm sorry, why would you want *me* to come?"

Juniper rolls her eyes. "Because you're the one who was there, genius."

I take a moment to weigh the options. On one hand, Juniper's intensity is terrifying, and I'm actively interested in doing pretty much anything other than spend more time with her. But on the other, the fact that she's changed her mind and believes my story is giving me hope that someone else might, too. Besides, I haven't heard any emergency alerts yet, so they might not even know Doctor Defect has escaped prison. And I definitely haven't heard anything about a new villain with the power to turn solid objects into pretzels. Someone's gotta tell 'em.

✖ TAYLOR SIMONDS ✖

I hold up my jar. "Can I bring my rat?"

THIRTEEN

I'M SURPRISED WHEN WE don't go to the police station in the center of town. Instead, the taxi Juniper hails for us drives along a stretch of road surrounded by dense forest for a good twenty minutes before pulling up in front of a glistening white building with a billion windows, what seems like hundreds of stories tall. It almost resembles a rocket erupting from the forest, its top ten or so floors partially concealed by clouds.

"Where are we?" I ask Juniper, but all she does is pay the driver and usher me out. Maybe this is some kind of headquarters.

It's a lot cleaner inside than I expected. It's all very white and polished, in a very bland sort of way. There aren't even any Most Wanted pictures on the walls. I guess I was expecting a lot of dark walls and cobwebs and prisoners crying at me for water.

Wait, that's a dungeon.

✖ COLLATERAL DAMAGE ✖

Listen, I try to avoid the police at all costs, so it's not my fault I don't know what their headquarters looks like.

After Juniper gets me a visitor's pass and pushes me through three separate security checkpoints, into an elevator, and out on the twenty-third floor, I start to wish she'd given me time to change into real pants. I didn't realize this was gonna be such a big thing. I thought we'd be in and out, you know? But between my loud boxers and my rat-jar, I'm attracting a lot of weird looks. I wonder whether anyone thinks I'm there to be arrested. I try extra hard to make my face have a "normal" expression, so no one will think I look suspicious, and try to hide the jar in the folds of my baggy sweatshirt. The rat, fortunately, has curled itself into a ball and gone to sleep, so I don't have to worry about it trying to chew through the glass again for the moment. To be honest, it actually looks kind of adorable like that. You could almost forget about its weaponized body parts.

"Sorry, am I walking too fast?" Juniper calls from down the hall, without slowing down for me.

I glare at the back of her head and speed up, but only because I'm worried I'm going to be lost forever in the maze of identical white hallways.

"Hey, so I thought we were going to the police," I yell in her direction as I start noticing that most of the rooms we're passing are overflowing with high-tech lab equipment.

"We are," she calls back without turning around, her shoes clicking sharply against the polished tile floor. I tramp after her in my oversized boots like an elephant.

"Uh, aren't they back in town?"

"Wrong division of the police. We're going to the division responsible for the SuperVariant Program, led by—oh! Sir! Dr. Crenshaw!" She smooths her hair with one hand and offers the other in what looks more like a salute than a wave toward a gray-haired man down an adjacent hallway who I instantly recognize from countless ads and interviews on TV.

"And make sure that I get those by—" I can hear him saying to a small cluster of lab-coated staff as we draw nearer. It's weird seeing him in person. You always expect the people you see on television to be like, twelve feet tall in real life, but he just looks like a normal, albeit slightly bug-eyed, doctor—a lot like my old pediatrician, actually. He cuts himself off as he notices Juniper and greets her with a wide smile. "Still here, Jensen? I would have thought you'd be asleep at home by now. Weren't you here on overtime all night?"

"It's an emergency, sir," she replies, grabbing my arm and pulling me along after her as she closes the distance between us and him. "Sir, I—"

"Well, if you're still working," he continues, adjusting his glasses and speaking over her, "perhaps you could take a look at the serum for the next SuperVariant Four. I gave Mike the project, but you know…" He gives her a conspiratorial sigh, shaking his head. "I'm starting to think he lied on his resume, if you know what I mean."

"Dr. Crenshaw," Juniper persists, although I can tell from the slight shift in her facial expression that she's pleased that he thinks her more capable than whoever Mike is. "I have to confess something. And I might get in trouble for this, but I know Three's secret identity. I know his real name is Sam Rowan. And he—"

Dr. Crenshaw laughs. "Juniper, the past Three's term has ended. It doesn't matter if you accidentally found out his secret identity—when did this happen, last night, by the way? I know you wouldn't put him in jeopardy by telling anyone. And besides, Sam Rowan no longer has any connection to SuperVariant Three. In fact, we're in the process of selecting his replacement as we speak."

"No, you don't understand." She stumbles over her words. "I've known who he was for quite some time, and he—he was attacked. He might have been—" She cuts herself off, unable to bring herself to say the word *killed*. "I'm certain it was Defect, possibly working with someone else, someone new. And his serum—"

"Oh, dear." Crenshaw puts a hand on Juniper's shoulder and shakes his head. "You know, this is why we stress to our Supers that they keep their identities secret. When did you find him like this?"

I cut Juniper off before she can answer. This is what she brought me for anyway, right? "This morning. Like, two hours ago. Maybe less."

He looks at me like he hadn't noticed I was even there. I hide my jar behind my back in an attempt to look less weird than I already do, feeling my face grow red as he takes in the koala-print boxers.

"Hello," he says amiably, "and who are you?"

I point at Juniper. "Neighbor. I found Sam in—"

"So you found him this morning, after his term had ended and he'd relinquished his superpowers? Is that right?"

"Yeah, but—"

"Girls," Crenshaw pushes his glasses up his forehead as he wipes his eyes with the back of his hand, "you really ought to take this as a lesson in rule-following. Sam clearly did not do an adequate job of protecting his secret identity, and Doctor Defect must have taken advantage of that in order to get revenge after Sam lost his powers."

My ability to form words evaporates. We're talking about one of Dr. Crenshaw's own employees here—okay, former employee, but still—and it's like he doesn't care. Worse, he's confirming Juniper's worst fears, as overheard through the wall just last night: that Sam should have been more careful, that he *deserved* what he got.

Juniper's mouth is slack, fledgling specks of tears forming in the corners of her eyes. I somehow thought the problem would be fixed as soon as we told somebody more powerful, but now I see how stupid that idea was.

"Of course, I'm terribly sorry that this happened to your friend," he continues, the sympathetic tone of his voice doing nothing to counter how unhelpful he's actually being. "But he just isn't one of us anymore." He holds his hands out apologetically. "What would you like me to do, exactly?"

Uh, find out who Doctor Defect's new accomplice is? Warn the other Supers that their former partner was murdered, and they might be next? Get back the stolen serum before Defect uses it to make himself even more powerful?

"You're not listening," I try furiously to explain. "The problem isn't Sam, the problem is—"

Crenshaw is already talking again. "I'm sorry I can't help more, but there is still a lot of work to be done for the next SuperVariant—one who, hopefully, will be much more cautious. I suggest you both return home and get some rest."

And without another word, he turns and practically evaporates, sweeping down the hallway toward whatever his next point of business is. Gone.

He's just *gone*.

My voice is gone too, swept away in a tide of numb, hysterical disbelief. He wouldn't even *listen*. Okay. That's fine. When this whole city goes up in flames courtesy of whoever this new Big Bad is, I'm going to sit on a hill eating popcorn and yelling *I told you so*.

"Sam didn't bring this upon himself," Juniper snarls, clenching her fists so hard, I worry her nails are going to puncture right through her palms. Her tears have evaporated. "This wasn't just about petty revenge. There's something bigger going on. The stolen serum proves that. We have to do something."

I can't believe she has enough self-control to do anything but cry over her lost boyfriend, but then I realize what she's said. "Wait—*we*?"

"Of course." She looks annoyed that I'm asking. "You're a part of this now, too."

"Whoa, whoa, whoa." I hold my hands up. "You said all I had to do was tell the police what I found. I *tried* to tell the police what I found, and they wouldn't listen to me. What do you

✖ COLLATERAL DAMAGE ✖

think two girls with no powers are going to be able to do? Take out Defect and his new accomplice? Get back the stolen serum ourselves? How are we supposed to do that, exactly?"

Juniper eyes widen. "We don't have to. All we have to do is warn the other Supers about the threat, and tell them what happened to Sam. They can handle the rest."

"Oh, yeah? And what happens when they don't listen to us, either?"

She sets her mouth in calm determination and starts striding down the hallway. "We have to try."

Out of all possible plans of action, I guess I should be glad she picked an option that doesn't involve confronting a bad guy myself. Warning the Supers still falls under 'tell someone more powerful to fix the problem for you.' It's the bare minimum of effort. I'm good at bare minimum.

I jog to catch up with her.

"Okay. There's only three other Supers," I pant, "So how hard can that be? You work here. Don't you know all their secret identities?"

She pauses long enough to flash me a condescending look. "Are you joking? Of course not. That's proprietary information. I've never even met one in person before. All I do is formulate the serum."

I'm sorry, does Sam not count as a person?

She must be able to read my mind, because she flushes. "It wasn't like that. I knew Sam before he became Three. I figured out his secret on my own."

I groan. "So you really have no idea who the other three Supers are?"

"No. But this city isn't that big. We can find them." She starts speed walking up the hallway again. "The tough part is going to be actually getting them to listen to us. Supers never pay civilians very much attention, unless they're saving them. Maybe, during the next crisis, we could make sure we're in a situation where we need help, and then—"

"Are you *crazy*?" I interrupt her, then look around furtively to make sure none of the other staff are paying attention to us. "*Are you crazy?*" I repeat in a whisper. "Sure, let's go put ourselves in danger. That's a great idea. Let's go hang off the side of a building, and when One comes and mind-levitates us down, we can say 'Hey, thanks! By the way, someone is trying to kill you!' That'll go over well."

Juniper's cheeks flush crimson again. "Fine. Let's hear your brilliant suggestion, then."

I take a second to think sincerely, only because I really, really want to one-up her. *Come on, brain. Be useful for once.*

I try to find a blank spot on the wall to stare at so I can concentrate, but it's hard to find a spare inch that isn't covered in holographic screens, each flashing a bright headline/photo combination detailing one of the current team of Supers' accomplishments. "SUMMER SOLSTICE GALA THREAT STOPPED BY SUPERVARIANTS"; "SCHOOL BUS CRASH PREVENTED BY SUPERVARIANT TWO"; "SUPERVARIANT TWO SAVES CHESS CLUB TEAM FROM DEATH—AND DEFEAT!"

I squint at the final screen. SuperVariant Two is visible for once, posing with his thumbs up in front of a tall brick school building, his blue supersuit concealing every inch of him from head to toe. He's the only SuperVariant whose costume covers their entire body. I heard once it's because the suit is the only article of clothing that turns invisible along with him; otherwise, he's like a mass of floating fabric.

As I look at the building behind him, though, something clicks in the back of my head, fuzzily. I look back at the "school bus crash" article.

"Juniper, what if—" I say, not wanting to jinx it by getting excited too quickly. "Hang on. Look for other headlines about SuperVariant Two."

"What?"

I start speed walking up the hall, scanning the walls. "Look—right here. 'SUPERVARIANT TWO PREVENTS ASSEMBLY SHOOTING.'" I switch sides and find another screen partially hidden behind a trash can. "DRAMA CLUB DRAMA HALTED BY SuperVariant two—attack during school play stopped in action." I look back at her. "What if he's a *student*?"

Juniper looks skeptical instead of impressed. "They wouldn't give a teenager this much power. It'd be insane. And can you imagine trying to balance this kind of double life with normal school? What teenager would even want that?"

"Uh, all of them! *All* of the teenagers would want this much power!" I motion to the screens surrounding us. "Look at this! Most of the time the Supers work as a team, but every time SuperVariant Two works alone, it's at this school. And I'm pretty sure there's never been an age restriction on being chosen as a Super." I lean closer to one of the screens to check for a location, then compare it against the other headlines mentioning Two. "Look. Saint Charles's Academy for Science and Technology. That's where every single one of these disasters took place. It can't be a coincidence."

She looks a little less skeptical, but I'm pretty sure that the only reason she's not agreeing with me is because she doesn't want me to be right. But I know I'm right. I can feel it.

"Look, it's the best lead you've got right now," I insist. "Why don't you go check out that school; see if you can figure out who seems like, I don't know, like a nerdy loner who could potentially moonlight as a superhero—someone who misses a lot of classes and doesn't have a lot of friends."

"Don't be ridiculous," she snaps. "I can't just go case a high school. No one would believe I was a student. I know in movies nobody bats an eyelash when a twenty-year-old plays a teenager, but people notice in the real world." She looks me up and down, then cracks a conniving smile. "You're the right age, though."

Oh no.

"No, no," I say, crossing my arms into an X. "Absolutely not. No way. I am *not* going back to high school. There's no way you can make me."

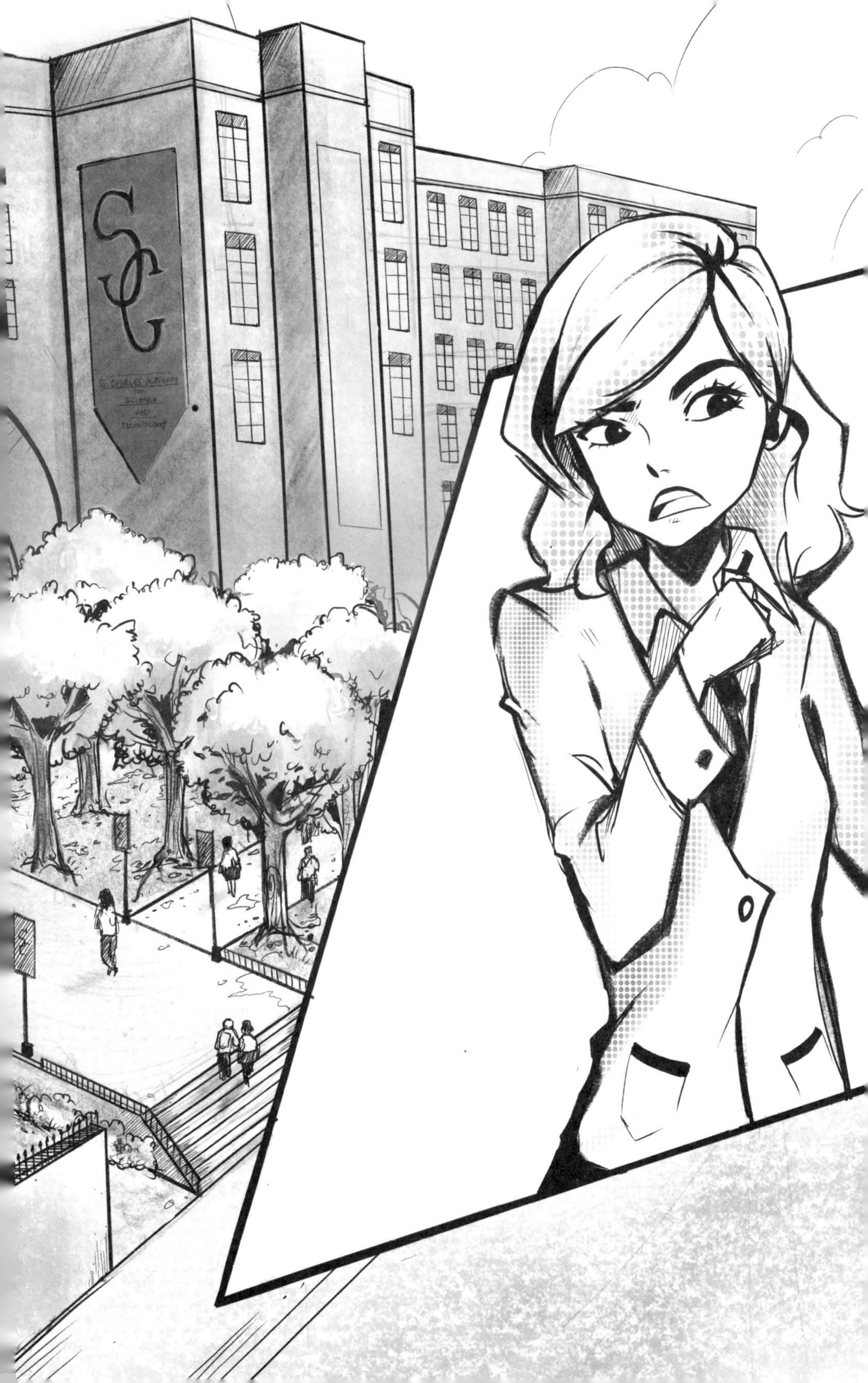

FOURTEEN

I TUG AT THE COLLAR of my starched white button-down blouse, wondering how long it takes to die from suffocation. I didn't even want to know how Juniper had a prep school uniform all ready to go so quickly, or how she got her hands on the high-tech earpiece that's now hidden underneath my hair.

"This is never going to work," I hiss into the tiny mic clipped to the inside of my collar while climbing up the steps of Saint Charles's. "I look ridiculous."

"*You do not.*" The words reverberate in my eardrum. I wince and discreetly adjust the volume. "*You look fine. Just stop fidgeting.*"

I do *not* look fine. I look exhausted and tense, if anything. Fortunately, that seems to be helping me blend in. The sea of identically uniformed students around me swarms up the stairs in bleary unison, a couple of them inhaling coffees out of thermoses. I have to actively stop myself from snatching one out of their hands. I miss my free The Pure Bean coffee. I'd had to beg for another day off from work today in order to be an undercover spy, probably leaving Carly to run the café by herself on a Monday. I wonder how far away from fired I am right now.

"Bare minimum," I mutter to myself as I step through the school's entrance. "I'm doing the bare minimum. I can last one day back at school."

"Excuse me, young lady!"

I ignore the calling of the dark-haired, middle-aged teacher, assuming that she must be talking to the girl next to me, who's doing a really terrible job of hiding the fact that she's copying her friend's chemistry homework letter for letter.

Then the teacher cuts in front of me, arms folded, and I realize that she's actually talking to me. "Young *lady*," she repeats.

Oh boy. They caught me. How am I going to get out of this? *Deny everything*, I tell myself.

"What's your name?" she demands.

My name? I made a student ID for myself last night, but I can't for the life of me remember what pseudonym I put on it, and it's not like I can dig it out in front of her to check. It wasn't "Meg Sawyer;" I know that much. And in my panic, I've also forgotten every other name in existence. *Come on, brain, think of something.*

"Violet!" I blurt out. I'd always thought it was a cool name. "Violet...Green." *What? Kill me.*

"Okay, Miss Green." The teacher doesn't seem to notice that my made-up name is two crayon colors. "I'm not sure what gave you the impression that the dress code policy vanishes after the first month of school, but you've been sorely misinformed." She points at my hair and whips a slip of paper out of god-knows-where faster than I can blink. "Detention, and the next time I see you, your hair had better be a natural, non-distracting color."

My mouth falls to the ground, but before I can say anything, she notices a boy wearing headphones snaked up the sleeve of his jacket and darts away to admonish him, another slip of paper clutched in her hand.

I can hear Juniper snickering in my earpiece.

"*Oh, shut up,*" I hiss and cram the paper into my backpack, nearly crushing the mutant rat, who I forgot was hanging out in there with an assortment of cardboard and cardboard-esque snacks to keep him busy. In all the emotional chaos of our trip to the lab, I never got the chance to turn him in to somebody, so I guess he's mine now. Besides, what else am I supposed to do with him? I can't just set him loose on the city, and I'm sure as heck not leaving him with Juniper.

I direct my attention back to the main entrance of the school, which feeds into a maze of hallways with six identical archways. I notice that there are carefully placed flyers, school spirit posters, and bulletin boards coating as many surfaces as possible, but there's still not enough to hide all the spots where the walls are singed, stained, or missing chunks completely. One particularly large banner hangs parallel to the railing on the tall staircase in the main hall, hiding an eight-foot gash in its side. I notice that there are at least five janitors positioned within my viewpoint alone, waiting for a crisis to happen for them to clean up after. I wonder why a prep school this prestigious can't afford proper maintenance. I guess all the money goes to athletics no matter where your school is.

"Where am I supposed to go now?" I whisper, surveying the hallway options. None of them look distinctly appealing.

"Homeroom. Haven't you ever been to high school before?"

"Thank you, genius, but *which* homeroom?" I look around in a mild panic. The bell is going to ring any minute. We really didn't plan this well.

"I don't *know*," Juniper replies. "I can't see. Look, just look around and see if anyone looks like a geeky loner."

I pick a hallway at random and scan it furtively, trying to blend in with the wall.

A small cluster of kids is playing some kind of board game

✖ COLLATERAL DAMAGE ✖

with pieces shaped like mythical creatures on the floor under a wall of lockers. A tiny girl with a prominent retainer leans over them—"sorry, sorry"—to pull one massive textbook after another out of her locker until she's carrying at least six. Another girl leans against a door next to a water fountain, muttering to herself in French, a four-inch stack of color-coded flash cards clutched in her hands. The door suddenly flies open, sending her stumbling into the water fountain. She moans sadly as the cards on the bottom of the stack get soaked. The boy who's opened the door doesn't even notice her, too intent on maneuvering a rolling cart topped with some kind of complicated, 3-D printed, scientific-looking model down the hallway. Another boy almost knocks the cart over, trying to walk, scribble a formula in the margins of his calculus book, and hold his calculator between his teeth all at the same time.

"Yeah, bad news, Juniper." I whisper. "'Geeky loner' is gonna be a little harder to narrow down than we thought."

"What do you mean?"

Beeeeeeep. Beeeeeeep. Beeeeeeep.

There's a noise like a smoke alarm. I immediately duck, flinching away from the screechy sound. Everyone in the hall starts stampeding for the classroom doors.

"What's happening? What's happening?" I try not to sound shrill, but I don't think it's working. "Is it a crisis?"

"That's the *bell*, dingus. Pick a classroom."

"You should be nicer to me; I'm the one in this stupid skirt," I mutter, scanning the crowd for somebody, anybody, who might be superhero material.

"And *you* should stop talking to yourself. People are gonna think you're nuts."

"What do we have this mic for, then?" I whisper-shout.

"*Less talking! More investigating!*"

I'd better have a lead by the end of the day. I can't take much more of Juniper's voice in my ear.

I finally give up on looking for one specific person, and instead follow a small group of kids who look stressed out, but not stressed out enough to be juniors, to what I'm hoping is a senior homeroom. I make it through the door behind them just as the bell rings. Unfortunately, every empty desk I try to beeline for is almost immediately filled by another student, until there are no desks left and I'm left standing awkwardly in the middle of the classroom.

I freeze. What am I going to say when the teacher notices me? *New student*, I think to myself. *I'm a new student, and my name is Violet—something better than Green.*

The ancient teacher at the front of the room slides the book she's reading down a hair so that her puffy eyes stick out from over the top. "Remember, no cell phones," she mutters before she turns her eyes back to her book. Huh. I had worried that these crazy-elite prep school teachers would be more attentive than the public school ones I had, but I guess not.

The other kids, however, don't suffer from the same lack of attentiveness. Everyone is still talking to one another, but I keep seeing eyes take turns darting in my direction, mostly with looks of confusion or suspicion. I clutch my backpack straps and book it to the back of the room.

"What's going on?" Juniper's voice crackles into my head. "I can't see anything, remember?"

"Juniper, I really, really don't think this is going to work." I shrink against the wall, trying to make myself as small as possible. "There are like, three thousand kids at this school. What am I supposed to do? Go around with a megaphone saying, 'Excuse me, but do any of you happen to put on some blue spandex and fight crime after school?'"

"You're telling me that there's *no one* in this room right now who looks even the *slightest* bit different from everyone else?"

I scan the army of faces. What does "different" even look like? "No, I…"

"*Thomas!*"

The furious exclamation makes me flinch, and my brain's

first—completely illogical—reaction is to think the girl responsible for it is talking to me. She comes barreling right at me in a flurry of dirty-blonde hair and rage-filled blue eyes, somehow making the act of carrying three textbooks look aggressive, and I swivel in confusion, positive that despite my glaring lack of caffeine, I have not yet introduced myself to anyone here as Thomas. But then she elbows right past me, and I realize that I've been standing in front of somebody's desk: a very bland, unassuming-looking kid with unstylish brown hair, large square glasses, and a frame that can only be described as "average." He's looking up at the shouting girl in a clear blend of terror and bewilderment, as though he'd very much like to go hide in the supply closet behind him. I'm baffled that I've practically been standing on top of his desk this whole time, to say the least. I didn't even see him.

I didn't even see him.

"Where were you on Saturday?" the girl demands, and I shuffle out of her way, keeping an eye on the boy's reaction. "I had to outline the entire Chem proposal myself. What part of 'group project' is confusing to you?"

He turns around, as if hoping she's yelling at the wall behind him, then sinks into his shoulders with evident embarrassment. "Sorry." I can barely hear the words; I have to read his lips to be sure of what he's saying. "I was sick."

"What, the way you were sick the time I got stuck with you for the Shakespeare literary analysis?" she fumes. "I'm not doing this again this year. If I'm going to keep getting stuck with you for projects, then you're—"

Saturday. Saturday was the robot attack. It could be a coincidence. It could mean nothing at all. But 'uses poor excuse to disappear during time of crisis' does fit the possible-superhero criteria.

"Okay, forget what I said," I whisper into Juniper's mic. "There might be someone. Maybe."

"Who? *Who?*" Juniper shrieks. "Describe them! Meg? Meg,

what's happening? Meg, who—"

With a tinny pop, I disconnect the earpiece from the base, then turn the entire thing off, wrapping the wire around the mic pack and throwing all of it in my backpack. Yeah, I can't do this. I can't listen to her voice all day.

The bell rings again. Jeez, homeroom is short here. It's okay, though. I have a target.

I follow the boy to his next class, making sure to keep a few people behind him so that I don't seem creepy, even though I am definitely feeling extremely creepy.

I wonder what his first class is. I hope it's something easy and subjective that I can fake my way through, like art or philosophy.

I look at the whiteboard.

Biology. Great. Just great.

"Excuse me?" *Oh no.*

I look up to see a balding teacher with a prominent paunch and absurdly small glasses standing in front me, arms folded. "Can I help you with something?"

New student, new student.

"Hiiiii," I say brightly, adopting an over-the-top, cutesy sort of voice that I immediately regret but am now forced to commit to. "I'm a new student. My name is Violet… Green." *Dammit.*

He lifts an eyebrow several inches above his doll-sized glasses. "And you've been assigned AP Biology? This is a very rigorous course. Are you sure you'll be able to keep up with the work this late into the semester? Perhaps you would prefer something easier, like theater studies."

Theater studies? *Excuse* me? I bristle, but keep my fake smile plastered on. "No, thanks! I was top of my class at my last school. I probably like, already know all this." Oh, boy. Why did I say that?

The bell rings, and the teacher looks back at his desk with a face that indicates that he wishes he'd eaten his granola bar instead of bothering to talk to me. "Well, I didn't receive any communication about a new student, but you're welcome to sit in until you're officially registered with administration, as long as you can keep up."

What is *with* this guy? Like, I know I suck at anything related to science, but *he* doesn't know that yet. How dare he assume I'm the moron I probably am.

He gestures wordlessly at a vacant table near the back of the room, two seats diagonal from Thomas, and I stumble over, fishing the mic and earpiece out of my backpack as quickly and surreptitiously as possible. I plug everything back together and jam the earpiece back under my hair and into my ear.

"Hello? Meg? Hello?"

I wince and turn the volume down. "Have you just been sitting there screaming my name for the last five minutes?"

"Did you hang *up* on me?"

"Shhh," I whisper, hoping the light buzz of chatter is distracting enough that no one can tell that I'm talking to myself. "I'm in a biology class. He's gonna call on me, I know it. Any good at high school-level science?"

"Am I *any good at science*?" Juniper practically screams. "Do you know what my *job is*?"

"Great, awesome, just feed me the answers if he asks me a question."

"I don't know," Juniper ponders, sounding genuinely doubtful. "Cheating is never a good idea. You don't learn anything."

"I am not a real student!" I hiss.

"I guess, but this could be a really good opportunity to—"

"Juniper!"

"Okay, fine."

But I end up not needing her help. The teacher—whose name I discover on a corner of the whiteboard to be Professor Gullet—ends up producing an African bullfrog and droning on in a monotone tinted with mild personal enthusiasm about the possibilities of human-frog gene splicing for medical purposes, which feels pretty advanced for a high school bio class. When I was in school, all my teachers ever did was give us practice standardized test questions.

Instead, I spend the class trying to stare at Thomas without *looking* like I'm staring at him. By all accounts, he seems completely ordinary, and I start to wonder if I've jumped to conclusions too quickly. What if he really was sick on Saturday? What if the only reason I didn't notice him in homeroom is because I'm just plain unobservant? The only suspicious thing he's done so far is sneakily use his phone in class, which isn't really suspicious or out of the ordinary for a student.

I squint at the screen from the few feet of distance, as though it's going to turn red and start flashing with a summons from the mayor. It doesn't, though. It just stays open to the news site the kid is looking at, the tiny words too small for me to read. But then he scrolls up, and the headline comes into focus: *Inter-City Drug Bust; 20 Face Charges.*

I'd heard about that. Sometimes, in the midst of the rotation of attacks from Doctor Defect and other weekly terrors, I forget that *normal* crime does still exist. There are still your average robbers and criminals dumb enough to keep breaking the law right under the SuperVariants' noses, hoping they'll be less of a priority if there's a bigger villain bothering the city that week. They're not as common as they used to be, but there's still some out there. This particular drug bust happened last month, but the people caught by the Supers were just dealers, not the supplier. Why would Thomas be looking at this article now, a month later?

Because he's personally interested in the case. Because he's trying to catch the supplier himself. Because he's the Super, my desperately optimistic brain provides.

Or maybe he's just interested in month-old news, I fight back with, but it's hard to ignore the number of coincidences stacking up. Besides, I don't have anyone else to stalk at the moment. This Thomas kid is the best bet.

✶ COLLATERAL DAMAGE ✶

I follow him to his next three classes, which, fortunately, have less neurotic teachers than the biology professor. The English literature teacher goes, "How fun, a new character," in a dreamy, vacant kind of voice, and then doesn't address me again. The Philosophy 101 teacher doesn't even seem to notice I exist. The next class is yearbook, which appears to be self-run, but there aren't enough students to blend in casually, so I hide in a supply closet until the bell rings for lunch. Wow, this school has a lot of bleach.

"Has he done anything yet?" Juniper asks into my ear for the eightieth time.

"Have *you* done anything yet?" I snap. "Or have you been sitting there eating popcorn and listening to me retake high school all morning?"

"For your information," she sniffs. "*I* am at the lab, trying to find out if we have any paperwork about the secret identities of the other Supers."

"That's... actually a pretty good idea," I admit begrudgingly. "Do you? Have any, I mean?"

"If we do, it's hidden pretty well. Which makes sense given the phrase 'secret identity.' But if it's here, I'll find it."

"Okay. Don't get caught." I poke my cafeteria food, which consists of a puck-like burger and a "side of vegetables" (the vegetables turned out to be French fries), and feed a fry to Trashface—I spent my time in the supply closet coming up with a name for the demon rat—who's still hiding in my backpack. I steal a glance at Possible Superhero Kid, who's eating by himself on the floor in a corner of the cafeteria. I wonder if he thinks it makes him look edgy. All I can think about is how disgusting the tile here probably is.

"This is getting boring," I whisper into my mic. "I'm not going to know whether this kid is a Super or not until something bad actually happens. And yeah, those things tend to happen pretty frequently, but I don't know how many more AP classes I can sit through. What if we make it through the whole day without a crisis?" I've never been disappointed in a lack of chaos before. Everything feels upside-down.

Juniper doesn't respond. I tap the mic impatiently. "Juniper? Hello?"

"How do you feel about *causing* a crisis?" she asks slowly.

"'Scuse me?"

"You heard me. You could stage something, and see how he reacts."

I blink. "That's *genius*."

"Yes, I know. Is there anything nearby that you could—"

"Way ahead of you, my friend." My eyes dart around the cafeteria walls until I find what I'm looking for, then seat hop as furtively as I can until I'm at the edge of the lunch table closest to the fire alarm. "I'm turning you off. It's gonna get loud."

"Wait, but—"

Pop. I disconnect the earpiece again. It doesn't get less fun.

Okay. I glance around. No teachers or monitors are paying attention. Superhero Kid is still within my eyesight, and I have a clear view to see if the sound of impending crisis makes him react suspiciously.

One...

Two...

"Are you *following* me or something?"

I nearly leap out of my chair. A startled snap of my head to the left reveals the source of the question—a lanky boy with gold-brown skin and a short crop of dark curls, sitting two stools away from me.

"*What*?" I reply, genuinely confused.

He starts counting on his fingers, and I realize that the question was asked curiously, not aggressively. "You've followed me to every single one of my classes this morning. I saw you in that closet, you know. And now you're following me at lunch? Look, I don't know who you are or why you just showed up out of nowhere, but I don't have time to deal with this right now." He turns a page in the thick textbook open in front of his lunch tray forcefully. "My uncle says if I can't keep my grades up, I'll have to quit yearbook."

"I—" My mouth falls open, dumbfounded. "I'm not *following* you," I manage to get out irritably. "It's not my fault my class schedule is the same as yours. Haven't you ever had a new student before?"

"No, I haven't." He flips a page without looking. "Not many people move here."

"Right," I swallow, examining the fire alarm again. "Well, I moved here for… um… my dad's work. He's a…" *Pick a job, pick a relevant job.* "…a reporter." *Oh, good one. Nice. Good job, me.*

He doesn't respond, so I turn back around, expecting to see an expression of bored disbelief on his face. Instead, his face is planted firmly in the middle of the textbook lying on the table.

"Uh…" I poke him. "Hello?"

His head whips back up and I jump, startled. "Huh? I'm awake! I'm awake!" he cries, looking around frantically.

Wow. I've never met someone who could fall into that deep of a sleep in less than ten seconds. I'm impressed.

"Sorry." He rubs his eyes, blinks them wide open, and refocuses them on the diagram on the page. "My uncle always tells me that I don't sleep enough. But I have to study."

"It's, uh… it's fine. Good luck with the studying." I fix my attention back on Possible Superhero. He's sketching something in a notebook. Of *course* the invisible one is artsy. I follow his line of vision and realize that he's drawing a pretty girl with auburn hair a few tables behind me. It's kind of cute, but mostly creepy. I mean, I'd be creeped.

"I'm Sanjeet, by the way."

I turn back around. The boy has diverted his attention from his biology book long enough to stick out a hand in my direction.

"Violet Green," I reply, shaking the proffered hand. I have to commit to the dumb name; it's too late now.

"Nice to meet you." He picks up the book and holds the

open pages a few inches from my face. "Quiz me?"

Seriously? "I…"

Beep. Beep. Beep. Beep.

The bell. Crap. Well, there went my fire alarm opportunity.

"I have to go to class!" I announce, throwing my backpack over my shoulder and leaping out the chair. I crane my neck, just barely catching the back of Superhero Kid's head as he vanishes through the door at the other end of the cafeteria, making a left. "Bye!"

"Wait, but—" The end of Sanjeet's sentence is lost in the air behind me as I push my way through the crowded cafeteria, jamming the parts of the earpiece back together.

"You *really* need to stop doing that." Juniper's voice immediately fills my ear.

"Sorry, sorry." I weave in between the mass of students, nearly knocking over a sky-high tower of textbooks that's standing twice as tall as the freshman carrying them. "I got sidetracked. I'm gonna have to try again."

"You didn't even do it yet?"

"I'm working on it, okay?" I finally spot the boy's off-brand backpack disappearing into a classroom with a crepe paper banner hanging from the archway. It flutters, revealing that the top of the doorway is jagged and broken up in several places. It looks like bite marks from something huge. I don't even want to know.

I duck through the door under the crepe paper and straighten up, looking at the board.

Chemistry 4 is written in scrawling, uneven letters across the top-left corner.

I look at the board, back at the boy I'm supposed to be following, and back to the board. Without turning around, I retreat three steps until I'm back outside the classroom, then turn and walk purposefully toward the nearest bathroom, locking myself into the stall nearest the door. "Nope," I mutter. "Hard pass. Absolutely not."

"What happened? What's going on?" Juniper asks frantically.

"No chemistry. I draw the line at chemistry. I am never doing that again."

"*Meg!*"

"No, listen, it'll be okay. I can pull the fire alarm from outside the classroom, and wait to see what he does when he comes out. It's fine. This'll work." I hope none of the girls crammed around the dirty mirror outside the stall can hear me. If they can, maybe they'll think the pressures of school have made me crack and leave me alone.

Juniper doesn't respond.

"Juniper?"

"Fine, but this had better work. If you get caught pulling the fire alarm, this is all over."

"I know, I know," I say impatiently, watching the other girls' feet trickle out the door.

"Are you going? What's happening?"

"Hold on, I have to wait until the bell rings and the hall's clear. Just give me like ten minutes, okay?" I whisper.

"Right. Okay. Sorry."

I wait for the sound of clattering footsteps to wind down, then sit down on the floor cross-legged. "So, how about you?"

"How about me, what?"

"How about you, did you find anything at the lab yet?" I fish Trashface out of my backpack, thinking he might need some fresh air, and set him on my lap, where he starts running in tiny circles. I guess I shouldn't have left him cooped up in there for so long.

"Not really. Just a bunch of stuff I already knew. I'm just lucky that no one's onto me. I told the lead technician that I needed the old files as a comparative base for developing new serum."

"Why would you need the old serum files?" I put a hand down and let Trashface run up my arm and onto my shoulder.

He's actually pretty cute. I'm starting to feel glad I didn't get rid of him. "Didn't you like, invent all of them?"

"How old do you think I am? I've only been here for a couple of years."

"But how hard is it to make new serum? Isn't it just refining what's already in it for the next person?"

Juniper hesitates. "Sort of, but there are always lots of things that need to be altered. We learn from any weaknesses demonstrated in the previous version, and try to limit them in the redesign. Plus, the chemicals for the serum that neutralizes the *original* serum, which the Supers are injected with at the end of their term, sometimes react differently based on the updates, so there are some other elements that have to be adjusted."

"Wait, *what*?" I straighten up, nearly launching Trashface off my shoulder, where he's curled up into a furry black ball. He squeaks in aggravation and sinks his claws into my skin.

"Yeah, you know, everyone's DNA is obviously very different, so—"

"No, not that, I'm not an idiot. *That's* how the Supers lose their powers? They literally drain it out of their bloodstream?"

"Well, sort of. It's more like shocking the genetic enhancements with one final boost that forces them to their maximum capacity, then unbinds them completely from the Super's genetic code, turning them back to normal." Juniper's voice is actually taking on a bored sort of quality, like she considers this to be the least interesting part of her job. "But I don't do a whole lot with that right now. I mostly work with the failure graveyard."

"Oh my god, how did you know what I call my house?"

"What?"

"Sorry." I stifle a snicker. "Remind me not to joke around with you. What's the failure graveyard?"

"It's… well, basically, I'm on a team that's been trying to develop new powers. You know, other than the four that already exist: telekinesis, speed, strength, and invisibility." She pauses.

"You know, I'm probably not supposed to be telling you this."

"Who am I gonna tell?"

"I don't know. Someone."

"I have exactly one friend, Juniper." I pry Trashface's paws from the shoulder of my private school blazer, leaving a bevy of snags, and return him to my lap. "And I won't tell. I haven't even told him about all of... well, all of this."

"Seriously? Why not?"

I shrug before remembering that she can't see me. "I don't know. It feels like we might be messing with something dangerous, and I don't want anything else bad happening to him."

There's a very meaningful pause, and I realize that Juniper is probably thinking about the person that she hadn't wanted anything bad happening to, and how wanting that hadn't mattered in the end. I clear my throat and try to get her back to the topic of the failure graveyard, which still sounds like a more fun topic than death. "So, the failure graveyard?"

"Okay." She sighs. "The failure graveyard is what my team calls the underground storage bunker out back where we keep the experimental versions of new serum ideas. Literally none of them have worked so far."

"What kind of new serum ideas?"

"Oh, *so* many. Shape-shifting, teleportation, phasing, force fields, ice powers, pyrokinesis—"

"Pyroki-what-a?"

"Like, fire powers."

Wow, screw that. If we get fire-powered teenagers, I am *definitely* moving.

"But none of them worked?" I've never been so relieved to only have four superheroes in the city. I had no idea it could have been so much worse.

"No." Juniper sounds dejected. "We can't make them react properly on a molecular level during the experimental stage yet. Not people," she says hurriedly. "Just rats. They're our primary test subject—they share a lot of genetic information with humans, but they react to the serum much more slowly, so they're easier to observe. That's why I was so shocked when I saw that rat in your jar. I thought you'd managed to replicate the serum on your own."

"Girl, I can't make toast," I say.

"Anyway," she continues. "It's not like we can just throw it away. It all goes in this giant, super-secure storage unit underground, behind the rest of the facility."

"That sounds safe," I say blandly.

"I just told you, it's secure."

"That's not *really* the same thing..."

"It's safe," she insists. "Trust me; anything that goes in there isn't coming out."

"Okay, okay." I hold my hands up defensively even though I know she still can't see me. I can't believe there's a whole toxic warehouse of prototypes for other Supers. Who knows how much data and research the LCPD lab has about genetic enhancements in their facility? If I were Doctor Defect, I would have gone right for the source and stolen the data from the lab itself. Although, I guess targeting one single Super is a lot easier than breaking into a highly-protected government facility, especially when he's just had a lose-your-powers appointment. Even I could probably take out a former Super who'd just—

Wait.

"Oh my god!" I yell, the echo reverberating around the tiled walls of the bathroom. I clap my hand over my mouth. "Oh my *god*," I say again in a muffled whisper.

"What? What is it? What happened?" Juniper screeches.

"When the Supers get the injection that makes them lose their powers," I say slowly, trying to keep my voice even, "how does that work? Do they go to the lab?"

Juniper snorts. "Are you kidding? Don't you think it'd be a little obvious if someone flew into the lab as a Super and then walked out the front door as a citizen? All their enemies would be waiting out front to attack them. No, one of the SuperVariant agents brings the gene-reversal serum into the city and meets them at a secret location and—" She stops talking, and I know we're on the same page.

"What if—" I whisper, just to be sure, "—what if the serum I found in the van wasn't the one that gives the Supers their powers? What if it was the one that takes them *away*? What if whoever killed Sam found out where he was going to be meeting the agent bringing him the gene-reversal serum, and—"

"And intercepted him and stole the serum," Juniper finishes. "Replicating the serum that gives the Supers their powers isn't the plan. The plan is to get rid of the Supers' powers completely."

I feel like someone has inserted a countdown clock into my brain. The "somebody's trying to replicate the serum and create their own army of Supers" theory obviously wasn't preferable, but at least I knew it might be some time before a plan like that could actually be carried out. But if whoever killed Sam—whether it was Doctor Defect or someone else—collects the serums that reverse each of the four genetic enhancements, he can take away any new SuperVariant's powers and murder them immediately. The city won't be able to replace them fast enough, assuming anyone even wants to be a Super anymore.

All they have to do is intercept the agent bringing the serum into the city every time a Super is scheduled to be relieved of their powers.

And it's almost time for the next one.

Also, I'm a *genius*. I should be a detective. I'm gonna quit my job at the café and be a detective.

"Four is next," Juniper says, a tremor in her voice. "Four always gets replaced after Three. And it's at the end of this week."

The news goes through me like an electric shock. "This *week*?" I yelp. "What do you mean, this week? Who scheduled two replacements so close together?"

"I know, I know!" She sounds like the verbal equivalent of

wringing your hands together. "The dates vary every year, remember? The only rule is that it's in the fall!"

"I know, but they're not always back-to-back like this! There's usually, like, a *month* in between SuperVariant replacements!" I scoop up Trashface and leap to my feet, tipping him back inside my backpack. "Okay. It's fine. It's fine. We just have to find one of them before the end of the week. We were already trying to do that. It's just more, you know, urgent now. It's fine. Okay. Wow, we have to do something, like, *now*."

And built up on a massive spurt of adrenaline and horror, I charge out into the hallway.

I barely even check to see if the coast is clear. Who cares? As long as I can pull the switch, it won't matter if I get kicked out of this school. I just need to see how Superhero Kid reacts.

In one aggressive motion, I skid into the wall, lift the plastic case protector, slam the switch down, and clamp my hands over my ears.

Nothing.

I cautiously take one finger out of my ear canal and look up at the ceiling.

What's going on? Why is nothing happening?

"What's going on?" Juniper asks. "Why is nothing happening?"

"Mind reading, now?"

"What?"

"It didn't work," I say in disbelief. "I—"

"Well, of course it didn't work," I hear a voice behind me say matter-of-factly. "Have you looked at this school? Nothing works."

FIFTEEN

I SPIN AROUND, feeling like a burglar caught in the act. I don't know who I'm expecting to see—a teacher, a hall monitor, one of the Super-killing bad guys. Instead, Sanjeet blinks at me from the archway leading to the boys' bathroom, clutching a hall pass.

"Sanjeet!" I exclaim, hiding my hands behind my back like it'll make him forget that he just saw me attempting to break school rules. "I wasn't... I just... uh..."

"I *knew* you were acting weird," he says, eyebrows furrowed in suspicion. "What I *don't* understand is why. Why would you try to pull a fire alarm on your first day at a new school? Especially one that's already known for havoc?"

"I... uh..."

"You're not really a student, are you?" he says bluntly. I freeze, too off-guard to think of a counterargument fast enough.

"What happened? Who's that talking?" Juniper pipes up in my ear.

"I noticed that you don't have a class schedule. You also don't have a comprehensive safety guide, which all students are given as soon as they enroll." He scratches his wrist under his watch, like the metal is chafing his skin. "Of course, I've memorized mine, but I doubt you've memorized yours as quickly. Have you?"

"Is it that boy? Are you finding out whether he's the Super?" Juniper is still talking.

"I can't imagine why you would sneak into a high school just to pull a fire alarm. Is it a trap? Do you have accomplices waiting in our designated emergency locations waiting to ambush other students? Is that who you've been talking to on your earpiece all day?"

Crap, he even noticed the earpiece? I try to back away, but he's inching closer and closer as he lists off accusations in an unperturbed, logical voice. Juniper is still freaking out in my ear, trying to get me to tell her what's going on. It's too much noise. I give up.

"Okay!" I yell. "Okay. You're right, I'm not a student."

"What's happening?" Juniper shrieks. "Why are you telling him that?"

"It's okay, he already figured it out." I exhale and hold my hands out defensively. "Listen to me, okay? I'm following one of the students here. We think he might be in danger."

Sanjeet wrinkles his nose, looking at me skeptically. "Danger?"

"Yes." Boy, do I hope this doesn't end up being a mistake. "You know that quiet boy with the square glasses you have every class with?"

"Thomas Reed?" He looks confused, like he's never given much thought to the boy before now. "What about him?"

Thomas Reed. He has a full name now. "Does he ever, like... disappear out of nowhere?"

His forehead crinkles up like an accordion as he thinks. "I never really noticed, but... yeah, I guess he does. He does miss a lot of classes."

"Okay." It's a struggle to keep my voice calm. It's all adding up, just like I thought. "And he doesn't really fit in with everyone else, right? Pretty quiet? Keeps to himself?"

Sanjeet is looking more and more confused. "I guess. I don't really know," he says. "I've honestly never even noticed him before. I think I heard his parents died last year, and he stopped talking to everyone."

So he's an orphan, just like Sam was. A quiet, class-skipping, crime-tracking orphan. That's too many commonalities to be a coincidence.

"I knew it," I say to Juniper through the mic. "I was right. I'm going to warn him."

"Wait, *what* are you talking about?" Sanjeet asks. "Warn him about what?"

"We think…" How do I explain this? "We think some bad people might be after him." Out loud, the explanation sounds even more lame.

"And how would pulling the fire alarm help with that?" Sanjeet still looks a little skeptical, like he's considering calling the principal or an insane asylum or something.

"I don't know, okay?" I throw my hands in the air. It had felt like a good idea at first, but now I'm not so sure. "I just need to talk to him."

"But if you just want to warn him," he says logically, "why don't you just talk to him in class like a normal person? If he's not the person you're looking for, you still won't lose anything."

I blink.

"Wow, that's a really good point," Juniper agrees.

"Hey, our idea was great, too," I grumble.

Sanjeet manages to look even more confused. "Who are you *talking* to?"

"Don't tell him who I am! You already blew your own cover; do not drag me into this!" Juniper shrieks, overhearing him.

I roll my eyes. "Juniper, he's not going to report you."

"Did you just tell him my name? Thanks. Thanks a whole lot."

I turn back to Sanjeet. "So listen, just don't tell anyone I'm not supposed to be here, okay? I promise, as soon as I talk to Thomas, I'll be out of your hair for good, and you can go back to napping your way through high school. Okay?"

He still looks slightly wary, but he nods. "I guess. But if you—"

Before he can finish his sentence, all the lights go out.

The echo of screaming reverberates up and down the entire hallway.

I reach for my umbrella instinctively, but before I can pull it out of its clip, I realize that the screaming isn't terrified or panicked or even mildly concerned. It's *joking*. They're just yelling for the sake of yelling in the face of something out of the ordinary happening at school. I can even hear taunts from some of the students mixed in with the gleeful screeches.

"Hey, who turned out the lights?"

"Knock it *off*, you creep!"

"Wait, does this mean the test is cancelled?"

I look at the blurry shape of Sanjeet in the dark. The blur shrugs. "This happens all the time. Just give it a second."

The emergency power comes on with a click, bathing the hallway in a creepy red light.

"See?" He almost looks bored, but I can see the slightest twinge of concern in his eyes as he glances back down the hallway toward the chemistry classroom. Or maybe that's just the light. "I'd better get back to class. Maybe you should hide again until they run the all-clear."

I look down the hall in the other direction. "All clear? So is it a real crisis or not? How do you know if—" I turn back around, but he's already gone. He probably wants to get another nap in before class resumes. I can't blame him.

"Meg?" I'd forgotten Juniper was still plugged in. "What's happening?"

"I don't really know," I say, barely able to hear myself. An emergency siren is now going off, and the ringing feels like it's coming from inside my brain. "I have to get out of here." I disconnect Juniper; all she'll be able to hear is the blaring alarm anyway.

But I don't know where else to go, and if it's really an emergency, I don't know where I *should* go, because I don't have that stupid handbook that I was apparently supposed to have to survive being in this school, so I run back inside the bathroom and curl up into the tiniest ball that I can behind the sink farthest from the door, hands over my ears, trying to shut out the noise that always sounds like impending death no matter how many times I hear it.

Err. Err. Err. Err. Err. Err.

Finally, right when I feel like the noise is going to bore a hole right through my skull, it stops. I cautiously pull my hands away from my ears.

"This has been a test of our emergency alarm system," drones an older man's voice over the speaker system. "Please resume all class activities. Thank you for your cooperation." The lights flick back on casually, like nothing has happened at all, and I forcefully plug my earpiece back in.

"Meg?" Juniper asks. "Are you okay?"

"I hate this place," I whisper angrily. "I hate this stupid place. I'm finding Thomas and I'm telling him what's going on, and then I'm never coming to this absolute torture chamber of a school ever, ever again."

Juniper lets out a light, tinkling giggle. "You sound like everyone who's ever been to high school."

I don't respond, launching myself up off the floor. Forget waiting. Who cares if I look like a crazy person? I'm going right into that chemistry class and telling Thomas that I need to talk to him right now. And then I'm going back to my life. This is ending today.

My drive lasts as long as it takes to get from the bathroom

to the classroom. I grab the handle and throw open the door. Immediately, every head in the room snaps toward me; most in confusion or mild interest, but a few in fear. I guess I do look like an absolute lunatic, and now I'm bursting into their classroom right after an emergency warning, even though it ended up being a fake one. But I don't have time to worry about looking weird right now.

"I need to talk to…" I scan the room. Then I scan it again.

No. No, no, no, no, no.

He's gone. Thomas Reed is gone.

Goddammit.

He must have turned invisible and gone to investigate the source of the emergency before they announced that it was just a test.

I don't believe this.

"Never mind," is all I'm able to mutter before swiveling as fast as I can and retreating out of the classroom.

"Um… still can't see what's happening, over here," Juniper says nervously.

"Okay." I run my fingers through my hair. "He has to come back. There wasn't really an emergency, so he has to come back. He'll show up again. It'll be fine."

SIXTEEN

IT'S NOT FINE. HE DOESN'T COME BACK.

I follow a resigned-looking Sanjeet to the rest of his classes after he tells me that, incredibly, their entire course schedule is exactly the same, but he doesn't show for the rest of the day. I do learn a lot about how to conjugate verbs in French, though, and also get to spend most of the last period being harassed by a small army of a cappella performers insisting that I join their club because I would "really even out their sound," whatever that means.

Then the final bell rings and I'm done, no closer to warning the Supers than I was at the beginning of the day.

"I can't believe this," I mumble sullenly into the microphone I still have attached to the underside of my collar. "I can't believe he just disappeared. Actually, I can, given the circumstances. This is ridiculous. No one even noticed. If I went to the *bathroom* for too long in high school, I got reported."

✖ COLLATERAL DAMAGE ✖

"Stop sulking," Juniper says, but I can tell that she's a little worried that this isn't moving fast enough too. "You'll just have to try again tomorrow."

"No way!" I yelp, bounding down the stairs to the front of the school two at a time, anxious to get my feet off the property. "I'm not coming back here. We have to think of something else."

"Meg, you can't give up now." Juniper's voice suddenly sounds like it's coming from two different places at once. I look up and realize that she's physically there, waiting for me at the bottom of the steps. Her lab coat is tucked into her tan tote bag, the edge not-so-accidentally sticking out, like she wants people to know how cool her job is. I jump off the second-to-last step and land in front of her.

"I'm not giving up," I snap. "I'm switching tactics. This plan isn't working. All I learned today is that the mitochondria is the powerhouse of the cell." I throw my arms wide. "How is that going to help me with anything? I also think I might have joined an a cappella group."

She looks bewildered, but recovers quickly. "Look, I know today sucked, but I *know* tomorrow will be better. You just have to go home and rest and—"

"I can't go home!" I snatch the yellow slip I'd gotten this morning out of my front backpack zipper and wave it in the air. "I have detention!"

Juniper slaps the slip out of my hand. *"You are not a real student!"*

"Yeah, and pretty soon someone else is going to notice that, too," I retort. "That Sanjeet kid already noticed, and he was asleep for most of the day! This isn't going to work. There has to be a better, faster way to do this. What's the point of wasting another day here?"

"It's not a *waste*, Meg! And today wasn't a failure. You got a lead, didn't you?"

I did. I did do that.

"Besides," she continues, "you don't have to spend an entire second day here tomorrow—you only have to stay until you find him again. Which, you know, could happen before homeroom is even over. Right?"

Dammit. She's right. It still forces me to wake up earlier than should be legal for a second day in a row, but she's right. Technically, tomorrow's undercover mission will only take ten minutes—assuming Thomas Reed even shows up.

"Fine." I glare at her. "One more day. But if this doesn't work, then I get to pick the new plan."

I DON'T FEEL LIKE going back to Oliver's empty apartment and waiting there for three hours for him to get home, so I bike to -o's Pizza, which is significantly farther from Saint Charles's than I'd expected. By the time I get to the door, my legs feel like jelly.

Oliver swivels toward me mid-bite from behind the counter, a half-eaten pepperoni slice in one hand. He looks me up and down with a very lost expression plastered across his face, and I suddenly remember that I'm wearing what has to look like a pretty cheap schoolgirl costume. I pull my too-short skirt down reflexively.

"What in God's name are you wearing?" Oliver asks through a mouthful of pizza.

"It's, uh…" I look down at myself. "Just… trying something out for Halloween."

"It's the middle of September."

"Is that Meg?" Carly's head pops in through the hole in the wall. "I wasn't aware that you still knew where this building was, seeing as how you haven't been here in two days."

"Hey!" I point a finger at her, using my other hand to snag a slice of pizza from the open box on the pickup counter. "My house burned down."

"Big deal! My house burned down three months ago." Oh, yeah. I'd forgotten about that. Carly had jumped out a second-story window to escape the flames and limped to work on a sprained ankle. "And if you have time for Halloween costumes, you have time for work."

"Wait, are you gonna tell me what's really going on, or what?" Oliver interrupts. "What's with the getup?"

I look at him. He's an entire world away from everything that's been happening to me over the last two days. Has it only been two days? It feels like I've been hiding this for *months*.

I didn't want him to know. I didn't want him to be involved. I thought it would be fine; that I would tell the police and be done, and it wouldn't matter that I was lying to him. But now I'm about to start on my third day of keeping this giant secret from him—Sam, the weapon, the serum, the threat to the Supers, everything—and I can feel the desperation to vent all of it out boiling inside me. Besides, he's my best friend, my partner, the only person I can count on.

And secrets are just so much work.

"I..." I begin, but Carly is still staring at me through the hole. "Do you *mind*?"

She vanishes, grumbling. "And I need tomorrow off, too!" I add. "Oh, I don't *think* so—" Carly starts, but I grab Oliver's wrist and pull him into the kitchen before I can hear the end of her protests.

"Don't mind us," I announce to Artie and Daniel, who are manning the ovens, then push a bewildered Oliver into the walk-in pantry and shut the door behind us.

"Should I be scared?" he demands as I flick the light on. "Because I'm scared. What is going *on* with you?"

What's going on with me? Where am I supposed to even begin?

The one thing I know for certain is that I'm tired. I'm tired of handling this by myself, stuck only with Juniper for support. I didn't want him to worry, but now, after a day of being nervous and alone and tense, I'm desperate for it—desperate for the attention and support that comes with letting someone who cares about you worry. And maybe that makes me selfish; maybe the difference between me and the heroes I'm trying to help save is that they know how to keep the people they love away from their problems, and I don't. But I'm not like them, and I shouldn't have tried to pretend I was.

And before I can change my mind and talk myself out of it, I blurt out, "Someone killed one of the Supers and stole the serum that drains their powers, and I have to warn the others before they get killed next."

Not one millimeter of Oliver's face shifts. "What?" he says blankly.

"Wow, it really sounds crazy when I say it out loud like that," I observe. "But you believe me, don't you? Doctor Defect is almost definitely involved, but we think there might be someone helping him this time—someone more powerful who the SuperVariant Program doesn't know about yet. And they're going to use the serum to take away the next SuperVariant Three's powers, and then kill SuperVariant Four and steal his serum and take away the next Four's powers too and—"

"*What?*"

"Aren't you listening? They're gonna kill all the former Supers and then kill all the replacement Supers and—"

"What?"

"—and we have to find just one Super to warn before Four gets replaced this week so that they can tell everybody else, but it's basically impossible—"

"What?"

"And we thought Two was in high school, but then I lost him, and I might not even be right about who it is, but I have to go back tomorrow anyway—"

"*What?*"

"Will you pick a new reaction word?" I yell.

"This is a lot to process!" Oliver yells back.

✖ COLLATERAL DAMAGE ✖

"*I know it's a lot to process, I've been processing it for two days and my brain still hurts—*"

"Listen, I get that, but this is a lot of information and—"

"WILL YOU KNOCK IT OFF OVER THERE?" Carly's voice comes bellowing through the shared wall, into the pantry. "YOU'RE SCARING THE CUSTOMERS."

Oliver has his hands so deep in his hair, his hat is teetering off his head. "I don't understand. Doctor Defect is targeting the Supers? Isn't he *always* targeting the Supers? Isn't dealing with him sort of part of their job description?"

"Yeah, but it actually worked this time. I mean, the last Three is *dead*. And apart from the one I accidentally stole, I'm positive he has the rest of those serum vials by now. I tried to tell Dr. Crenshaw—you know, the head of the Supers—but he wouldn't listen. So now I have to tell them myself."

"This is nuts," he mutters.

"Trust me, I know," I reply sullenly, but a lot of my heaviness already feels like it's dissipating. Somehow, talking to Oliver about this makes the entire situation feel more manageable.

I look over at him only to find that he's propped himself up against the door, like his legs don't know how to work.

"Oliver?" I ask tentatively. "You okay, buddy?"

"It's cool," he mumbles. "Lot to process. Dead Supers. You trying to *help* the Supers. Remind me, don't you hate them? Did I make that up?"

I play with a loose thread at the bottom of my blouse uncomfortably. "I mean, they're really destructive and irresponsible, but they don't deserve to *die* like this. Somebody has to tell them."

"Huh." He pushes himself away from the doorframe. "Okay. Still processing, but I'm okay." He looks at me, his eyes suddenly wild. "So, what do we do?"

"We?" I don't know what I expected. All I really wanted was to vent. But I should have known Oliver wouldn't just leave his involvement at sympathy.

"Obviously I'm helping. You had to know that I would help you, and I'm assuming that's why you didn't tell me before. Didn't want me to get involved, right? Too dangerous or something?"

I stick my hands in my pockets so I can stop fiddling with them. "I know that sounds dumb…"

"No, it doesn't," he cuts me off. "I would do the same thing for you. Trust me. But you did tell me, so I'm not going to just hang out here while you risk your life getting involved with the Supers. Besides, if I help, it might get done faster, which will get you out of harm's way faster, too. Right?"

I feel like I'm going to collapse from sheer relief. "Have I ever told you you're the best?"

"It's always been implied. Look, weird things always happen at one point or another while I'm out on my deliveries. I'll just follow the next one and yell at the nearest Super until he listens to me."

"That was Juniper's original idea." I frown. "I still think intentionally going to a crisis is crazy. What if something falls on you, or hits you on accident?"

Oliver waves his hand dismissively. "That could always happen no matter where I am. It'll be fine."

I'm not sure. I'm starting to get anxious again. If something happens to Oliver because I brought him into this, I will never, ever forgive myself.

He must see how skeptical I look, because he goes, "I'll be fine; I promise. First sign of a real problem, and I'll be out of there. Look, I'll even wear my safety helmet and everything."

"Yeah… okay." I nod my head reluctantly. "Just, you know. Don't die."

"Not today," he says automatically. "Or tomorrow, I guess."

"So, you'll do that, and then I guess I'll go back to the school and—"

"Ah… right." Oliver ruffles up the back of his hair. "I don't know if that's a good idea."

I wrinkle my forehead, confused. "What do you mean, that's not a good idea? Juniper's right; it almost worked today. One more day there, and I'm sure I can find the Super and warn him."

"I don't know." Oliver won't meet my eyes. "What if that kid ends up not being the Super after all? You know, a lot of weird things happen at that school. You could get hurt."

"Yeah, and you could get hurt chasing a Super down the street into some kind of crisis tomorrow," I reply angrily. "I'm not going to sit at the café all day while you take this over. That's not why I told you. I'm going back."

"I'm not taking this over, I just think maybe you should—"

"I don't need your permission, Oliver!" I cry out. Why is he fighting me on this? I didn't even want to go back to the school before, but now that he clearly thinks I'm incapable of doing this on my own without dying, I feel the irresistible urge to prove him wrong. "I can do this."

"It's not that I think you *can't*, I just—" He cuts himself off and takes a deep breath. "What-if-something-happens-to-you-and-I'm-not-there?" It spills out all at once, like one giant word.

My irritation evaporates. I can't be upset that he's worried about me. "Oliver, I'll be fine," I promise him. "Tomorrow is going to be a ten-minutes-tops mission. I swear."

He sighs, not looking completely convinced. "Well, you know what I'm going to say."

"I know. 'Don't die.'" I grin. "Do I ever?"

SEVENTEEN

WHEN I CLIMB THE STAIRS up to the school the next day, Sanjeet is sitting on the third-from-the-top step, leaning against the railing, an unfinished practice sheet covered with mathematical formulas open on his knees. "You're back again," he remarks.

"Very observant." I continue through the main entrance without stopping.

"Hey, wait," he calls from behind me, leaping to his feet and staggering up the remaining steps with the paper clutched in his hand. "Did you happen to get the calc homework done? I didn't have time last night."

"I'm not a real student," I remind him.

"Oh... right. So, are you back to stalk Thomas Reed again?" He looks me up and down. I'm wearing my The Pure Bean t-shirt underneath my button-down/blazer combo and dark jeans instead of the skirt, planning on getting in and out fast enough to make it to work this afternoon. Carly flatly vetoed a third day off. "You're not blending in as well today."

"So? The worst they can do is give me another dress code violation. And I'm not *stalking* him." I scan the hallways, hoping I can find Thomas before class so I don't have to even go to homeroom at all. "I told you, I'm trying to warn him."

"Right, about the bad people that are after him?" Sanjeet scratches his wrist. "You know, I could just, like, tell him for you. You don't have to stick around. Why don't I just pass on the message?"

"It's more complicated than that," I say. *Why do people keep offering to handle this for me? Where have all of these helpful people been during the rest of my life?*

Sanjeet is still scratching his wrist. I squint down at it. "What's going on, do you have chicken pox or something?"

He flexes his fingers and hides his hands behind his back. "Huh? No. I'm fine. How are you?"

I raise an eyebrow. What a weird kid.

The bell rings, and I follow him to homeroom, having forgotten which door in the maze of hallways I went into yesterday. My heart leaps as we walk through the doorway: Thomas is in his chair, staring out the window. *Thank god. This is almost over.*

I practically sprint toward his desk. I'm four steps away... three steps away... two...

"Are you Thomas Reed?" I ask, suddenly very conscious of how fast my blood is pumping through my body. He looks up from his notebook in surprise and peers at me through his absurd glasses like no one has ever intentionally addressed him before. "I need to talk to you. I think someone is going to try to kill you."

That's what I open my mouth to say, at least. But all that comes out is "I need—" before the rest of my sentence is eaten by a massive, resounding *boom* that rattles my bones and makes the entire floor suddenly feel like I'm standing in one of those freaky tilted carnival houses. Everyone standing jolts with a collective shriek that ends with half the kids on the floor. I only prevent myself from joining them by grabbing the edge of Thomas's desk and throwing my other leg out wide like I'm surfing the unbalanced floor.

The power cuts out for a split second, then switches back on with the same eerie red light as yesterday. Then the alarms return.

I clamp my hands over my ears and swivel frantically. Everyone in the room is scrambling for the door. The homeroom teacher hasn't moved from her chair yet, but she has produced a megaphone from out of nowhere and is lazily droning, "Everyone remain calm and proceed to your emergency stations in an orderly fashion…"

"No chance this is another practice drill, is there?" I shout over the noise to Sanjeet, who's offering a hand to a girl that's still trying to get back up from the ground. She ignores him, using the side of a desk to haul herself up, and books it for the door.

"No," he replies, dejectedly sticking the rejected hand back in his jacket pocket. "Come on, we have to get out of here. Do you know where your emergency location is?"

"Of course I don't!" I unhook my umbrella from my backpack, clutching it so hard my knuckles go white. "*I am not a real student!*"

Another titanic boom shakes the floor again.

"Come on!" Sanjeet repeats, dodging behind me and shepherding me toward the door, where the final few students are vanishing through the archway. "Down the hall to your right, second stairwell, out the door, and across the street. Got it?"

"Wait!" I freeze, scanning around myself frantically. If I lose Thomas now, I'll have to start this all over again. I can't let that happen. I finally spot him fighting through a sea of students elbowing each other toward the exit. As I expected, he's going the complete opposite direction from everyone else, heading toward the source of the noise instead of away from it. He hunches over, looks around furtively, then ducks around the corner.

"Gotcha," I mutter. I turn to announce an excuse to Sanjeet, but he's already gone, probably stampeding toward the emergency meet-up location along with the rest of the school. I don't blame him for giving up on me. He probably doesn't want to risk getting killed over my inability to do the smart thing and run for my life.

This'd better work, I tell myself, before unhooking my umbrella from my backpack, swinging it out to the side, and charging after Thomas.

EIGHTEEN

"GREAT. I'M OFFICIALLY the type of person who gets killed first in a horror movie," I mutter as I follow the flickering red lights down the hall. "Awesome. I've peaked."

The only response I get is a gravelly sort of croaking sound, which begins to overlap with the rhythmic blaring of the emergency alarms, like the world's worst orchestra.

Errrrrr. Errrrrr. Errrrr. CRIIIIICK. Errrrr. Errrrr. Errrrr. CRIIIIIICK.

I lift my umbrella over my shoulder with both hands, ready to swing it like a steel baseball bat if need be. I just hope that I'm faster than whatever caused the alarms to go off.

I take a massive breath, like it'll help, and round the corner. Nothing.

No monster or supervillain. But also no Thomas, either as a student or as a Super.

Oh, no. What if he's already turned invisible? I'll never find him. I bounce from foot to foot nervously.

This was such a stupid idea. I should have just gone to the emergency station with everybody else, waited for the crisis to end, and caught up with him afterward. But no, I was so impatient that I had to run in here without thinking. Now I'm probably going to get eaten by whatever set off the alert, and the Supers still won't know about the threat. I should—

Before I can finish the thought, a door halfway down the hall suddenly closes. It closes so imperceptibly that I never could have heard it click shut over the noise; if I hadn't happened to be looking right at it, I wouldn't even have noticed.

I get a tiny bit of hope back. Thomas. SuperVariant Two. It has to be him.

Maybe he snuck in there to change into his supersuit or something. I always assumed that they all wore their costumes under their clothes, but I guess that would get pretty itchy after a while. Not to mention the smell. I wonder how often they have to wash those. How *do* you wash those?

There's another resounding *boom* from around the end of this hallway's corner.

Maybe now isn't the time for these kinds of deep thoughts.

I dash for the door and realize as I close in on it that it's attached to a supply closet. *Please be him, please be him,* I pray desperately, then grab the handle and throw it open.

The good news: Thomas is inside, just as I'd hoped.

The bad news: he is not wearing a supersuit. He's not in the process of turning invisible. He *is*, however, pulling a very ordinary-looking box of index cards off a shelf of school supplies. When I whip the door open, the motion startles him so much that the box flies out of his hands, dumping its contents all over the floor. I look down to see that the grimy linoleum is now littered with clear plastic bags full of pills.

I make eye contact with Thomas Reed, who's practically paralyzed. "What are you doing?" I ask calmly. It's not really a question. I know what he's doing. There's just an infinitesimally small part of my brain that's really, really hoping that maybe he'll respond with, "Oh, these are special government-supplied pills that make me fight better," instead of, "Oh, I'm actually the school drug dealer and that's why I miss class all the time."

"Saving my stash," he snaps defensively, and the last shred of hope goes flying out the window. "What are you gonna do, tell on me?"

I don't believe this. Wait, yes I do. Who am I kidding? This is exactly the type of thing that would happen to me.

I was wrong. Thomas wasn't the Super. All of this has been for nothing.

"Are you kidding me?" I yell as he stoops to shovel the bags back into the index card box. "You're a *drug dealer*? That's the big secret?"

"They're not drugs!" he snaps angrily. "I'm not some kind of crackhead. It's a special formula I created myself, to enhance focus and knowledge retention. AP classes are no joke."

"You're describing drugs!" I shout.

"Why do you even care?" he retorts. "Who *are* you?"

I push my bangs back with my free hand. This isn't happening. "It's over. You're not the Super," I whisper.

"Super at *what*?"

I scream in frustration and slam the door back shut. Abort mission. I have to get out of here.

Boom.

My feet are wrenched out from beneath me as everything tilts sideways again. As I hit the ground, I lose my grip on my umbrella and it spins away, ricocheting off the opposite wall and lying still four feet away from me. I flip my head up, sending my curls flying away from my face, and suddenly see the thing that caused all this chaos.

I want to gag and scream at the same time, but it's like my body has forgotten how to do everything. I can't even move.

It's Professor Gullet, from yesterday, only not. His bald head now sticks straight upward from a twisted, warty, puce-green torso, which is pressed horizontally against the ground. His limbs, also puce-green and covered in tiny knobs of wrinkled flesh, crack at horrendous angles upward at the joint, and then back down to connect with four long-fingered, webbed hands. His eyes stare without seeing. His gaping mouth leaks spittle.

Every blood vessel in my body runs cold.

Thomas finally emerges from the closet, a box-of-pills-shaped lump in his jacket. He rubs his eyes. "You can see that too, right?"

I finally get my voice back. It comes back much shriller than I remember it ever being. "What *is* that?" I shriek in a hysterical tone that I'm not proud of. "What the hell is it?"

The creature's head snaps to the left. Its bloodless eyes bore into mine. *Frogs*, I realize. *He was studying African bullfrogs.* This is why people really need to stop messing around with genetic experimentation. Whatever powers he was trying to give himself by blending frog DNA with his own have clearly, atrociously backfired. It would be pathetic if the results weren't so unbelievably terrifying. If I live through this, I'm going to have nightmares forever.

The monster looks at me for a moment longer. I'm scared to even breathe.

And then it starts moving.

If you're wondering whether it walks like a frog or a human, the answer is both.

It's knobby, impossibly-angled legs windmill one after the other—left, right, left, right—with a sickening plopping sound, faster than I can blink. Its eyes continue to bore through me as it propels itself down the hall, toward the wall opposite me. *It doesn't know how to steer*, I think desperately. *It's not going to be able to—*

I spoke too soon.

Using its momentum from barreling down the hallway, the frog-thing manages to get all four appendages onto the wall, and pushes off with muscled limbs bigger than my head. It rockets through the air, aiming right toward us.

"Holy—" I manage to get out before rolling out of the way at the last second. The impact it makes when it lands on the ground where my head had been seconds earlier creates another resounding, earth-shattering *boom*, propelling me right into the other wall. "Ow..." I groan, rubbing the back of my head as I pull myself up into a seat, then immediately cringe against the wall as I see the creature, which is now just a few feet away from me.

The thing's head is still right side up, but its body is now flat on its back. As I watch in horror, it extends one leg at a time back onto the ground and rotates its entire body like a wind-up toy until everything is back in place, never moving its head or breaking eye contact. I let out an involuntary whimper. It inches forward, one windmilling leg at a time, and slowly opens its cave of a mouth until it looms just a foot away from me. It leans in and...

Thwack!

It lets out an angry, guttural croak of pain and flinches away from me. I pant heavily, my steel umbrella open to full-protective ability and held out in front of me with two hands, the edges still quivering from the brunt of the impact it made when I expanded it right into the creature's mouth.

Thomas looks at me with something like awe. I leap to my feet. "Run!" I yell. "*Run!*"

We run.

I don't bother to look behind me to see if Thomas is following, but the sound of his shallow breathing trailing a few steps behind me as I sprint down the hallway as fast as my shaky legs can take me proves that he's done what I said.

There's another crash behind us, and I instinctively turn in time to see the frog man overshoot as it rounds the corner, unable to slow down in time to prevent itself from crashing into the adjoining wall. A flurry of school spirit flyers rains down around it, revealing a brand new, car-sized crater in the graying brick. It shakes its head twice, still not blinking, then starts bounding after us again.

I don't get it, I think frantically to myself, fighting through a growing stitch in my side as we slam through the doorway to the rickety stairwell and start leaping down them two at a time. *Why is it chasing us? What does it want? Since when do frogs eat humans? They don't. But they do eat...*

"Oh, *dammit*!" I howl. "Trashface, you stupid animal." There's a faint squeaking sound from inside my backpack in response.

"*What*?" Thomas finds time to look at me in pure confusion mid-jump as he throws himself off the stairs onto the ground floor.

"My rat! In my bag." I gasp for air. "I think it wants to eat it. African bullfrogs—they're carnivorous."

"So it's after *you*?"

Crash.

The frog man breaks through the second-floor doorway and rolls like a gigantic, knobby bowling bowl down the first half of the flight of stairs, colliding with the wall on the landing. I've already seen where the door is behind me, so I launch myself backward into it, expecting it to fly open. Instead, I'm rewarded with a sudden stab of pain erupting from my lower back, and I'm jolted forward again. *What the—*

I swivel around in confusion just in time to see Thomas's face on the other side, bent over something attached to the door. I press my face to the glass and look down; he's finishing fiddling with the lock. My eyes widen in horror. "What are you doing?" I scream, straining against the push bar. "Let me *out*!"

"Sorry." His voice is faint through the thick wood as he starts to back away. "I'm not going to die just because you're trying to save a *rat*."

"Thomas!" I yell, pounding on the door with all my might. "I will *kill* you! Open this door! Open—"

But without another backward glance, he runs away.

Oh my god.

Oh my *god*.

I can't believe I thought the Super was that cowardly, evil—

But I don't have time to waste hoping that something rips his limbs off. The frog-thing is already recovering, creeping down the stairs one spiraling foot at a time.

I raise my umbrella, which is back in rod-mode, over my head, turn my face away to shield myself, and smash it through the window as hard as I can.

Crack.

The sound is promising, but when I turn to look, I'm still met with a solid window. Seriously? Shatterproof glass is usually my best friend, but now is not the time. I raise my umbrella and try again.

Crack.

Nothing.

Come on, I think desperately, stepping back to get a running start this time. *Please…*

There's another one of those guttural croaks behind me, and I turn just in time to see that the frog-man has given up on going down the stairs one at a time. With an almost graceful leap, he vaults over the rest of the staircase, aiming straight for me.

I abandon the window and dive out of the way underneath the stairwell, then cover my head with my arms and wait for the inevitable *boom* of a landing.

But it doesn't come.

I peel my arms away and look out in confusion.

The frog-man is suspended in mid-air, limbs flapping in bewilderment, held up by absolutely nothing.

Nothing visible, at least.

Took him long enough, whoever he is.

"Get a little carried away with your research, Mr. Gullet?" calls out a disembodied voice. "Did you start *jumping to conclusions?*"

Oh, god. Puns. I changed my mind. Just let it eat me.

✖ COLLATERAL DAMAGE ✖

The frog suddenly flips upside down in midair and slams down onto the floor. I flinch away from the earthquake-inducing collision. The air around the creature's front legs shimmers, and then, in one swift motion, it's flipped back over with its two front legs wrenched behind it. A thick rope—the kind I used to refuse to climb in gym—appears out of nowhere and wraps around the legs, pinning them together at the joint.

"Ha!" calls out the same voice again. "Gotcha!"

Okay. Now that I'm not about to be eaten, my blood pressure is calming down. This could work. The real SuperVariant Two showed up after all. As soon as he has this creature subdued, I can tell him what I know. Everything will work out after all.

The frog-man, however, has other plans.

Its front legs might be out of service, but its back legs are still fully operational, and it launches itself sideways into the stairwell wall, then bounces off. A spot by the floor of the wall shimmers, and then Two materializes, upside down, his legs sticking straight up the wall at a right angle to his back on the floor. He cocks his head in something like vague puzzlement, then rolls over in an awkward sort of half cartwheel and grabs the end of the rope right before the thing can escape. "I don't think so!" he mutters through his teeth, straining with his heels pressed into the ground like he's trying to wrangle a bull.

I give him points for effort, but super strength is not Two's thing. He can clearly tell that he's not going to win this game of tug-of-war either, because he turns his face toward every inch of the stairwell in rapid succession, looking for a new plan. He pauses as he settles on the railing of the second-story platform. "Got it!"

I crane my neck out to see where he's looking and see him throw the end of the rope up so that it loops over the railing. He uses the writhing frog-man as a springboard to launch himself upward, catch the end, and land clumsily back on the ground. I watch him crouch, his arms poised to pull, and hear a *crack* shudder through the platform above me.

"No!" I shriek as I realize what's about to happen. "It's not strong enough to hold the weight! It's going to—"

I don't get to finish the sentence.

Two doesn't hear me. Before I have time to think to run out and do anything else to either stop him or get myself out of the way, he flexes his arms and *yanks*.

The railing gives way under the weight, and the rest of the already-damaged platform, like it had been waiting for this last Jenga piece to be pulled, collapses inward over me.

I have just enough time to throw my arms over my head and shield my face, and then everything goes black.

NINETEEN

"MEG? MEG!"

Everything seems to be ringing faintly, like I'm listening to a very persistent bell from the end of a miles-long tunnel. Mingled with the ringing is a dull, pained, groaning sound, like someone dying.

Then I realize that the sound is coming from me.

Opening my eyes feels like it takes as much strength as deadlifting a truck, and doesn't ultimately make a difference. Everything is still impossibly dark.

Assess the damage, I think vaguely. *I have to…*

But even thinking about checking to make sure I'm not dead proves to be too straining, and I let myself remain collapsed under what I have no doubt is a massive pile of rubble. Besides, what would be the point? Why bother to check to see what hurts? I already know the answer. It's everything. Everything hurts.

"*Meg?*"

Someone's loud, grating voice is getting closer. I don't know who's looking for me, but it can't be someone from the school. They don't know what my real name is.

I hear a massive creak as someone opens a door, setting off a loud protest from its squeaky hinges.

"Meg? Are you in here?"

This time, the voice isn't muffled, and I know that it's in the room with me.

Help, I think weakly. All that comes out is another pained groan.

"Hello?" the voice responds, and I breathe a sigh of relief that I instantly regret, as sharp bursts of pain shoot down my ribs. "Is anybody in here?"

I wait for the debris crushing my body to start lifting away, but it doesn't happen. There are a few seconds of silence, and then the door begins to creak open again.

Oh, no. No, no, no.

"Wait." I muster up all of my remaining strength and manage to croak out the word hoarsely. "Help."

"*Meg!*"

A massive amount of pressure suddenly leaves my legs, then my stomach. I gasp for air. The final two sections of platform miraculously propped up against each other when they fell, creating a tent just over my head, which is probably the only reason I'm not actually dead right now. But most of the pain in my extremely painful body is coming from my left arm, where the lower edge of one of the platform sections had planted itself, and that's what I'm most worried about right now.

There's a grunt of effort from my rescuer, and then both sections of platforms go crashing to the side, clearing my vision. The movement jostles my arm, and I scream as sharp knives of pain shoot through my elbow.

A heart-shaped face framed by a familiar sheet of pale hair suddenly comes into focus, kneeling over me with a concerned expression. I feel myself flood with relief. I've never been so happy to see anyone in my life as I am to see Juniper in that moment.

"Well, aren't you a sight for sore everything," I groan with extremely false cheer.

"Oh my *god*, Meg, what happened? Are you okay?"

"Oh, yeah, this is great," I gasp. "All according to plan. I *meant* for this to happen."

Juniper ignores my sarcasm, covering her mouth as she looks down at me. "Oh, god, your *arm*."

That doesn't sound promising. I don't want to look. I just want to lie here forever and not think about how much everything hurts.

I peek. "Oh, *Jesus*..."

I shouldn't have looked. Why did I look? The bone is sticking out of its joint, erupting from a frothy mess of blood and dirty skin and jagged white spears. It's the most disgusting thing I've ever seen, even counting frog-man. My stomach lurches. How is that ever going to go back into place? Are they going to have to amputate it? I can feel myself getting hysterical, so I turn my eyes back to the ceiling instead.

Juniper dashes around me and lifts me under my arms, trying to help me up. I groan again, and give up once I reach a seated position. I cradle my left arm gingerly, but nothing I do stops the pulsing stabs of pain. *Don't you freaking faint, you wimp*, I order myself angrily, and survey the rest of the damage.

In addition to my arm, which I don't even want to think about, my entire body is stiff with dull aches. I'm going to have so many bruises tomorrow. My head is still ringing a little bit, but when I touch it with my non-broken hand, I don't feel any blood, so that's a good sign.

"How long have I been here?" I ask, squinting around at the lightless stairwell. All concept of time is gone.

"A couple of hours." She looks uncomfortable.

"A couple of *hours*? You mean nobody at this dumb school

even checked to make sure their students weren't dead?"

"Well, you weren't technically registered, so they probably thought they had everyone accounted for."

"Unbelievable." I shake my head and wince when my sore neck protests loudly at the movement. "How did *you* even find me, then?"

"Well, I noticed that you hadn't moved in a while, so I turned on the news, and as soon as I realized what had happened, I ran over here and—"

"Wait, what do you mean you noticed I hadn't moved in a while?"

"Oh, um..." Juniper fiddles with the end of her hair and doesn't meet my eyes. "I, um... I sort of put a tracker on you."

"You *what*?"

"Just in case!" she cries. "And look! It ended up being useful!"

"Juniper," I grit my teeth. "If there is a tracker *inside of my body*, I swear to god—"

"Calm down!" she scolds defensively. "It's the size of a pea. And it was to *help you*—"

"I don't care what size it is!" I snap, my joy at seeing her quickly dissipating. "Here's an idea, genius. Don't put trackers in people without telling them!"

"I didn't think it was a big deal!" she retorts hotly, then pushes her hair back, exhaling again to calm herself down. "Did you at least," she asks, "find the Super?"

I look at her incredulously. "*No, I didn't find the Super,* Juniper. I was a little busy being *crushed under a falling building*!"

"But you could have before—"

"Well, I didn't!" I don't believe this. I can't believe she's asking me about the Supers instead of helping me get to a surgeon. I'm losing words to describe just how much my arm hurts. It's getting hard to focus on anything else. I squint around and manage to spot my backpack, with the umbrella miraculously still unbroken just a foot away from it, and drag both of them to me. A quick look inside reveals that Trashface is still alive, without even a scratch. Unbelievable. He squeaks and scurries up the side of the backpack and up my arm, perching on my shoulder.

I manage to push myself up off the ground with my free arm, away from her, and immediately gasp in pain again as my right leg threatens to give way underneath me. I lean against the wall and curse my body for not being more damage-proof.

"Okay. It's okay." Juniper straightens up, too. "We still have time. The next replacement is still three days away. We'll just have to—"

My mouth falls open. It takes me a few seconds to fully process what she's just said. "*What*?"

"Of course, infiltrating the school clearly didn't work, so you'll have to try something else. I still think my original plan could work. There's bound to be another crisis soon, right? Maybe you could write the information down on a note or something, and give it to a Super while he's—"

"Is that a joke?" I let out an involuntary laugh of disbelief. "Juniper. Please tell me you're joking."

She plows through, ignoring me. "…and maybe I can borrow some better protective gear from work. We'll just have to be more careful this time."

Everything suddenly feels like it's on fire, and not just because of the shooting pain in my arm and leg. My head feels like it's going to explode. "*We*?" I manage to get out.

"Of course, 'we;' we're in this together." She looks surprised. "Now, here's what I'm thinking for your next try—"

"No." The word is out of my mouth before I even realize I've said it, but as soon as I do, I wonder why it took me so long.

She stops mid-word. "What?"

"I said no."

The pain in my body is still there, but my focus has now been replaced. I can feel myself shaking, both from my anger and my inability to stand up properly. Screw her. Screw all of this. My arm is in about ten different pieces. I could have died. And yet, here she is, already talking about sending me back into battle.

"We are *not* in this together." I take a shaky, limping step toward her. "*I* found Three. *I* got shot at. *I* had to go undercover to try to warn the others at this school. *I* almost got eaten by that freak science teacher-turned-amphibian. *I* almost died under a falling staircase today." I can feel my eyes watering from the effort, but I fight through the pain long enough to straighten up and look straight at her. She suddenly looks so helpless and confused, and I don't care. I hate her, I hate her, I hate her.

"I didn't even want to come back today, remember?" I snap. I feel like everything I've been feeling is finally draining out of me. It's both exhausting and freeing at the same time. "I wanted to try something else. Preferably something we could *both* be involved in. *You* made me do this. And look!" I point to my arm. "Look at this! What's next, Juniper? My leg? My head? Sure, let me just race off into the next collapsing building while you sit in your lab doing *nothing*."

She flares up. "I am *not* doing—"

"Oh, save it!" I snap. Angry tears are threatening to embarrass me by spilling out down my cheeks. I can't believe I let her convince me to be a part of this. It was stupid to think I could be some kind of hero. This isn't my job. I wish I'd never gone with her to the LCPD lab in the first place. *If I got killed trying to find these Supers, she wouldn't even care.* I grit my teeth.

"I'm not going to die for them, or for you. You want to save the Supers? You can do it yourself." I limp to the door and press my aching back against the push bar. "I'm done."

TWENTY

THE NUMBER OF PEOPLE outside handling the damage is minimal, which is the best indicator of how much time I was trapped under that staircase. A few police officers are still milling around, keeping people off the sidewalk, and a cluster of school janitors stands to the side, glaring at the citywide cleanup crew like they're encroaching on their territory.

I make it to the edge of the staircase leading up to the school entrance and look down at it, then at my incompetent leg. Yeah, that's not happening.

"Help," I demand sullenly, hoping someone at the bottom will hear me. Fortunately, the emergence of a girl with ripped clothes, bloody limbs, and a general coating of dirt is apparently enough to grab some attention. At least ten heads swivel my direction.

"Someone was still in there!" somebody shouts, and then a bunch of people come stampeding at me all at once. I flinch away reflexively, but they all stop short inches away from me.

"How did you survive in there for so long?"

"Are you all right?"

"Stay calm, miss, everything is going to be okay."

"I'm fine, I'm fine! *Ow*!" I cringe as one of the policemen picks me up to carry me down to the sidewalk, unintentionally jostling everything that hurts.

A microphone gets shoved in my face the second I'm set back down. A brunette reporter shadowed by a man whose entire top half is covered with camera equipment peppers me with, "Do you blame Saint Charles's for their negligence in failing to ensure your safety? Will you be pressing charges against the school?"

"What? Uh, no, I—"

"As the records will state," an older man whose voice I recognize from the morning school announcements cuts in angrily, "All students were in fact accounted for. I'm sure there is a reasonable explanation for this student's absence that you will find has nothing to do with the school."

"In that case, could the blame be placed with the LCPD, for not conducting a thorough enough sweep of the school after the tragedy?" the reporter pushes on eagerly, leaning across me to stick the microphone in a police officer's face.

"Can we maybe do this later?" I ask as a cop snaps back at the reporter with something generic and defensive that doesn't really answer her question. "Hello? Person probably dying of blood loss over here."

"I couldn't agree more," says a forceful female voice, and I turn as I feel a light hand on my shoulder. A thin, dark-haired woman in scrubs flashes the kind of glare I would never want to be on the wrong side of toward the other people surrounding me. "This girl needs a hospital immediately. Your questioning will have to wait."

"But we—"

"I *said no*," the woman commands, and the reporter shuts

up.

I let out a breath of relief so huge, it makes my ribs feel pinched. The woman in scrubs quickly puts a protective hand around my shoulder without touching my injured bone and steers me down the sidewalk toward the one ambulance still parked out front. "Now, just stay calm," she says. I feel a light pinch in my upper arm, and think that her grip must be so firm that she's poking me with her nail. "You're going to be okay."

As a rule, I've never liked hospitals, but right now, nothing seems more tempting than a bed and somebody to numb my entire body. For the first time in at least three days, I start to feel more relaxed. *It's over. It's done. No more undercover missions. No more risking my life. At least, no more than usual.* Even my body starts to relax, giving way to the exhaustion that I've clearly been building up since this whole mess began. My eyes start to droop pleasantly as two male nurses gently help me into the back of the ambulance.

"Thanks," I say, yawning as I'm seated in a hard-backed chair attached to the wall. I look around the back of the ambulance in a sleepy haze. I can't remember the last time I was in one, but I feel like they usually have more stuff—gurneys and portable IVs and walls of first aid materials, and such. "Budget cuts?" I ask the nurse to my right sympathetically.

He doesn't answer, but he presses a button on the wall behind me, and before I can react, thick, unyielding straps have wrapped around my waist, pressing me against the chair. *What?* I can hear my own breathing, ragged and shallow, as I immediately try to push against the restraints, but it's as though someone has drained the muscle from my body.

"Oh, no…" I continue struggling weakly as both of the nurses jump down out of the fake ambulance, but both my tongue and my limbs feel like they're made of lead. I catch a glimpse of the first nurse's face as she holds her watch face up to her mouth and says something into it, and then the door slams closed. "Wait—"

�֍ COLLATERAL DAMAGE ✖

But before I can do anything else, whatever I've clearly been drugged with finally kicks in. All the energy drains from my body, and for the second time today, everything goes black.

WHEN I WAKE UP, I'm genuinely surprised I'm not tied to a table, my legs being sawed off or something. Instead, I'm in a pretty normal-looking stretcher, in a pretty normal-looking, although drab and bare, room. There aren't even any torture weapons on the walls or anything.

"Hello?" I call. The echo reverberates around the polished white walls.

Something feels weird. I mean, apart from the whole kidnapping thing. I can't put my finger on it.

I use my legs to propel myself into a seated position, and that's when I realize what's different. The pain in my leg is gone. Actually, the pain pretty much everywhere is gone. It doesn't hurt to breathe, and I can move my leg without feeling like I'm being stabbed with a billion knives. I look down at my arm and gasp. My blazer and button-down have been removed, leaving only the T-shirt, and there isn't a scratch or a blemish on the freckled skin apart from a small Band-Aid the size of a dime on the inside of my elbow. I peel up the corner and find a barely visible pinprick of a hole, like the kind that gets left over when you get a flu shot. But a simple shot wouldn't explain how I've been cured so magically. *What is going on?*

I push the bandage back down and flex my arm experimentally, expecting pain to shoot up from my wrist, but the pain doesn't come. It's like the damage never even happened. As I stare at my limbs in shock, there's a faint chittering sound, and Trashface crawls out of my nest of hair and onto my shoulder.

"*Hello?*" I shout again, kicking my legs free from the starched white sheets and swinging them off the side of the stretcher and onto the floor.

I spot my backpack on the ground next to my feet, snatch it up, and quickly rifle through it. Nothing is missing—although there's a small hole in the top of the bag that Trashface must have gnawed his way out of—and my umbrella is still clipped to the side. None of this makes any sense. Where am I? Why am I here, being healed, and not being murdered somewhere?

I push myself off the stretcher and am at the door in three quick strides, but before I can reach the handle, it erupts open on its own. I leap back, startled, with just enough time to prevent my feet from being crushed by the thick, heavy metal. I look up and see a face framed by angular glasses and sleek white hair towering over mine. Several more questions add themselves to the list of things confusing me, and I finally vocalize one of them.

"Dr. Crenshaw?" I blurt out. "What are you doing here?"

Trashface squeaks and burrows himself behind my neck, using his claws to grip onto my shirt.

"Hello again, Meg!" the department head of the LCPD SuperVariant Program greets me, closing the door behind him. "Why don't you have a seat?"

I don't move. I don't like it when people tell me to do things. "What's going on?" I ask suspiciously, backing out of his way as he enters the room. "What am I doing here? Is this a hospital?"

"The hospital? No, this is the LCPD lab." He smiles broadly with a twinkle of mischief in his eyes, like he has a secret he can't wait to share. "Can you guess why?"

Well, my original guess was going to be, *I've seen too much and now I'm finally going to be murdered for it,* but that doesn't seem to add up anymore. If I was going to be murdered, I'd already be dead. "I don't know," I say warily.

His already broad smile widens. "Oh, I love when it's a surprise. You know, I really wanted to tell you when you came to the lab with Miss Jensen, but then she would have known, too.

✖ COLLATERAL DAMAGE ✖

Which would have defeated the whole purpose, of course."

Huh?

He's still talking. "You wouldn't believe how hard it was to track you down without being conspicuous! Especially after your original address burned down. This is why we have change-of-address forms, Miss Sawyer!" He winks at me, letting out a conspiratorial chuckle, and glances at my arm. "You seem to have healed nicely, by the way. Your cells took to the recovery injection remarkably fast."

Recovery injection? Oh, no. The knockoff invincibility serum used to heal citizen injuries. I can't afford that kind of medicine. I'd rather have kept the broken arm. "I can't pay for a recovery injection," I blurt out. "I don't have health insurance. I have twelve dollars, max."

Dr. Crenshaw's sharp burst of laughter in response startles me so much, I flinch backward. "Don't worry about it." He chuckles again, pushing his glasses back into place. "We're considering it a good investment."

A good investment? "What are you *talking* about?" I ask in unmasked confusion. "Are you going to keep speaking in riddles, or are you gonna tell me what's going on?"

Crenshaw takes his glasses off and rubs the bridge of his nose, tucking his clipboard under his arm. After a dramatically long pause, he looks at me again. "You've heard of the Genetically Enhanced SuperVariant Program, haven't you?"

"Well, I live here, so I'd say I have," I retort, but I can't ignore the feeling of dread creeping into my stomach.

"Then," he continues, ignoring my tone, "You may know that we are currently seeking a heroic young person to replace one of our SuperVariants."

I blink and say nothing.

A hint of vague annoyance creeps onto his otherwise amiable face, like I'm missing something I should be getting faster. "Meg, we want you to join the SuperVariant team for the next two years, taking on the mantle of SuperVariant Three."

I'm laughing before I can stop myself. Actually, I'm laughing before he even finishes the sentence, somewhere around the words "SuperVariant team."

"Yeah, okay." I nearly choke, trying to talk and laugh at the same time. "Good one, Dr. Crenshaw. Why am I really here?"

He looks bewildered, like no one has ever reacted this way before. "I assure you, Meg, I would never joke about this. We've been watching you for a while, and we really think that you're the best possible option."

My eyes are literally watering at this point. I must be on that gas they give you at the dentist that makes you hallucinate. "Okay," I manage to get out. "Thanks, but no thanks. I don't—"

"Your modesty is truly a testament to your character," Crenshaw interrupts me, smiling kindly. "It's one of the many reasons we knew you'd be a great fit. There are others, of course. Your ability to stay calm in the face of crisis, consistent examples of quick thinking. A defensive wit, which we have often observed to translate into strong defensive fighting strategies. Even as recently as this weekend, you've proven yourself to act with compassion and generosity, when most would be selfish."

Compassion? When have I ever— A cold stab of incredulity slices through me as I realize he has to be talking about that kid I gave my tip money to. Had somebody been watching me? They must be really hard-pressed for heroism, if that worked as some kind of qualifier.

"Something about a homemade shield was also mentioned."

I instinctively reach behind me to push my umbrella out of view, but Crenshaw notices the gesture and reaches out a hand. "May I?"

"It's nothing," I say, reluctantly unclipping it and handing it over. "It's just an umbrella."

He examines the shaft with interest, presses the button to expand the frame, then retracts it. "Crude, but not unimpressive," he says as he hands it back. "Really, I'm surprised that you weren't on our radar sooner. Nevertheless, we do have an opening, and—"

"Okay, you gotta stop." This is unbelievable. This is all nuts. "Please stop. Even if I accepted that you really think *I'm* the best person for the job—which is a whole other issue that I could refute for hours—you must be insane to think I would ever sign up to replace SuperVariant Three when—"

And then I remember that he doesn't know. That he never let me tell him. Dr. Crenshaw's forehead is wrinkled in bewilderment, like he's offended that I'm not jumping up and down, offering him my firstborn child in exchange for this miraculous gift he's trying to grant me.

"When what?" he demands. "Why would you never sign up to replace SuperVariant Three?"

"Because it's a *death sentence*, Dr. Crenshaw." The words explode out of me before I can even think about handling the announcement with subtlety or grace. It doesn't matter. He just has to know. "It's what I tried to tell you on Sunday. When I found Sam dead, it was in a van, and he was all blue and veiny and surrounded by the SuperVariant serum. Somebody stole it after he got his powers stripped, and then they killed him. It wasn't an accident. It wasn't because he let his secret identity leak. You wouldn't listen before, but you have to now. You can't replace him as a Super until you get that serum back."

The pen falls off Dr. Crenshaw's clipboard and onto the ground.

He does nothing to pick it up. He doesn't even seem to notice that it's there. He just stares right through me, his already buggy eyes bulging like ping pong balls out of his sockets, unable to speak.

"Uh… Dr. Crenshaw?" I step an inch out of his line of vision and wave a hand to see what will happen. He doesn't move. He doesn't blink.

Oh my god, I think I broke him.

"Should I, uh, call someone?" I offer.

His unfocused eyes flicker. "I can't believe this happened."

I can't tell if he's talking to me or to himself. "This program has existed for twelve years, and no one has ever—" He cuts himself off and turns his glassy stare on me, as if remembering I'm still there. "Thank you for telling me this. I should have listened to you before, but don't worry. This will be dealt with immediately."

I chew on the inside of my cheek to stifle my grin, because now probably isn't the time. But I can't help the feeling of victory. I did it. I told someone more responsible, and they're going to fix the problem. Mission accomplished.

I can't *wait* to rub this in Juniper's face.

What I say out loud, though, is, "No problem. I was just trying to help."

Part of Crenshaw's face relaxes a little, and he flashes a thin, paternal smile. "Which is exactly why we picked you." He takes a few steps toward the door, his hand outstretched, but then he pauses and turns back around. "You know, once this situation is handled, assuming you feel safe enough… the offer still stands. You're more than you think you are. We still want you to be a Super."

No, you don't. The inner response comes easily, naturally. *You couldn't. Why would you?*

It doesn't make any sense. You don't get to be a superhero just because you're quick and defensive, not when you're also the kind of person who abandons their partners during important missions, like I did today. That's not how Supers act. I don't deserve that kind of power.

But you could get better, a tiny voice in my head says. *You could do it. You could learn how to be a Super. What's the harm? They think you're special. If you say yes, you could be.*

"Well," I start to say, "maybe if—"

But before I can say anything else, a set of tiny claws sink themselves into my neck.

"*Ouch*! What the—"

Something writhes on my shoulder, and I manage to reach

✖ COLLATERAL DAMAGE ✖

over and catch Trashface in my palm before he falls off and hits the floor. His small body shakes in my hand. "Hey buddy, what's going on?" I ask.

"Is that a *rat*?" Crenshaw looks at me with unmasked confusion and disgust.

"Yeah. I sort of accidentally jacked it up with some of that serum I told you about. Long story. Juniper told me rats react to it a lot more slowly than humans, so he must be finally losing his powers," I explain, peering at Trashface, who I'm having trouble keeping in my hands because of how intensely he's twitching. "It's okay, little guy. You'll be a normal rat again soon."

Suddenly, a hand darts toward mine. I clamp my palms together and leap to the side before it can reach me. "What are you doing?" I demand.

"That rat has been contaminated by government property, and therefore is government property," Crenshaw says authoritatively. "You need to hand him over."

"What? No way!" I sidestep him and Trashface's tail whips against my wrist, searing a thin red welt into the skin. I wince, but refuse to let go. Getting the superpowers drained from your body must not feel great. "He's mine! Besides, he's not even going to be a mutant anymore in a couple of seconds!"

"This is not up for debate," Crenshaw barks, advancing closer. "Give it to me right now!"

"What's wrong with you?" I duck under his outstretched arm and run for the door. "It's just a rat!"

I get the door open about two inches before it slams closed. I look up to see Crenshaw reaching over my head, his palm flat against the door. He grabs my wrists with his other hand. "Ow!" I shriek as his pincer-like fingers squeeze tighter. Why's he acting like this? He'd been so kind and welcoming less than a minute ago. "You're insane! Let go of me!"

"Give me that *vermin*!" His calm, pleasant tone has been replaced by something scarily frantic and intense. His eyes suddenly look wild and unbalanced. He uses his other hand to peel my fingers open.

"Give me back my blood circulation!" I shout back, lifting my knee up and kicking sideways, right into his stomach. He barely flinches, but the surprise of being kicked causes him to lose focus on my wrist, and I manage to wrench it away. Now that all of our motion has stopped, I suddenly realize that I can't feel any twitching anymore.

"Trashface?" I say, opening my palms. I gasp.

He's lying on his side, his legs curled inward uselessly, his eyes wide in paralyzed shock. His tail is back to its original, pink state; no longer armored. His teeth are more yellow, more jagged, the way they were when I first found him.

He's dead. Unquestionably dead.

And across his body, glowing through the matted black fur, is traced a grid-like network of neon-blue lines.

The same blue veins that stretched over Sam's dead body the day I found him.

And suddenly, I understand everything. The serum was never stolen. It worked exactly the way it was supposed to. The driver of the van I found Sam in wasn't some new villain who was stealing the serum from an agent; the driver was the agent.

And Sam's final serum was never meant to merely drain away his powers.

"You." I look up at Dr. Crenshaw in horror. "It was you—you and your agents? You killed Sam?"

Crenshaw pants, smoothing down a hair that had gone astray in the struggle, and looks at me wordlessly.

I don't believe this. It makes no sense. Dr. Crenshaw is the head of the SuperVariant Program. He invented the serum. He picks the Supers. Why would he be working to destroy them? My head is spinning.

Crenshaw takes a step closer to me, putting his hands out as if he's trying to calm me. His kind, paternal tone returns. "You're confused. You don't know what you're talking about."

✖ COLLATERAL DAMAGE ✖

"Like hell I don't!" I seethe. "You added something to the serum. I know you did. Why? Why would you kill one of your own Supers? You *created* him!"

Crenshaw's expression shifts again, and he looks down at me like I'm a bug he wants to crush under his shoe. "Fine. You're right. I did," he says silkily, and my jaw drops. Isn't he supposed to be convincing me that I'm wrong? "What are you going to do about that, exactly?" he asks.

Why isn't he trying to make up an excuse? "Well, I'm going to…" I begin confidently, then trail off. ". . . tell the police?" I realize how dumb that sounds as I say it.

Crenshaw must recognize how dumb it sounds, too. "I *am* the police," he says, the left side of his mouth turning up into an unconcealed smirk.

Crap.

"You're not going to get away with this," I start to say, instantly hating myself for saying something so cliché. Fortunately, I don't get to finish the sentence, because Crenshaw cuts me off.

"Much as I would love to explain everything to you…" he says drily. His eyes are cold and emotionless. I miss sweet, harmless, Program Director Crenshaw. This new Crenshaw is freaking me out. ". . . I simply don't have the time. And neither" —he rolls his sleeve up over his watch, traces a circle on the screen, and presses down on the center—"do you."

"Wait, what?" I panic.

Alarms sound around me.

And that's when I realize why he didn't bother lying. He doesn't intend for me to be alive long enough to tell anyone.

"Now, I wouldn't try running. Don't worry, I promise this will all be over soon," Crenshaw says, adjusting his tie calmly.

He's right; there's almost no point in trying to escape. I have a pretty good idea that whatever button he just pushed has triggered some kind of "kill the intruder" alert, and an army of agents are going to storm in here any second. I can't outrun a turtle, let alone a squadron of armed professionals. But I'm also not going to just stay here and wait for them to come for me.

I grab my umbrella rod and swivel toward Crenshaw in one fluid motion, cracking him across the face with it with a satisfying crunch. I get a single moment of brief satisfaction as he staggers backward, before I turn and book it out the door to finish a race that I've never been so certain about losing.

TWENTY-ONE

THE HALLWAY IS STROBING with flashing red alarm lights. It's the third time I've seen them in the last two days, and my tolerance of them has about peaked. I quickly sprint toward the nearest door with a picture of a staircase next to it and tumble down one set of steps after another. The decreasing numbers marking each floor that I stagger past feel like they're counting down to my death.

Predictably, as I burst out of the stairwell on the first floor, the first of the agents responding to the alarm rounds the corner. I skid to a stop. He looks at me, with my torn clothing and my frantic expression, and raises his gun.

I barely get the button on my umbrella pushed in time, but as I duck behind it, I hear the loud crack next to my ear that indicates the bullet has ricocheted off the titanium. Without pausing for another second, I swerve away in the other direction, the sound of bullets still flying behind me.

✖ COLLATERAL DAMAGE ✖

They're really going to kill me. Oh my *god*.

There's a door to my right with a narrow window in the center, giving me a view of an adjoining hallway. As I rush past it, I kick it open, hoping the officers following me will think I've gone through the door, then crouch down and press myself against a spot farther down the hall, behind an abandoned cart of cleaning supplies. I try not to breathe, which is pretty hard considering that my lungs feel on the verge of spontaneous combustion.

Through the space in between several bottles of toilet bowl cleaner, I see the agent who shot at me rush down the hallway, joined by four others. I silently pray that they'll be stupid enough to take the bait and go through the door.

"This way!" the agent in front calls, and barges through it.

Idiots.

I wait for the door to finish closing completely, then, heart still pounding, clamber back up to my feet and streak toward a doorway on the opposite wall, ready to run down a different hallway. I open the door as quietly and as minimally as possible, sidle around it, and turn the handle so it won't make a sound when I close it, then press the lock button. Behind me, the motion detector lights snap on. I turn, expecting to see another hallway, but the pit of my stomach jolts when I realize that I've trapped myself in another room. I'm about to open the door to pick another exit strategy, but then my peripheral vision is caught by a foot lying prone, sticking out of a cubbyhole in the wall on the other side of the room.

No more dead-people feet, I tell myself forcefully. *That's how we got into this mess in the first place.*

But I look anyway. What if they're covering up another murder in here?

All I can see is the foot. The rest of the person attached to it is on a roll-out shelf pushed into the wall, like the kind they put corpses on in morgues. There's a white placard with some writing scrawled on it underneath the pull handle. I walk toward the wall to get a better look, noticing that the rest of the room looks, inexplicably, like some kind of weird art studio. There's a table in the center covered in paint stains, and peach-colored shavings of something all over the ground. A couple of cans with spray nozzles filled with red and brown liquid rest on the end of the table. I flinch in disgust as I pass a cabinet full of drawers labeled with things like *hair: dark brown* and *eyes: blue/green. Eyes?*

I crouch down until I'm eye level with the sign underneath the feet, and read the slanted, loopy handwriting.

"*SuperVariant Four,*" it says, and underneath that: "*3:48 p.m., September 20. Shooting.*"

Even though I'm supposed to be running for my life right now, I freeze. My blood runs cold for at least the eightieth time that day.

The decoy. The fake Sam the fire department showed Juniper after my apartment building burned down. I was right; it was planted there by the people who killed Sam, so that she would think he died in the fire instead of being killed by the serum. And they're going to do it again. Whoever Four is, they're going to inject him with the same serum, and plant this fake version of him at the site of a crisis—a shooting, I guess, just a few days from now—and let everyone who knows his secret identity believe that he died from a gunshot wound, while the real Four gets carted off somewhere to be hidden from the world forever.

This is sick. I *feel* sick.

I can't let this happen again. Juniper was right. I have to warn Four not to take the final serum, or he'll end up just like Sam.

I grab the handle and yank the rolling tray open, my eyes traveling upward across a pair of dirt-stained jeans and a white T-shirt punctuated with spots of deep red near the chest and stomach areas, the fake blood sprawling over the dirty cotton like an outstretched hand. Nauseated, I look at Four's face.

✖ COLLATERAL DAMAGE ✖

I almost scream. I clamp my wrist over my mouth just in time, my hand still clutching my umbrella. I can't scream. They'll find me if I scream. But as I look at the skin peeling away from the gaping bullet wound in his forehead, the dried blood running down in thin rivulets into his vacant, staring eyes—his eyes, how did they get his eyes so accurate?—all I want to do is curl up into a ball and scream forever.

This is too much. It was one thing to almost die under a staircase, and then to be kidnapped. And then to find out that Crenshaw and his agents were behind Sam's death. And that now they were after me, literally trying to kill me. I didn't think I could take any more shock.

I was wrong.

I should have known it could always be worse.

I look down at Oliver's face, and inside my head, I scream, and scream, and scream.

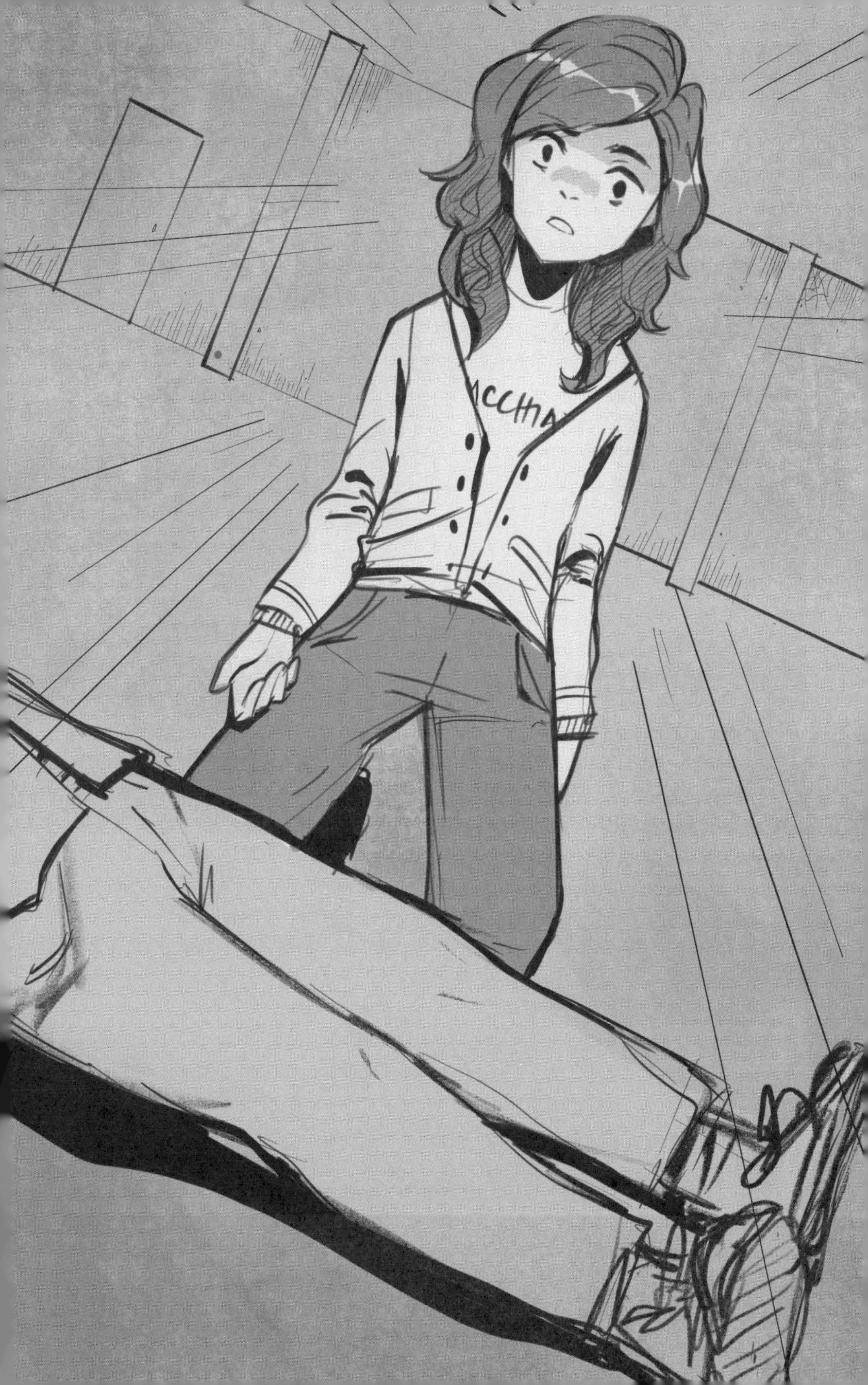

TWENTY-TWO

OLIVER'S A SUPER.

Oliver. My best friend. The person I care about most in the world. A Super.

My head is going to explode. My brain tries to think of too many things at once: mixed in with a still-frantic desperation to get out of here alive so I can warn Oliver about Crenshaw, and general shock about the revelation that my best friend in the entire world is a superhero is a numb, indistinct feeling of inexplicable sadness. How did I miss this? Am I really so selfish that I spent the last two years completely oblivious to the fact that Oliver was moonlighting as Four every day?

His delivery routes, I suddenly realize. *He was stopping crime while out on his delivery routes.* Four is the fast one, after all. It's not like he wouldn't have enough time, going two hundred miles an hour.

And no wonder he wanted me to let him handle warning

the other Supers after I told him about what I'd found, instead of going back to the school. He probably told them all immediately.

But they don't know who's really behind it. They don't know that their entire employment is a trap.

The sound of heavy feet outside the door snaps me out of my thoughts and forces me to get back to the more immediate problem—not being shot. The handle jiggles, and I hear muffled shouting.

Crap, crap, crap.

I slam the shelf back closed after taking one last look at fake Oliver's face. *You're not going to end up like this*, I silently promise. A quick look around the room confirms that there's no other exit door apart from the one that the security team outside is currently trying to break down.

There is, however, an air vent in the ceiling.

Well, I think, *it works in movies.*

Slam! The door suddenly shifts slightly off its hinges, pumping me full of terror and adrenaline. They're going to get in here any second, and then I'm a goner.

I clamber up onto the table that I now realize was the workspace used to create the fake Supers, grabbing a chair on the way. Fortunately, the ceiling is low enough that standing on the chair is enough to get my head and shoulders inside the vent, and I scramble inside, kicking my legs in mid-air to propel myself forward until I'm rolling like a beached whale away from the opening. Just as I clear it, the door gives way completely, and a tiny army of agents storms into the room. Without hesitating, they send a barrage of bullets toward the vent. I yank my head out of view just in time and crab walk backward as fast as I can.

I have a brief moment of relief, but it vanishes almost as quickly as it comes. My heart nearly stops as an agent's burly head and shoulders appear through the opening in the vent. If I can use a chair as a ladder, so can they. I'm such an idiot. All I accomplished was trapping myself in here like a rat in a maze.

I look at him pleadingly. *I'm not a criminal. I'm just a person. Please don't kill me.*

He lifts himself up even farther, and I practically collapse in fear. This is it. I'm so dead. *Oliver,* I remind myself, *I have to save Oliver.* It's not too late for him. At least I can try to get him the message.

But before I can find my phone in my backpack, the vent rattles. I look back at the agent, who's looking down at his torso angrily. I want to laugh and cry in relief at the same time as I realize what's happened. His shoulders are too broad, and he's gotten himself stuck. "Ha!" I cry out with undisguised glee, and scurry away from his retaliatory glare as he tries to wiggle himself free. I'm not looking anymore, but it must have worked, because a few moments later, a bullet ricochets off the wall next to my head, nearly slicing off my ear and wiping the grin off my face. I catapult myself around the corner, hoping a smaller agent isn't going to try to follow me.

"She's in the vents!" I hear someone shout. "Go back to the west hallway!"

The tunnel I'm faced with when I turn the corner splits off into three adjoining ones. I have no idea which one is going to put me directly above the agents and which one will get me outside, and I don't have time to try to rationalize an answer, so I guess the hallway to my right and start scrambling down it. The movement is the most un-stealthy thing I've ever done, and the vent echoes with the clanging resonation of my boots on metal.

The clanging is interrupted by a deafening *crack,* as a bullet cuts through the vent about ten feet behind me and disappears through the ceiling.

Dammit. I picked wrong.

The gunshots fire again, this time breaking through a few feet closer to where I'm crouching. "You're destroying your own building!" I taunt. "Your insurance isn't gonna cover that!"

✖ COLLATERAL DAMAGE ✖

Another gunshot resounds behind me in response. I try to clap my hands over my ears to block out the head-splitting reverberation, but I can't protect myself and crawl at the same time, so I resign myself to the impending headache and keep going.

There are a few more moments of aggressive shooting, and then, suddenly, it stops. *I must have crawled out of the area above them*, I think triumphantly. Even more miraculous is the light I can see shining through a vent cover to my left. Outside? Did I actually make it outside? There's no way. Everything feels like a trap now.

Suddenly, there's a sharp hiss from behind me, like air being let out of a can.

I turn around and peer back down the vent. Several thin green tendrils without form snake their way around the corner, just a few yards from me, and then the rest follows: a dense, acidic green fog, spilling into every corner of the vent like water from a broken dam.

"Gas?" The word comes out like a hoarse gasp. "Are you *kidding*?"

I don't have a choice. I slide toward the vent opening feet first and kick the cover off, then push off with my elbows and roll out of the vent onto the hard, grassy ground.

"Ow," I groan as my shoulder takes the brunt of the fall. I blink, trying to focus on my surroundings through the bright outer lights of the building, then widen them as I see where I am.

I'm outside, sure, but in a lawn that's more dirt than grass, caged in on the two sides not connected to the building by a tall wire fence. I freeze in terror as a door bursts open on the other end of the lawn, and five agents in bulletproof vests come stampeding out.

I look around desperately for an escape. Behind me is a solid wall. To my left is the fence, which I'd be willing to bet all of the twelve dollars I have to my name is electrified.

The agents raise their guns.

I put my hands up to shield myself, like it'll help, too panic-stricken to remember to grab my umbrella from its clip. It doesn't matter. That wouldn't have helped for long anyway, either.

I'm so sorry, Oliver, I think, closing my eyes, and then they fire.

TWENTY-THREE

I HEAR THE RECOIL, smell the smoke, flinch as the bullets whistle through the air. But they don't hit me. I'm still alive.

I open one eye in confusion.

All five agents' guns are pointed straight at the sky. They all wear expressions of bewilderment, but before they can reposition their weapons, there's a blur, and suddenly three of them are on their backs on the ground. Less than a second later, the other two sail through the air and collide with a sickening *crunch* with the side of the building. They fall to the ground too, and don't move. The agent in the middle tries to stagger to his feet, but then there's another blur and his head snaps back like he's been kicked in the face, and the gun practically leaps out of his hands.

I have exactly enough time to think one word—*What?*—and then I'm sucked into a void.

✖ COLLATERAL DAMAGE ✖

I FEEL LIKE I'm on the inside of a tornado. Something is pressed around my middle tightly, almost suffocating my breathing. Sharp wind bites through my exposed skin like tiny arrows as I'm jerked backward, and my legs slice through the air in front of me.

"What's happening?" I want to yell, but the howling wind whipping against me from all sides is so forceful, I'm afraid it'll cut through my tongue if I open my mouth.

And then, as soon as I think I'm going to be squeezed in half completely, it stops.

I immediately lose my balance as my feet reconnect with the ground, almost falling over in dizziness. I can sort of make out a glimpse of a dark cityscape in the distance, peppered with lights, but everything still feels like it's spinning around me.

As I stagger, something shoots out an orange-clad arm and steadies me. I look down at the arm, then at its owner, and feel like someone has cut all the strings from my limbs. I collapse against Four's—Oliver's—torso, flooded with relief, and squeeze it as hard as I can.

He tenses, like he doesn't know how to react, and takes a huge gasp of air. "Miss, I cannot breathe," he says formally, and I remember that he doesn't know I know.

"You're alive!" I gasp, straightening back up and getting a better look at him. I'd never paid much attention to Four. Actually, I'd never paid much attention to any of them, because if they were close enough to look at, then I probably had a bigger problem to deal with. But now I'm looking at him and trying to figure out where the Oliver I know is hiding under there. He looks taller than normal; there must be lifts in his boots. The rust-orange supersuit is an uncomfortable level of skin-tight, accentuating muscles that I never would have known existed underneath the baggy clothes he usually wears. His eyes are covered by sleek metallic goggles, probably to prevent the wind from slicing his eyeballs in half while he runs, so I can't really see the top half of his face. But as I narrow in on his cheeks, I realize that he's done something to his face to make his cheekbones look sharper, making his whole complexion appear older and more chiseled. It's not my fault that for two years I didn't realize who he was. He looks totally different.

"You're okay!" I continue, actively restraining myself from hugging him again. "Oliver, listen, you have to—"

He freezes. "I… what?" he stammers. "I'm not… what? Who's… I mean, uh, who's Oliver? Not me, that's for sure." He lets out an awkward laugh.

I hook my fingers through the goggles over the bridge of his nose and pull back, exposing his eyes. He looks down at me sheepishly. I release the rubber and they snap back into place, smacking him in the face. "Ow!" he yells, massaging his nose and moving the goggles up to his forehead. "How the hell did you find out?"

"Because I saw you! Dead you! Oh, we don't have time for this!" I grab his arm as he looks at me blankly, trying to examine his wrist through his supersuit. "Did you take the final serum? Did they inject you yet?"

"Meg, no, listen to me! You can't know! No one can know!" Oliver grabs my scrabbling fingers and holds them still, looking panicked. "They told me when I started two years ago that the only way I could keep the people I cared about safe was to make sure they never found out about this part of my life. You can't let anyone find out that you know. Promise me."

Something about his words, tinged with regret, and the realization that he's been doing this for almost exactly *two years* clicks together. "Wait," I say hesitantly. "When you got this job, did your mom—?"

"No. I wasn't Four yet when—" He looks down. "—you know. They asked me right after. I hated the Supers as much as you did, before. But I thought that I could do better... stop the bad people who caused the problems in the first place, prevent the same thing from happening to more kids. I just felt so useless, and I was so angry..." He trails off. I'm angry too, that the LCPD took advantage of a sixteen-year-old kid's loss in order to warp his emotions into a weapon. It's vile.

"I should have convinced you to stay out of this when you told me what happened yesterday," he continues, panic electrifying his features. "Because if something happens to you because you got involved..."

"Hey," I interrupt him, trying to calm us both down. "Things always happen to me. That's my life. And right now, I'm trying to prevent something bad from happening to *you*, okay? Just calm down and *listen* to me for a second."

He exhales, still looking anxious. I'm about to start explaining everything I've found out, but I suddenly realize that we're standing on the roof of a building at least fifty stories tall. I look down in terror, my stomach dropping out from under me. "How do I feel about heights, Oliver?" I say, my voice high-pitched and squeaky.

"Well, sorry!" He looks offended. "I thought they wouldn't be able to find us up here!"

"Well, you're not wrong," I say, focusing on his face and trying to ignore the swirling clouds around us. *You're not going to fall. If you fall, he'll catch you. Don't look down. Don't look down.*

"Meg, what's happening?" He grips my shoulders, looking confused and intense at the same time. "Why were those agents trying to kill you? What were you doing at the lab?"

"Um..." I say. "I sort of got asked to be SuperVariant Three."

"*What*? Meg, that's amazing! We'll get to—" He looks excited for a moment, but then his face falls. "Oh. I was going to say that we'd get to be Supers together, but... well, I keep forgetting that I'm being replaced this week." He laughs. "How's that for irony?"

I shake my head. "They're not going to replace you. They're

going to kill you."

He takes a step backward, and I have to grab his arm to prevent him from falling off the side of the roof. He lets out a short, disbelieving snort. "What? What do you mean, kill me? Meg, come on." He looks at me like he's waiting for the punch line to a joke.

"I'm serious." I pull him back away from the edge, then release his arm. "Remember how I told you someone had killed Sam and stolen his serum?"

"Yeah, of course. And don't worry, I told the rest of the team. Everyone's on alert."

"Well, get on higher alert, because it wasn't him. It was Dr. Crenshaw."

"*What*?"

I nod. "I don't know why. I don't know if they're working together, or it was a coincidence that they were both out that morning, or what, but it's true. And that serum he's going to give you at the end of your term as a Super—it's not an antidote to the one that gives you powers. It's poison. It'll kill you." I suddenly remember my original concern. "And you haven't taken yours yet, have you?"

I watch all the color drain from Oliver's face, and numb paralysis washes over me like a shroud. *He's taken it. It's too late.*

Then, "No," he says, and everything starts working again. "So what, you found out and now they're trying to kill you?"

"Exactly."

"This is insane." He runs his fingers through his hair, which has settled into a sleek, pointy wave over his forehead from speeding across town. "I don't understand. Why would they want to kill me? I work for them." He starts pacing, and I have to grab his arm again to prevent him from walking right off the side of the building. "I don't know," I say. "It doesn't make any sense to me either. But you have to tell the others."

"You mean *we* have to tell the others," he corrects me, "unless you want to go walking around on your own with the entire police force looking for you."

"Yeah, hard pass." I brave another look down at the river of traffic below us, half-expecting a squadron of agents to come speeding by. "So what, do you have a secret hideout or something?"

"Uh, obviously."

"*Ew*, I was kidding. You're such a dork."

"It's not dorky. It's awesome. You're jealous."

I frown. "Wait, you sure the others are going to let me into a secret hideout? Doesn't it sort of defeat the purpose?"

"They're going to have to," he says confidently, but then his face twists in discomfort, and he slumps his shoulders a fraction. "Are you mad?"

I'm taken aback. "Mad? About what?"

"You know." He shuffles from one foot to the other. "That I didn't tell you."

"Mad" isn't the right word at all. I do feel stupid, and selfishly, inexplicably betrayed that he kept such a huge thing from me for two years. But that's silly. I know he couldn't tell me. And besides, stronger than any of those feelings is the feeling of relief that I got to him in time to save his life, and even a tiny hint of pride that the SuperVariant Program director, even though he turned out to be evil, saw in Oliver what I always knew about him: that he's pretty much the greatest person in existence.

"Of course, I'm mad." I grin at him and nudge his arm. "Mad that we've been taking your filthy truck everywhere when you could have been super-speeding us places."

"Hey, don't insult the truck!" he protests, but his face breaks into a relieved grin as well. "Come on, let's go. I know how much you hate heights."

"Well, you don't, or you wouldn't have made me come up here." I look over the edge fearfully. "How are we gonna get down?"

"Uh, hello?" Oliver flexes his muscles. "Superhero."

"Put your arms *down*." I roll my eyes. "Is this what it's gonna be like, now that I know? This doesn't make you cool."

"It makes me so cool."

"Nope. Besides, that didn't answer the question."

"Sure it did." Suddenly, he's leaning over, with one arm underneath my knees and the other wrapping around my shoulders. "Hey!" I shriek. "What are you *doing*?"

"Getting you down, genius." He knocks my legs out from underneath me and swings me up into his arms. "Got a better plan?"

I don't, but I also don't like him holding me like this. It's weird.

"Fine," he teases in response to my glare. "I'll just leave you up here."

"I'm thinking about it."

"You're such a *baby*." He rolls his eyes and backs up a few steps to get a running start. "Hold on."

"I hate this," I mutter, and then I'm sucked into the speed void again.

TWENTY-FOUR

AFTER ANOTHER TORNADO-LIKE experience, we jerk to a halt. Oliver puts me down, and I push my uncooperative hair out of my face again. It looks like we're in a normal alleyway, wedged between a cluster of foul-smelling trash cans and the bottom step of a fire escape. It doesn't seem very secret hideout-ish. I look at Oliver and realize that he's lost the supersuit, and is now in the combo of faded jeans and T-shirt that I'm more used to. I wonder if he was wearing it underneath or just changed absurdly fast. "Where are we?" I ask.

"The closest entryway, I think." Oliver stares at a storm drain in the middle of the street, then peers up at the buildings around us and nods. "Yeah, I think this is right." Before I can ask any more questions—*What? Entryway? Closest to what?*—he's grabbed my hand and pulled me onto the grate. "Hold on," he says as we struggle to occupy the same two square feet of space. He loops his arm around my neck. "I've never done this with another person before. Hopefully it works."

"Are you going to explain *anything* to me today, or—" I begin, my voice muffled against his arm, but then my words get sucked away as the ground drops out from beneath us.

The scream that's wrenched out of me lasts about two seconds—the same amount of time that it takes the elevator we're apparently standing on to shudder to a halt somewhere at the bottom of a chute. It's impossible to tell how far underground we are; the storm drain has sealed itself closed again on the ground level, plunging us into darkness.

A dim blue stripe of light flicks on along the walls to either side of us, illuminating a path that seems to stretch on forever, splitting off into three different directions.

"Wait, are there tunnels under the whole city?" I gape, awestruck, as I let Oliver lead me off the platform, down the narrow, metallic hallway. The sound of both my voice and our footsteps echoes around us, enveloping us in a cocoon of sound. "That's how the Supers get to a crisis so fast without being seen or stopped, isn't it?"

"Yep," Oliver confirms, grinning proudly. "There are entry points all over the place, in spots ordinary citizens wouldn't think to go into—sewers, unfinished buildings, a few bathrooms that have been closed permanently. And they all lead back to—"

He rounds the corner, and I pull up short behind him, narrowly avoiding slamming into his back. I peer around him, but it's a dead end—just a blank, metallic wall inset with a single gray screen about the size of my hand.

"Wait, don't tell me." I take a step forward and lean in to examine the screen. "Facial recognition? Voice matching? Wait, no… it's a secret password, isn't it?" I look back at Oliver, but am startled to see that he's in his supersuit again. "How are you doing that?" I ask, looking with undisguised curiosity at the marbled orange fabric.

"Oh, the quick change?" He glances down at his clothes

too, then presses a button on his watch. Suddenly, the entire suit retracts in a matter of seconds, refitting him in his baggy T-shirt and jeans. He presses it again, and metallic orange particles drift out from the watch face, expanding to form panels that unfold across his body until he's coated in the familiar armored supersuit.

"*Ew*," I say, squinting at his arm. "Was that inside your skin?"

"I think it folds up into the watch somehow?" He looks uncertain, like he's never really thought about it. "I don't know. All I know is I push a button, and boom, instant suit."

"Nifty. Do they make those for pajamas?"

"I wish, right? Come on."

He presses the watch to the screen, and it scans his watch face with a low humming noise. Predictably, the wall slides open.

My nerves return as I peer inside. I guess I thought the secret hideout would be fun, cozy—the kind of place three young superheroes could hang out in between saving the city. But it's... well, *intimidating*, to say the least. Every inch of it is some shade of monochromatic gray, from the few couches arranged in a semicircle around the center of the room to the large display of TV monitors coating the wall opposite me. Upon further squinting, I realize that each shows a different part of the city, with the labels in the bottom-right corner of the screens dividing everything into sectors. The adjacent wall is hung with dozens of unfamiliar, lethal-looking weapons—coils of rope, swords, throwing knives, shelves of dark objects in angular geometric shapes. The floor and ceiling are just as cold and metallic as the hallway outside, giving the entire room an eerie, prison-like sort of vibe. It's not someplace I'd want to hang out in permanently.

"The decorator's got a thing for gray, huh?" I observe, stepping warily into the room. "Don't you—"

And then I'm in the air.

"What the—" I screech as I try in vain to free myself from whatever's holding me. I can't move at all. It feels like something unseen is pressing in on every inch of my body at once. What is this, some kind of weird security system? "*Oliver!*"

"No, no, no, no!" Oliver shouts, racing through the entrance behind me toward the other end of the room. "One, put her down!"

A spot of purple appears against the gray landscape. Super-Variant One streaks out from behind a wall, her cape trailing like a dark shadow behind her, a scowl distorting her face under the mask. Her right hand is extended toward me, gloved palm out. "Who are you?" she barks. "How did you find this place?"

"I said put her down, One!" Oliver repeats. "She's with me! It's fine, it's fine, she's with me!"

One directs her glare at Oliver instead. The tendrils of brown hair escaping from her braid ripple away from her face like they're caught in a gust of wind that I know for a fact doesn't exist down here. "And what are you doing bringing a non-Super into the hideout, then?"

"It's—she's—listen, we'll explain everything, but just *put her down*!"

One gives Oliver one last suspicious glower, then strikes her palm downward through the air.

I rocket toward the ground, barely getting out a screech of terror before there's a flash of orange, and Oliver is beneath me, trying to catch me before I'm shoulders-deep in pale concrete. But he doesn't get his arms up in time, and I shoot straight into him, barreling him over.

I sit up with some effort, having landed on his back, and shake my dazed head. "Good pillow, Oliver," I say, patting his hair amicably.

"Ow," he groans, his face mashed into the ground.

"Wait, why did she just call you that?" One interrogates him, not addressing me. "Did you break the identity rule?"

"No, he didn't." I push up off the ground and stomp toward One. "And don't *levitate* people," I order. "Especially when they're people who are here to tell you that—"

"Wait!" Oliver interrupts, scurrying up behind me. "I don't want you to have to tell this twice. Where's Two?"

One scowls again. "I'm not his babysitter."

Oliver shoots her a look before catapulting over the couch with one arm and starting to wave his hands crazily over the cushions.

"Uh... what are you doing?" I ask, raising an eyebrow. "Why are you putting a magic spell on the couch?"

"I'm not," he says, switching to the other couch and flapping his arms near those cushions too. He looks like a bird trying to dance, or someone doing really terrible karate. "I'm checking for Two. He always forgets to go un-invisible and then falls asleep over here—"

"Hey, what's going on?" a voice behind us says, and we all swivel.

A boy mostly concealed by marbled blue fabric appears in the archway. The bottom half of his mask is lifted up, leaving his mouth free to munch on a bag of take-out French fries. As I recognize both his voice and his gold-brown skin, I gasp in recognition. He freezes mid-bite, his cheeks bulging.

"San*jeet*?" I exclaim in astonishment.

There's a faint *pop*, and he turns invisible, leaving the bag of fries floating in midair. "No," he says, forcing his voice into a deeper octave.

"You know him?" Oliver asks me.

"No!" Sanjeet repeats loudly, still invisible.

"It was *you*?" I can't believe this. I deserve an award for my ineptitude. "All that time, it was *you*?"

Sanjeet reappears with another pop. "What do you mean, 'it was you?' Is that what you were doing at my school? Looking for Supers? I knew there was something weird about you—"

"Did you just come in here to expose our secret identities?"

One interrupts him. Her heeled boots threaten to puncture the cement floor as she stomps toward me. "Do you know how much trouble you could get us in?"

I open my mouth furiously. "No, I came here to—"

"Because we could get in major trouble for this. And if you think this is a game—if you're some kind of fangirl who thinks it's *fun* to mess around with our lives, with our *jobs*—"

"Yeah, let me tell you about your jobs!" I seethe. "Because I think you might want to hear this."

"She's telling the truth, One," Oliver backs me up. "I wouldn't have brought her here if it wasn't life or death."

One's eyes are still narrowed into slits beneath her mask, but she at least lets her hands relax a little, putting me out of danger of being thrown across the room again for the time being.

"Okay," I begin. "Remember how Three had his last day over the weekend?"

For what's starting to feel like the seventy-eighth time, I recap everything that has happened in the last three days, with Oliver interjecting every so often to explain along with me, even though he wasn't there for almost any of it.

I'm about to start on the part that really matters, about how I was taken to the lab and discovered that Dr. Crenshaw was actually behind it all, when there's a loud grating sound behind me. The door is opening again.

We all turn, immediately on guard. Sanjeet turns invisible; Oliver crouches into a runner's stance; One extends both hands out in front of her toward the exit. I grab my umbrella out of its clip and hold it out to the side, finger on the expand button.

There are a few moments of tense silence, and then the door finally finishes opening, revealing someone tall and willowy with long blonde hair, gaping with an expression of combined confusion and awe into the room.

SuperVariant One raises her hand, but I grab it and pull it back down before she can use her powers again. "*Juniper?*" I ask, genuinely shocked.

"Meg!" she cries. She looks like she wants to run toward me, but doesn't. "Are you okay?"

"Uh... yeah, I'm fine." The last time I checked, she didn't care. "What are you *doing* here?"

"I was confused when you ended up at the lab instead of the hospital, and then you suddenly appeared on top of the bank headquarters, and then here." Juniper looks around the room, noting the wall of assorted throwing knives, bows and arrows, and other weapons hanging on carefully labeled hooks. "Where *are* we?" Then she notices who's standing next to me. "The rest of the Supers," she gasps. "You found them?"

"I'm sorry; did we just invite everyone in town to a party down here that I don't know about?" One snaps. "How did *you* get in here? You have to be a member of the LCPD to get through the entryway."

"I *am* an LCPD employee," Juniper shoots back, snatching her badge out of her pocket and holding it up. "The scanner must allow us through as well, in case there's ever an emergency."

"This is Three's girlfriend. She's a biogenetic engineering intern," I explain. "How did you even find *me*?" But I remember the answer before she even responds.

"Tracker," she says, at least having the decency to look embarrassed.

"Wait, how did you access my tracker?" Oliver asks in confusion.

I gape at him. "You put a tracker on me, too?"

"Uh, duh. I didn't want you to *die*. How do you think I found you at the lab?"

"I swear to God, if *one more person feeds me a tracker this week*," I scream, glaring at the ceiling.

"I already told you, it was to protect you—"

"It was in a brownie; what's the big deal? It's not like you can taste it—"

"Oh my *God*." I rub my temples, then cross my arms, looking back at Juniper. "Why were you even still tracking me?"

"Because I wanted to make sure you were safe." She looks at me defiantly, which is why her next words surprise me so much. "I'm sorry."

"For what, tracking me?"

"No." She clears the distance between us by half, her eyes wide and sincere. "For what I said. For everything. I shouldn't have made you risk your life like that. This was my responsibility, and I shouldn't have made you share it with me. And I'm genuinely, really sorry. I ran out to tell you almost as soon as you left, but you were gone before I got out of the school."

I'm so surprised, I hardly know what to say.

She's sorry? I'm the one who ran out on her. I'm the one who gave up. She was just trying to protect the people standing behind me right now. "Don't," I say, and her eyes widen in surprise. "You were right, okay? About everything. I shouldn't have left."

She shakes her head, the movement rippling her hair. "No, I should have listened to you. I put your life in danger; I took you for granted. I should have been the one at that school—"

"It's okay." I put a hand up, and she swallows the rest of her sentence. "None of that matters. All that matters is what we're going to do next."

Her face relaxes into a desperate, relieved smile, and she nods.

"Excuse me?" Sanjeet interrupts pointedly. "Are you going to finish telling us what's going on, now?"

"Right." I turn back around. "So, what happened is—and Juniper, you actually don't know this part…"

I finish telling them everything; about what happened with Trashface, how Dr. Crenshaw ordered the agents to kill me for what I knew without even telling me why he'd done this, about the fake Oliver I found in the craft-room-from-hell shelf.

When I'm done, everyone is silent, including Oliver. He'd

already heard most of the story, but I hadn't told him about his decoy yet. He looks like he's going to be sick.

"So, guys?" I glance with dismay at their shocked faces. I'd hoped for somebody to immediately have a solution, but that outcome isn't looking strong. "What do we do?"

"I don't understand," Juniper whispers, her face numb and impassive. "I don't *understand*..."

"We need a strategy," Sanjeet says, still clutching the empty bag of fries. His knuckles are white from clenching. "We can't just go running in there and confront him."

"Why not?" demands One. "We have *superpowers*. What are they for, if not to defend ourselves and others against evil? This is evil. Crenshaw killed Three, and it looks like he was planning on killing Four next. Even if Oliver refuses to take the final serum, do you really think that'll stop him?"

Everyone looks at one another uneasily. Juniper is shaking, but I'm full of adrenaline and rage. Running in and confronting Crenshaw, forcing him to admit that he was planning on killing Oliver, and then letting the Supers bring him to justice is exactly what I want to do right now.

But I'm not a Super, so I'm pretty sure I don't get a vote.

"Yeah, I agree," Oliver speaks up, and I grin victoriously. "I'm not going to just sit here waiting for someone to come kill me. They know where our hideout is; they built it. Once Crenshaw knows that Meg escaped, he'll put together that she would go and find me. He has to know we're friends. We have to do something before he does." Oliver pauses, and his forehead crinkles up, puckering the edges of his rubbery goggles. "And since everything else is falling apart—" The inner war he's clearly having lasts only a moment longer, and then he presses a button on his watch. His orange supersuit vanishes again, replaced with his street clothes, and his sleek wave of hair deflates forward, falling into his eyes in a messy clump. I notice that the other two Supers take an involuntary step away from him, as though he's spontaneously transformed into an

✖ COLLATERAL DAMAGE ✖

alpaca instead of a normal citizen. "I'm Oliver. I'm eighteen, and I deliver pizzas when I'm not here." He shrugs as he looks from one startled teammate to the other. "We have to be able to trust each other."

No one says anything. I see a flicker of nervousness in Oliver's eyes, like he's terrified that he's misread the situation and wishes that he could fold up his secret identity and stuff it back in the watch. But then—

"You're right." Sanjeet slaps his own wrist, and the rest of his face comes into view as his suit dematerializes. He's still wearing his school uniform, although it's massively wrinkled and the shirt has come untucked from his pants. "Okay. I'm Sanjeet. I'm in high school, and I'm still pretty honored to be here."

Everyone turns to look expectantly at SuperVariant One, who's separated from the rest of us by one of the austere gray couches. She crosses her gloved arms over her chest, but she doesn't look angry. She almost looks *scared.*

"Is this really necessary?" she demands. "Can't we just—"

"Come on, One," Sanjeet wheedles. "Peer pressure. Peer pressure!"

She plays with the button on the side of her watch like it's a pin on a grenade.

"This is such a mistake," she mutters, but then she hits the button. The tight, deep purple fabric coating her body melts away, replaced by black denim shorts, tights with asymmetric holes, and a high school band polo. In grungy sneakers instead of heeled boots, she shrinks until she's almost an entire head shorter than me. Her whip-like brown braid recedes into her head and turns into a cloud of silvery hair—hair that I recognize. Hair that I've seen before, in the coffee shop, just a couple days ago.

"I'm Penny," says the girl, shoving her hands in her pockets. "I'm fourteen. And I—"

"Wait, I *know* you!" I gasp, disbelief and anger bubbling up inside me. "You're that girl who tried to steal my tip money! What kind of superhero commits robberies?"

"You did *what*?" Sanjeet echoes. The girl's olive skin grows pale, and she puts her hands up. I flinch reflexively, but then I realize that the action is defensive, not aggressive.

"No, it was an accident!" she stammers. "I really didn't mean to take the money, I swear. It's just that with these powers, sometimes all I do is *think* about wanting something and—" Her eyes flick at random to one of the weapons on the wall, an orb-like ball coated in swirling, grooved markings. It takes less than a second for the ball to rocket across the room and into her palm, as though yanked by an invisible string. She looks down at it apologetically. "See? I've only been a Super for six months. I'm still working on it."

"But why were you even *thinking* about taking the money? And why did you let me give it to you? Why would a Super need—" I stop short. The only explanation dangles itself in front of me, in the form of Penny's ripped clothing and the fact that she still has to live at the Shelter and Oliver's need for a stupid pizza delivery job. The whole murdering-people thing is bad, but if I'm right about this too, then the SuperVariant Program's deceit is even more layered. "Do they…" I can't believe I have to ask this. I can't believe there's a possibility this is true. "Do they not pay you? For being a Super?"

Penny looks horrified. "Of course not!" she exclaims. "We couldn't accept payment for our duties. It's about doing the right thing. The genetic enhancements and invincibility are payment enough. It's our responsibility to—" She frowns, the logic clicking its way into her brain. She's clearly never said the words out loud before. "That's not right, is it?"

"Yeah." Dawning realization is spreading across Oliver's face too. They both look like they're recovering from being brainwashed. "Why am I working at a pizza joint? If they're gonna kill me, they should at least *pay* me for it."

I can't believe this. No wonder they use kids. It had to have been so much easier to convince a teenager that free labor is for their benefit than an adult.

"Okay." I don't know why this makes me want to destroy Crenshaw even more, but it does. "Put 'force Crenshaw to buy all of you a house' on the confrontational to-do list."

Oliver laughs hollowly. "Okay, so the three of us will go to the LCPD station and—"

"Hold on, what?" I raise my hand. "What do you mean, the three of you? I'm coming, too."

"And me," Juniper interjects. Her voice manages to crack even with the two solitary words. I suddenly realize that she hasn't said anything since I finished telling her that Crenshaw was the one who killed Sam.

"Uh, no!" Oliver reaches up and pushes my hand back down. "You are *not*. You don't even have any powers. You would have died earlier if I hadn't shown up."

"Only because I was outnumbered! And unprepared!" I argue, then gesture to the wall of weapons. "Just because I don't have powers doesn't mean I can't be useful. I can fight. Let me borrow a knife, or something."

"You don't know how to fight with a knife."

"You don't know how to fight with a knife!" I retaliate.

"You're right, I don't. I don't think any of us do. They're really not the most effective weapon."

I stare at him blankly. "Then why do you have like fifty of them hanging from your wall?"

He shrugs. "I don't know. They look cool. Don't they look cool?"

"So cool," Sanjeet agrees.

"This is ridiculous." I try to get him back on track. "You're going to need a lookout. I can be your lookout."

"And me!" Juniper echoes again.

"And Juniper." I motion toward her, then say fiercely, "We're coming. If you think I'm just going to sit here and wait to find out whether you survive this or not, you're an idiot. I'm not leaving you until this over. Don't even *pretend* you wouldn't do the same for me."

I look at the other two Supers for support, but they avert their eyes, making it clear that they don't want to get in the middle of this fight.

He's silent for a few moments, but then he says, "If you die, I'm gonna be so mad at you. Like, I'll still avenge you and everything, but I'm still gonna be really, really mad."

"I won't die," I say firmly.

"Awesome," Penny interjects. "So we're doing this now, right?"

Affirmative echoes bounce around the room from everyone but Sanjeet. We all turn and look at him.

"Yeah, okay," he says, checking his watch. "Just not too late, okay? I have a chemistry test I need to study for."

TWENTY-FIVE

WITHOUT HESITATING ANOTHER moment, all three Supers start moving at once.

"Anybody want anything extra?" Penny asks, glancing toward the wall of weapons and scanning its contents. "Grenade? Laser blaster? Smoke bomb? Water bottle?"

"I could go for a grenade, just in case," Oliver leans over and plucks the grooved ball she's still holding out of her hands. "Meg, can you put this in your backpack for me?"

"What? No! I'm not carrying a *bomb* around!" I shriek, backing away.

"Please? I don't have pockets."

"Wait a second." Juniper takes the grenade out of Oliver's hands and examines it. "That's not a normal grenade. This is *my* design. I did some work for the weapons division on my first internship at the LCPD, before I switched to biogenetics."

Everyone looks at her blankly.

She shrugs and tosses the grenade in the air in a one-handed catch like it's a baseball. "It could probably collapse this entire tunnel."

"Who *are* you?" I yell.

"Well, if you're carrying stuff," Sanjeet interjects, looking hopeful. "Can you put this in there, too? Just in case we have any downtime." He holds up a chemistry textbook.

"I'm not your mom, guys! Just because I'm the only one with a backpack doesn't mean I have to be responsible for all your crap!"

"Hold on," Juniper says. "How are we all going to get into the building? I'm an employee, but what about everyone else? It'll be pretty suspicious if all the Supers show up at once. And Meg, isn't everyone in there trying to kill you?"

"Good point," I realize, my face falling. My red hair is like a beacon. I won't make it in the front door. And I don't really feel like crawling through the vents again.

Oliver, on the other hand, is wearing the type of expression cartoon characters get when a lightbulb goes off over their head, staring at Juniper's shirt. "What?" I narrow my eyes at him. "What are you so excited about it?"

"Crafting." He leans over and snags Juniper's ID badge off her collar. "*Hey!*" she protests, but he ignores her and throws it to me. I catch it one-handed, still confused. There's no way he can expect me to pretend to be Juniper. I—

But then I look up at him, at Sanjeet's full-coverage supersuit, and back down at the card, and a plan starts to click together. I feel myself grinning in spite of the tension.

"You guys got a printer in here?"

TWENTY-SIX

"VIOLET GREEN?" I can hear Penny complaining from the bed of Oliver's truck as we screech to a halt on the grass next to the LCPD lab, still examining the fake employee badge I'd whipped up for her back in the hideout. She's wearing Juniper's sweater over her T-shirt in an attempt to look more professional, and has a scowl on her face. "This is a *terrible* undercover name."

"Sorry." I twist my neck from my perch on the edge of the passenger seat to peer back at her. "It's kind of been a thing today."

"What about mine?" Sanjeet jumps out of the back of the truck and leans through the passenger window. He's wearing the plain white polo and black pants from his school uniform, but has lent his blazer to Oliver, who's struggling with the too-short sleeves. "'Clark Parker'? Isn't it a little—I don't know, on the nose?"

"Is everyone going to just insult my fake IDs? Is that really the priority right now?" My words are coming out muffled; Sanjeet's supersuit is way too tight on me, and the thick fabric over my face makes talking a pain. I jump out of the car and perform a few squats, trying to readjust the pant legs to a more comfortable position.

"You look great." Oliver smirks at me. "Very heroic."

"Oh, shut up." I pull the bottom of the mask up over my nose so I can breathe. "I don't have to look heroic. I just have to look invisible."

"This is gonna work, right?" Oliver's smirk turns into an expression of wariness. "Check it again."

"It'll be fine, Four. Look." Sanjeet sidles up beside me and grasps my hand. He makes his fingers vanish, and the invisibility spreads, coating the entire suit until I can look down at myself and see straight through to the ground. "See? Just like back at the hideout. As long as I'm touching the suit, it'll turn invisible along with my fingers."

"This is still so weird," I mutter, holding my hand up in front of my face. "I don't know how you do this every day."

"Okay." Juniper is out of the car too, standing next to Penny. "There shouldn't be too many people left inside this late at night. But just in case, everyone's clear on the plan, right? Try not to talk to anyone. Act confident. If anyone asks, you're—" She looks back in forth between the three Supers expectantly. "You're what, guys?"

"The new biogenetic engineering interns," Sanjeet recites, then frowns. "Don't you think people are going to ask why I'm missing my fingers first? Should I have an excuse ready? Did I burn them off in an experiment? What's my backstory?"

"You're overthinking this, buddy. We live in a city of daily explosions; I don't think anyone's going to notice or care that you're missing a few fingers." I try to look at the watch I've borrowed from Sanjeet, but it's invisible too. Whatever time it is, we need to get this over with before I lose my nerve. "We'll be fine," I try to reassure everyone despite the curdling feeling in my stomach. "Let's go end this."

I DON'T KNOW what I'm expecting when we walk in—warning bells, or black-suited agents descending from the ceiling to surround us, or the one or two people still at work in the vicinity of the entrance to snap their heads toward us accusatorially.

But no one says anything.

Juniper holds her badge up, opening her mouth to say something, but the bleary-eyed secretary at the desk doesn't even look at her. She clips it back to her collar, looking dejected, like she already had a story ready that she's disappointed about not getting to use.

When we go through security, nothing happens. No alarms. No random extra searches. Nothing.

Sanjeet and I stride wordlessly behind Juniper and the others as she leads them through the swinging door into the network of back hallways that I've come to be way too familiar with over the last couple of days.

Once Juniper guides us to the outside of Crenshaw's office, Oliver stops and leans down a little to whisper, looking intensely at a spot a foot away from my head. "Everyone be careful, okay? We don't—"

"Little to your left, bud," I say.

He follows my voice and ends up staring at a spot directly in between Sanjeet and me, then finishes, "We don't know what kind of security Crenshaw has."

"His watch has an alarm trigger," Juniper says. "You can start with that."

"Okay, good to know."

"Meg," she continues. "You record his confession, okay?"

I salute, then remember she can't see me. "Wait, wasn't I supposed to be lookout? Who's going to be lookout now? You?"

Juniper looks like she immediately regrets giving me a new assignment. "I don't think—"

"I think that'll work." Penny nods. "You're the only one who really looks like they belong here, anyway."

Juniper's cheeks redden in frustration. "You seriously just want me to be *lookout*? By myself? What do you want me to do, stand out here like an idiot and yell through the wall if I see a—" She straightens up, looking at a spot behind Oliver with widened eyes. "Doctor!"

"Yeah, just like that," Oliver approves.

"No, I'm serious!" she whispers, and we all turn. Every muscle in my body seizes up. He's there. Dr. Crenshaw is about fifty feet away from us, nose buried in a clipboard, striding up the hall. He hasn't seen us yet, but as soon as he looks up from his paperwork, we're dead. Why did we think he'd just be sitting in his office, waiting for us? We can't ambush him in the hallway. Someone else will see and stop us before we get a confession.

Before I can come up with anything resembling a plan, Juniper has turned the handle on the office door and pushed me and all three Supers inside. "*Hide*!" she hisses, and the door shuts without a sound.

Where? I immediately want to shout. The office is relatively furniture-less and only about three hundred square feet in size, so Juniper's order is definitely one of those easier-said-than-done things. Even the desk is facing the wall, meaning hiding underneath it would be pointless. I wonder briefly if Crenshaw designed the secret hideout, too. He seems like he's got a thing for minimalism.

Another voice is suddenly present through the door—a calm, deep, even voice. He's right outside, talking to Juniper. I can't make out any of the words, and wish my heart would calm down so I can focus. He'll be in here any second. What's going to happen when he sees us?

When he sees them, I realize with a wave of guilt. He won't be able to see me at all.

Without hesitating another moment, I rip Sanjeet's watch from my wrist. *"What are you doing?"* he whispers, horrified, as he tries to grab it and force it back onto my arm. "He's going to see you!"

"I don't care!" I grab Sanjeet's arm and snap the cuff around it, pressing the button. I catch a glimpse of his startled expression and open mouth before the suit materializes over his face. "You need this more than I do!"

"But—" he argues, then freezes. The door slides open a few inches. Without another word, he vanishes completely. Penny presses her watch too, transforming into her supersuit, then launches herself into the air and braces herself against the ceiling. I see a burst of orange in my peripheral vision, and turn to see Oliver flattened against the wall in the shadows next to the door, equally suited-up. I sidestep behind the door, hoping it doesn't crush me when he opens it all the way. *This was a mistake. This isn't going to work. Why did we rush in here? Why didn't we plan this better?*

I can hear Crenshaw's voice a foot away from my face, this insignificant slab of metal the only thing separating us. "I appreciate your diligence in working on your personal projects, Ms. Jensen, but I really don't have time to answer your questions right now. Why don't we set up a meeting for Thursday?"

"Yes… yes, sir," she says, and I hear the click of her shoes as she begins to retreat down the hallway.

The door opens all the way. I hold my breath, like the sound of my own airways is going to give me away, like he's going to notice the activity of my lungs before he notices the fact that Penny is *literally hanging from his ceiling.*

Obviously, he notices Penny first.

But he doesn't look shocked or defensive, or like any person being ambushed would normally look. He just looks mildly inconvenienced.

"Well," he says, and looks down at his watch, "you're a few

minutes later than I expected."

His fingers twitch toward the side button—the one that had called the agents on me earlier.

"*Move,*" I hear Oliver shout, and before Crenshaw can do anything else, he's been pushed inside the room. Oliver slams the door behind him and whips off Crenshaw's watch—then snags his belt too.

"What are you—" Dr. Crenshaw looks down at his pants, looking genuinely bewildered.

"You were supposed to just take the watch!" Penny shrieks, launching herself off the ceiling and aiming her open palms at Crenshaw. "Why'd you take the *belt*?"

Oliver waves it in the air defensively. "I don't know! I don't trust him; what if he has something on here he can use, too?"

"Use to what, hold up his pants?" Penny argues, throwing Crenshaw in the air without looking and holding him there.

"Are you going to keep yelling at me, or are we going to get him to confess?"

"And what," Crenshaw is calm almost to the point of apparent boredom. "Am I confessing to, exactly?"

"Oh, I think you know," Penny hisses, clenching her outstretched hand into a fist. An invisible force pins Crenshaw's arms to his sides, but Crenshaw doesn't even strain against it. He just floats in mid-air, looking irritated.

Oliver takes two furious strides toward Crenshaw. "We know you killed the last Three," he accuses him. "We know you were going to kill me next. The only thing that really matters is that we're not going to let that happen, but in the interest of personal curiosity, I *have* to know why. Why'd you—" He cuts himself off and looks back at the space on the wall near my head. "Meg, are you recording this?"

"Huh?" I step away from the wall. "Wait, am I supposed to be recording already? Nobody said anything. Hold on." I reach awkwardly down the neck of my T-shirt until I find my phone pressed against my chest, where I'd crammed it down earlier.

"Okay, now go."

"Should I just start over?"

"Yeah, if you want that part on the tape."

"Oh, okay." Oliver shakes his arms out, then turns back toward Crenshaw. "We know you killed—"

"Hello again, Miss Sawyer." Dr. Crenshaw talks over Oliver, smiling at me like I'm a disobedient pupil, then glances down at the others. "I see you brought backup. To be honest, I'm glad you're all here. There seems to be a little miscommunication."

"Miscommunication?" Sanjeet reappears. "Are you really going to try to tell us that you didn't kill Three—I mean Sam? That you're not working with Doctor Defect?"

"Working with—" Crenshaw's mouth falls drops open and moves without emitting sound, making him look some kind of confused fish. Finally, a deep, disbelieving laugh erupts out of him, and he shakes with mirth. "You think I'm working with Doctor Defect?" he manages to get out.

Everyone looks at me.

My stomach feels the way it used to when a teacher called on me and I answered wrong in front of the entire class. "You have to be," I say, my mouth dry. "It's the only explanation."

Crenshaw gets his laughter under control and sighs. "I assure you, I am not working with Doctor Defect. Quite the opposite, actually."

"Then why'd you kill Three?" Oliver demands.

"Think carefully before you lie to us." Penny flexes her hands, and Crenshaw's clothes pucker in rings, like he's being suffocated by an invisible python. I feel a flicker of relief that they still believe at least part of what I told them, even if my theory about Crenshaw being Defect's accomplice was wrong.

Crenshaw's only response to having his torso strangled is to let out a light cough. "Yes, I think I should," he says, and at first, I think my sleep-deprived brain has hallucinated it. *He's really going to tell us? Just like that?* "At this point, it's probably better that you know. Then you can make the choice for yourselves."

"What choice?" I demand, even though I don't think he's talking about me. But I got offered a SuperVariant position too, didn't I? I sort of count. "What are you talking about?"

Crenshaw ignores me, glancing at Penny. I hadn't noticed, but her hand is starting to quiver the way mine does when I've been carrying something heavy for too long.

"Would you like to put me down first?" Crenshaw asks. "I know how much concentration holding things in place takes for you. A quarter of the way through your service, and you still haven't mastered your powers."

Penny flushes red, and her hand shakes even more.

"If you put him down, and he runs," Oliver says warily, "I'm still faster than him. If you're getting tired, you can do it."

Without waiting for him to change his mind, Penny slams Crenshaw into the floor with a grunt of expelled effort. He straightens up and dusts off his pants.

"Now," he says. His voice is an even line. "Would you like me to start from the beginning, or work backward?"

All four of us look at him in confusion. I'm on edge, my flight response starting to hammer into my brain persistently. Something about this is really weirding me out. Why would he just tell us? Why isn't he fighting back more?

"From the beginning, I think." He nods to himself. "Things are usually easier to follow if presented chronologically." He pushes his glasses up his nose. "Once, this city was riddled with crime. Gangs prowled the streets, murders and robberies were commonplace, and even the police force was corrupted. The world felt dark and hopeless. But from that darkness came a spark—an idea, to push the boundaries of science and creativity in an effort to bring peace and justice to Lunar City. Some of the most brilliant minds in the city were hired by the uncorrupted members of the police force to create a new form of weapon, and thus, the SuperVariant Program was born."

"Did you *rehearse* this?" I interrupt, annoyed. "Did you really just have an evil monologue all ready to go? Besides, we already *know* all this."

Crenshaw presses on like he doesn't hear me. "Miraculously, the first SuperVariant—one of the scientists who had helped me craft the serum—was everything we could have hoped for. The serum was accepted into his bloodstream without issue. He became invincibly strong and fast, and his pure heart and desire for justice made eliminating crime easy. Most of the criminals in the city simply fled rather than face his judgment. The corrupt members of the police were replaced. Things finally felt safe.

"And then, after a couple of years, everything changed. He changed. Obsessed with his power, the first SuperVariant began to view himself as a god, above responsibility and above accountability for his actions. The police were no longer able to control him. Instead of working with them to stop crimes, he became a vigilante, answering to no one but himself as he killed petty criminal after petty criminal in an endless, desperate search for justice."

"Wait, I remember that," Oliver interjects. "I had forgotten. I think I was only like, five or six. Everyone was afraid to even shoplift." He furrows his brow, trying to bring the memories back into focus. "But then he was replaced."

"He was not replaced." Crenshaw continues, "Not in the way that Supers are replaced now. Horrified at the monster we had inadvertently created, my team and I tried to negate the effects of the serum, to drain the power from his system. But it wouldn't drain. The serum strain had fused to his DNA too tightly to separate. And killing him proved impossible; we had simply made him too invincible. He could heal himself from any wound within seconds."

"And, what?" Penny crosses her arms. "There weren't enough rooms left for you to lock him in a padded cell?"

"No cell would hold him." Crenshaw shakes his head. "Ultimately, we did decide that a better strategy might be to attack him psychologically, instead of physiologically. Rather than cell confinement, I was able to develop a chemical that could target specific memories, which was injected into his brain. It was successful. The subject lost all recollection of being a Super, and of having powers."

"Okay, great," I interrupt, still lost about how any of this is relevant. "So, what's the problem?"

"The problem," Crenshaw explains, "is that the chemical did not suppress emotion. Although he had no memories as to why, the subject still possessed a deep, consuming, hatred for the LCPD and all it represented, for keeping him from doing what he felt was his true calling. Ashamed to admit to the frightened public that we hadn't been completely successful, we announced that the stress of the job had simply become too great for him to continue, then created a new SuperVariant to replace him as the city's protector."

"You really made another one after all that?" I say, dumbfounded. "Don't you know anything about quitting while you're ahead?"

"It was necessary," Crenshaw says drily. "If the city lost its superhuman protector, the crime would have come back tenfold. Not to mention, we needed someone capable of protecting the LCPD from that first SuperVariant, who is still intent on destroying us."

"Wait, what do you mean, 'still?'" Sanjeet interrupts. "He's still out there?"

"Of course." Crenshaw looks both surprised and mildly disappointed that we haven't caught on quickly enough. "The man the public so reductively refers to as Doctor Defect... he's the original SuperVariant."

TWENTY-SEVEN

THERE'S A MOMENT OF STUNNED silence, and then everyone starts shouting at once.

"*What?*"

"He was a *SuperVariant*?"

"No wonder he's impossible to beat—"

"I don't understand; why isn't he being kept in a vault somewhere?"

"We *tried* to keep him in a vault." Crenshaw holds his hands up to silence the other Supers. "For quite a while, after his replacement was created. But then he escaped. And, as you well know, he's been intermittently recaptured ever since, between bouts of terrorizing the city."

"You still haven't answered the question," I continue, pressing through the feeling of sickness that's trying to prevent me from talking. "What does any of this have to do with *why you're killing the current Supers*?"

✖ COLLATERAL DAMAGE ✖

"I was just getting to subject retirement," he says calmly, and I boil. *Subject retirement?* The euphemism makes it sound like they're old versions of phones getting thrown out. "After the failures of the first SuperVariant, it was clear that it wasn't a good idea to create a human that powerful again. After experimenting with new types of genetic advancements, the responsibility was divided into four separate people, with four unique powers—telekinesis, invisibility, strength, and speed. We thought having fewer powers would make the subjects more controllable, more human, and more dependent on each other."

"Let me guess," I snap. "It didn't."

Crenshaw nods. "After about two years, the same amount of time at which Defect began to exhibit signs of instability, the new SuperVariant One began to act differently, too. She began to question orders, fight with the rest of her team, and act independently of authority. She had to be stopped. Fortunately, we hadn't repeated our original mistakes. She was nearly invincible, but her alterations came with a weakness. I invented a substance that could decay her from the inside, when injected."

"Your problem-solving skills need so much work," Sanjeet whispers, shaking his head.

Crenshaw continues without responding to him, a glazed look in his eye, like he's lost in the story. "It became clear that the Supers were incapable of keeping their powers for a span of longer than a couple of years, but we still had no way of separating the genetic enhancements from the host. And the citizens still needed their heroes. But we couldn't just keep killing them off. No one would ever want to join the force. So, we created the idea of replacements. We made the public think that the mantle of being a SuperVariant was passed on every two years. With the reveal of the new Super, no one wondered what had happened to the old one, especially with the help of secret identities. Then, the person who had occupied the role of former SuperVariant would be written off as having been killed in a local accident, with no one the wiser. It was a perfect solution."

He looks around at all four of us. I don't know what he's waiting for—for someone to say, "Oh, sure, that makes perfect sense, we totally get it," probably.

I can't breathe.

I can't believe how wrong my theory was.

Sam wasn't the first Super to be killed. I haven't uncovered some new plot, something that could be caught and fixed before anyone else got hurt. It's too late for that. It's already been happening, without anyone knowing, for the last decade.

"How could you?" Oliver gapes, finally finding his voice again. "Your entire program has been killing its own Supers for eight *years*? Citizens who just wanted the opportunity to help the city?"

"Well, exactly." Crenshaw brightens, like he's glad someone is catching onto his twisted logic. "They were people who wanted to help the city. They all—*you* all—agreed to the risks of potential self-sacrifice in order to protect this city and this department. You knew what you were getting into. Besides, it's not like you would be missed."

His forehead twitches. It's barely perceptible, but I see it. It's the first—the only—gesture he's made so far to indicate that he regrets one of the things he's told us. And that's when something else clicks. Oliver, alone in his mom's old apartment, with me as his only friend. Sanjeet, the invisible loser at his school of nerds. Penny, stuck at the Shelter for the Misplaced.

"Wouldn't be missed?" I echo, suddenly finding it difficult to breathe. "Dr. Crenshaw, why was I picked to be a Super?"

Dr. Crenshaw smiles, the crack in his facial armor repairing itself. "Why, just as I told you. Because of your courage, your selflessness, your—"

Oliver chokes back a snort of laughter, but I'm not offended. He's right. "No," I say. "That wasn't it." I turn to Penny. "Penny, what happened to your family?"

Her breath catches and she looks from Sanjeet to Oliver with confusion spreading over her face. "Why…" She swallows and glares at the ground. "Doctor Defect. Like everybody else."

"And Sanjeet?" I turn around so I can look at him next. I can't see his facial expression because his mask is on, but his whole body is frozen. "What happened to your—"

"They died," he cuts me off quietly before I can finish the question. "Radioactive gas leak. That's why I live with my uncle."

My heart is pounding. I didn't think I could find out anything worse, but I was wrong. I wheel around back toward Crenshaw, every nerve explosive. "You don't just care about courage or selflessness," I say quietly. "You pick people who are alone. Who don't have anyone left. It's just like you said—because no one would miss us." My clenched fists shake. I want to sink into the ground and let the horrified tears building up behind my eyelids drown me, but I don't. "And you pick people whose family were killed by Doctor Defect, too, so they'll already want to fight him. Don't you?"

The room is silent. The kind of silent that makes you feel like all the sound in the universe has evaporated.

And then:

"Yes," Crenshaw says simply.

Yes. One word to explain away years and years of murder and deceit.

This is worse, I realize dully. *This part is the worst.*

It would almost have been better not to know. To believe that the people picked to be superheroes—my friends, the people standing around me right now, and even me, I guess—were chosen because of their natural superiority, their inherent goodness, would have been infinitely better than the knowledge that the opposite was the real truth: they were chosen because of how replaceable the LCPD really believed they were.

No one moves. No one can find the strength to respond.

"So you see," Crenshaw finally says, "now that you know,

you have a choice to make."

I steal a glance at Oliver to see how he's reacting, but he looks like a mannequin. His eyes are cold and lifeless, like the ones on the decoy body I found. "What choice?" he asks, but his words are lifeless too. He sounds as though he's reciting lines from a script, as though he's only saying what he knows someone is supposed to say in response.

"It's simple." Crenshaw smooths out an imperceptible crease in his shirt. "You can continue the SuperVariant Program as scheduled and be retired at your completion. You can commit to keeping what I've told you confidential, to ensure the continuation of the program. You can continue to use your powers for good, to help this city, and you can finish your term as the heroes that I know you are. Or… you can be treated as hostile insubordinates and dealt with accordingly now. It's completely up to you."

The room, already too small for five people, feels even smaller. It feels like a casket with the top closing, trapping us all in.

"You can't," I manage to say even though it feels like all my oxygen is gone. "How can you do this? How can you possibly think this is the best way? You know how messed up this is, or you wouldn't have kept it a secret."

"We kept it a secret so that the city wouldn't interfere with its own protection on the grounds of some nonsensical moral dilemma," Crenshaw insists. "The numbers—the statistical proof that the Supers have lowered the presence of crime in the city over the last decade—are inarguable. The program must be continued. Sacrifices must be made."

Rage clouds my consciousness. "Easy to say when you're not the one making the sacrifice," I seethe. I look around at the Supers surrounding me, who appear to be something that I've never seen them be before: helpless. "You could try something different. You have all this power, all this technology. You could fix this city a different way."

"You're a child." Crenshaw glares at me. "Don't pretend to know how things work."

"She wasn't too much of a child to be asked to give up her life for this city!" Oliver snaps. "None of us were! We're done being manipulated by you. If you want to continue the program, that's fine, but good luck finding any volunteers once everyone knows what you've done."

Crenshaw sighs, looking irked rather than threatened. "I was hoping you would choose differently. It's not as though you can win against us, you know." His eyes glitter from behind his glasses. "After the first mistake, we built a fail-safe. Something to use in case any other Supers ever went rogue before we could inject them with the final serum."

My blood runs cold. *We have to get out of here*, I realize. *I knew he wouldn't tell us all this freely. There's always a catch.*

Penny finally shakes herself out of her shocked, overwhelmed reverie. "What's the fail-safe?" she demands, but I know as he says it what kind of trap we've walked into.

Crenshaw's smile widens.

"Me," he says, and then he vanishes.

TWENTY-EIGHT

"SHIT!" I BOLT FOR THE DOOR. "Move it, everyone!"

But before I can turn the handle, the lock clicks closed. I go to unlock it again, but as I stretch out my hand, Crenshaw re-materializes about two feet away from me, his face stony. Before I can even blink, he snatches the phone from my hand, throws it to the ground, and stomps on it. When he pulls his foot away, all that remains is dust.

"No, no!" I shriek. A new phone is going to cost a fortune. Besides, what did he think that would do? Delete the video? Idiot. "Uh, good try, but that video wasn't saved on my phone," I tell him, annoyed. "That was a live stream. It's already uploaded to the public. You owe me a new phone, moron."

His face darkens in silent, murderous fury, and my eyes cross as he extends his outstretched palm toward me, inches from my face.

And then there's a blur, and I'm forced to stagger backward

as someone pushes themselves in front of me, into the line of fire. Oliver only occupies the space for a moment before, as though he's connected to a tether being jerked across the room, he goes flying into the opposite wall. Small chunks of cement rain down around him as he falls to the floor. "Oliver!" I shout and try to run toward him, but Crenshaw seizes my wrist. Penny dashes over to help him up instead.

"You should have just stayed out of this," Crenshaw hisses, raising his other hand back into a fist.

My eyes widen, but before the punch can land, his head jerks straight backward. Blood seeps from both nostrils, and I take his loss of focus as an opportunity to wrench my wrist from his grip. He straightens up and tries to take a step toward me, and I'm horrified to see his broken nose has already reset itself in a matter of seconds, the blood draining backward into his head. It's disgusting. Before he can reach me again, he scissors in half, clutching his stomach. I suddenly realize what's happening.

"Nice one, Sanjeet!" I cry.

Crenshaw looks around him furiously, but even he can't see through invisibility. With a sound like a marble being sucked into a vacuum, he vanishes again.

"Shit, shit, shit!" I hear Sanjeet panicking somewhere near my right ear. "Where is he?"

Without responding, Penny telekinetically wrenches an entire cabinet from the wall, twisting the choppy wood, which groans and tears into a dozen pieces. She flings them around the room one by one, fast as lightning. I cut through the flying shrapnel like I'm in a particularly deadly game of dodgeball, sprinting toward Oliver.

"Hey—ow!" Sanjeet yelps as a stray cabinet door presumably hits him. "Watch it!"

"I can't!" Penny shoots back, continuing to fire chunks of wood in rapid succession.

"You dead or what?" I kneel over and help lift Oliver to his feet. "I'm fine," he groans in response, rubbing the back of his head. "'S just a concussion."

I glance around the room, trying to see if anything is moving suspiciously around the debris Penny is still throwing. Then I see it—a syringe full of blue liquid rising into the air. "Penny!" I shout. "He's got a—"

She whips around, stretches her hand toward it, and yanks, and the syringe goes shooting across the room toward her. But before it can reach her, it freezes in midair. Crenshaw, visible again, stares at it, his eyes a cold beacon of focus, his hand outstretched.

Penny's neck twitches as she strains, willing the serum to come toward her, but it doesn't budge. It hovers in mid-air, indecisively torn between the two telepaths. "After six months," Crenshaw admonishes. "Your abilities are still nowhere near the level of your predecessors. I'd thought you had a lot of potential, but your weakness is so disappointing."

"If I'm weak, how come you're not beating me?" Penny grunts, but I know immediately that she's spoken too soon. Her eyes widen as the syringe languidly turns in the air, the arrow-like tip pointed directly toward her.

Fortunately, both of them are so focused on their battle of wills, they don't see me as I grab my umbrella and run between them until I'm using it to hammer the syringe out of the air and into the ground. "Sanjeet!" I yell as it clatters against the tile. "Get it!"

"Already on it!" I hear, and the syringe disappears.

"No!" Crenshaw gives up on keeping his voice calm and free of rage and storms in three tile-shattering steps toward the door to block it.

Definitely still offended by the "weak" comment, Penny flings her hand out and in front of her and slices it to the side with enough force to cut my head off if I'd been any closer. The door flies off its hinges and slams into Crenshaw, hitting him so hard that he barrels into the adjoining wall and stays there, stuck in a Crenshaw-shaped hole.

The door shifts on the ground as Sanjeet, still invisible, clambers over it, and then the hall is filled with the echo of his feet as he runs the deadly serum away from us.

Penny, Oliver, and I—all panting—take several tentative steps toward Crenshaw. The image of him stuck in the wall would be pretty fun if we weren't all terrified from the fact that he'd just tried to kill us.

"What was that he said?" Penny seethes as she dusts her hands off against each other, glaring at the back of Crenshaw's head. "Something about us being weak?"

"You really think that killed him?" I ask, uncertain.

"Man, I hope so." Oliver rubs the back of his head again and checks his palm for blood. "I can't believe he gave himself all our powers. Did not see that coming."

"Come on," says Penny, grabbing my arm and pulling me over the door. "We have to get out of here before he—"

Without removing himself from the wall, Crenshaw vanishes.

"Before he does that!" Oliver finishes for her. "Get out! I'll cover you!"

I look back at him to argue, because no way in hell am I leaving him in here to fight an all-powerful maniac on his own, but as I open my mouth, Crenshaw reappears in front of his face, his fist drawn backward. I yell a warning, but it's too late. Crenshaw plunges the fist with all of his immutable force into Oliver's core, and he flies backward into the wall for the second time. He collides with the cement with a sickening crunch and rolls onto his back, where he doesn't move.

I try to scream and rush forward, but suddenly, neither my legs nor my mouth are working. I can't even turn my head. In my peripheral vision, I can see Penny, who's struggling against a similar unseen binding. The immobility is explained when I realize that Crenshaw has his palm extended toward us without looking, his eyes fixed straight ahead as he stalks toward

Oliver. "You should have just done your job." His voice has reverted back to a soft, paternal timbre. He leans down and picks up a cabinet door, the edges sharp and jagged. "I didn't want to do this this way. Everything was going so well."

"My job?" Oliver mutters, his eyes barely open. "In case it wasn't obvious, I quit." He pushes himself up onto his elbows, trying to get back to his feet, but Crenshaw plants a foot in the center of his chest.

"You were actually quite an exemplary SuperVariant. I hope your replacement will have a stronger sense of duty and sacrifice than you." And he raises the board above his head with both hands.

The hold that's been on Penny and me releases as his left hand goes up to support the door, but before either Penny or I can react, it's swinging downward like an unstoppable pendulum.

As the jagged side of the heavy wood slices through his legs, Oliver's scream of agony sets every nerve in my body on fire, and my own scream mingles with his. I leap toward Crenshaw, umbrella raised, but before I can drive the rod through his skull, there's a blur, and suddenly, he's on the other side of the room. The umbrella cuts through empty air.

"You take care of Oliver!" Penny orders, levitating a large piece of shrapnel and throwing it toward Crenshaw. He blurs again, landing four feet away. Penny lifts the entire chair in the center of the room in a fury and flings it at his head with a roar of frustration and rage. He blurs again, and then he's behind her.

"Penny, watch out!" I cry in warning. She wheels around, hands up, but that's what Crenshaw was waiting for. He grabs her by the wrists and, in a flash, cracks them both sideways at the joint. Her entire being seems to crumple along with her hands, which now hang uselessly from the broken wrists. With another swipe of his hand, he throws her backward, where she collapses a foot away from me and Oliver, her back against the wall.

"Penny!" I know I should go and help her too, but I physically can't pull myself away from Oliver, who's clearly in so much anguish that his body has shut itself down to prevent him from feeling it. He lies unconscious on the ground, blood blossoming through the part of the suit coating his thighs, staining the orange material a dark crimson. Something far back in my brain tells me that as long as we can get him out of here, he can heal himself, he'll be fine, but it's like we're in a tunnel, with everything else happening somewhere very far away. "You're okay," I whisper, shaking as I lean over him, pulling him into me. "Stay with me, Oliver, come on. Don't die, don't die." I turn around and look up; Crenshaw is walking leisurely toward us, straightening his glasses. I stagger to my feet. I'm trembling so much that I can barely hit the button to extend my umbrella, but it expands with a creak into a shield. I step in front of Oliver and Penny, still shaking, the umbrella forming a near-useless wall between me and Crenshaw. "Get away from us," I say as fiercely as I can, but my voice cracks. "Get the hell away from us."

Crenshaw stops and considers me, his head cocked slightly to the side. "You know that shield of yours will do nothing, and yet you're still trying to protect your friends with it. That's so… admirable."

"Am I supposed to say thank you?" I snarl.

He sighs. It's a bored, condescending sound. "You see, this is why we knew you'd make such a good SuperVariant. You just don't give up, even when you've already lost. It's unfortunate that you'll never get to utilize your full potential now."

Shit. I'm so going to die. I'd really hoped it would end differently. But really, considering where we live, I should have known that I would go trying to protect Oliver. I just wish it would make a difference. But I'm not leaving them. Either of them. I stand my ground behind the umbrella.

Crenshaw sighs again, and focuses his gaze on my forehead. "Suit yourself."

He draws his hand back, aims it toward my face, and—

And falls to the ground, his entire head on fire.

I scream and nearly drop my umbrella, leaping away from the flames. I peer around the smoke and see a figure in the doorway holding a massive cylinder on its shoulder, with the front end smoldering. The figure lowers the weapon, and I realize that her eyes are blazing nearly as much as Crenshaw's head.

"Come on!" Juniper orders me. "Let's get out of here. And don't you ever abandon me to be lookout again."

TWENTY-NINE

"WHAT THE HELL IS THAT?" I shriek as Juniper dashes toward me, the metallic cylinder tucked under her arm. Something unseen brushes past me, and I turn in time to see Sanjeet materialize inside the room, bending over to help Penny and Oliver. Juniper grabs my hand and starts to drag me out to the hallway, the clunky cylinder rattling prominently. "Where did you get that?"

"I raided the weapons division," Juniper pants as we sprint down the hall. "You didn't really think I was just going to stand there and wait for you all to do everything, did you?"

I glance back at the vacant doorframe we'd just run out of as we round a corner, half-expecting Crenshaw to burst through it with his head still aflame. "Is that it, then?" I gasp for air. "He isn't… is he dead?"

"No way," Sanjeet responds as he catches up to us. Oliver is thrown over his shoulders in a fireman's lift. Penny's face is ashen, but she doesn't make a sound as she cradles her hands against her chest, keeping up with the rest of us as we run. "He's like us. He's going to heal himself soon, and we have to get out of here before that happens."

"Where are we going?" Penny asks. "How do we get out?"

"We need to find—" Juniper's eyes dart around the hallway searchingly, finally landing on a door at the end of the hallway that reads, "East Wing Fire Exit—Emergency Use Only." Underneath that is another sign, this one saying, "Warning: Radioactive Environment. Protective gear must be worn at all times." "Ha!" she says triumphantly. "There!"

"You sure about that?" I pant, trying to keep up with the others. I'm not even injured or carrying another human, and they're still outpacing me. "Did you read the sign? I think I left my hazmat suit at home today."

Juniper says something in response, but her words are cut off by a loud, erratic screeching, which begins to echo around the hallway. Dozens of red lights flash above us, bathing the ceiling in an ominous crimson glow. "Alarms already? Really?" I say, my blood pressure optimistically pressing onward to never-before-seen levels. "Jesus, Crenshaw recovers fast."

"Crap, the alarm trigger," Oliver groans from over Sanjeet's shoulder. The flood of relief that he's awake again turns my next few steps into staggers. "I left it in Crenshaw's office."

"It doesn't matter!" Juniper responds, continuing to run forward. "We're getting out of here anyway!"

"How?" Sanjeet demands. "I'm the only one left with powers right now!"

"Trust me!"

I force my legs to speed up for the last few steps as we close on the door, so that I can get through it first and hold it open for the other two, who don't really have the use of their hands anymore. As the door opens, I'm legitimately expecting us to be met with some kind of post-apocalyptic wasteland, filled with chemical debris and visibly radioactive substances, but it just looks like a normal backyard, apart from the flat, wide cylinder jutting about two feet out of the ground, about twenty feet from the door. I try to peek at the glowing green keypad attached to the top of it to see what kind of crazy radioactive substance is being hidden in there, but I'm too busy being herded toward Oliver's mess of a rusted orange truck, which is parked out of sight on the far end of the grass.

"Get in!" Juniper yells, leaping into the driver's seat and throwing it into gear. She starts to move before Sanjeet has even finished setting Oliver down in the truck bed.

"Wait, you nutcase!" I howl as we all run to catch up, but the night air is split with a faint popping sound and clouds of dirt fly up in several patches around our feet.

"Dammit, the roof!" Penny cries, and I turn mid-run to look. Two SuperVariant agents are perched up top, firing at us. Out of the corner of my eye, I see Penny start to rise into the air and grab her leg. "Are you nuts?" I screech, pulling her back down. "Your hands are like pretzels!"

"They're almost better!" she argues, flexing her fingers experimentally, then wincing. Without letting her debate me further, I push her floating form forward so that she lands in the bed of the truck. Sanjeet gives me a hand up too, then leaps in after.

He crouches and loops Oliver's arm around his shoulder, pulling him against the side to ensure that his legs are straight out in front of him. "I'm fine!" Oliver insists, bracing himself with both arms against the sides of the bed. "Gimme like thirty more seconds!"

His exclamation is followed by more popping sounds, and sparks fly up as some of the bullets ricochet off the sides of the truck. More agents are streaming out a side door of the building as we whip past. I'm not worried, because Juniper has to be going at least a hundred miles an hour, until I see a tall figure that can only be Crenshaw push through the rest of the squadron.

✖ COLLATERAL DAMAGE ✖

"Crap, he's alive again!" I shout, flattening myself against the bottom of the truck. Crenshaw's regeneration powers appear to not extend to his hair; even from this distance, I can see the gleam of the building lights as they bounce off his newly bald head. His look has gone full mad scientist. "If somebody wants to finish healing right about now, that'd be awesome!"

"You think I'm not trying?" Penny snaps shrilly, still flexing her fingers desperately, like she can will her hands into working for her again. Crenshaw blurs and reappears fifty feet behind the car. Thirty feet. Twenty. His face is a perfect mask of calm victory.

And then he's in the truck.

I scream as his terrifying bald head becomes visible above me, his legs braced on the truck bed on either side of mine.

"*You will—*" he roars, probably about to say something cliché like, "You will pay for this," or, "You will die now," but he doesn't get the chance.

I reach for my umbrella, but Oliver reacts faster. He grabs his own useless leg like a club and, howling in pain from the effort, rams it into Crenshaw's kneecaps right as Juniper runs over a pothole. Crenshaw staggers and falls backward off the edge of the truck, but flips over and rights himself in midair without even touching the ground. His eyes narrow in frustration, and he streaks through the air toward us again, coming to a hover just a few feet away. He raises his hand, aiming straight for the wheels.

"*Juniper!*" I scream, and the entire car swerves so sharply that I roll right into Oliver. Crenshaw's aim is thrown off, and all his burst of telekinetic energy does is swipe a massive cloud of gravel off the side of the road.

There's no time for celebration, though. Crenshaw pauses, furious; but an army of white cars bursts over the top of the hill behind him, careening down the road after us.

The popping noise begins again, typewriter-fast.

Sanjeet lets out a stifled whimper and turns invisible. My

hand shakes as I scrabble for my umbrella, find the button with my thumb, and force it open, pulling Oliver and Penny behind it with me. It's not big enough to cover all three of us, but I have nothing else to contribute. I tuck my head and knees into my chest and listen to the horrifying sound of metal death clanging off metal as it drills itself into my brain.

Bratatat! Bratatatat!

I dare a look and see that the gunman is in a contraption that folds out from the side of the van, sitting in an angular black chair with a machine gun perched on his lap. He scans the gun back and forth, firing with no interest in accuracy, covering as much space in front of him as possible. My knuckles are already white and raw from clenching, but I refuse to let go, even though everything feels weak.

And then there's an agonizing scream, and Sanjeet becomes visible again.

"Sanjeet!" I look over at him wildly. He moans, holding a hand to his shoulder, which is now spurting blood, and sinks against the side of the truck.

"*NO!*" Penny screams, and the forest around us falls. It starts with a massive oak wrenching itself up and colliding with the gunman, crushing his entire car as though it were made of aluminum. One by one, tree after tree rips itself out of the ground and throws itself sideways. Dirt and debris choke the air. The white cars chasing us swerve frantically, desperate to avoid the rampage, but it doesn't take more than a few moments for the avalanche to bury them all.

Penny's eyes are blazing by the time she's finished. She blinks the intensity out of them as though waking herself up from a trance, then flexes her hands and directs her attention to Sanjeet. "You okay?"

Sanjeet pulls off his mask and grins at Penny from underneath a mop of messy curls. "That was *awesome*."

"Everybody alive back there?" Juniper calls out in a shaky voice, her hands practically cemented to the wheel. We're almost back in town by now. I can see the splintered, faded *Welcome to Lunar City*! sign less than a few hundred feet away.

"We're good!" I reply, leaning over to check on Oliver's legs. The blood has even disappeared from his suit. "We—"

A figure floats up from the wreckage of the forest.

Crenshaw.

"*No*," I moan. "Why can't this just be over?"

But he doesn't speed toward us, telekinetic hands flying. He observes us for a few moments as we drive past the city limits sign, then ominously sinks back into the coverage of the fallen trees.

"What the hell was that?" Oliver demands. "What happened to trying to kill us?"

"Right?" I agree, completely lost. It's not like the trees did anything to stop him. Why isn't he chasing us into the city, trying to… *oh*. Oliver jumps as I start laughing. "Oh my god. He can't attack us in front of other people," I explain. "Look at him! Look at his *head*." I snicker. "He's gone full-on bad guy, and he knows it. If people see him attacking their beloved Supers, they'll riot."

"That's not going to last forever," says Penny, gritting her teeth. "He's going to come up with a plan, and we need to come up with a better one first."

Sanjeet pushes his hair away from his face with both hands. "You mean, other than going into hiding forever?"

"Hello? Sorry to interrupt, but," Juniper interrupts from the front seat, craning her neck while keeping her eyes on the road, "is someone going to tell me whether you got Crenshaw to confess? Why did he—" Her voices cracks just the tiniest bit, but she powers through and says, "Sam. Tell me why he did this to Sam."

I freeze. I can't tell her. I can't. This will destroy her. It's bad enough that she lost Sam—I can't let her know that the Super-Variant Program has killed all the other Supers, too. I can't let her know what the serum she helped create is actually being used for.

But I also can't lie to her. So I really don't have a choice.

"Juniper…" I begin, turning around and leaning against the glass between us on my knees. "Before I tell you…you have to know that it wasn't your fault."

She shoots me a look of unmatched confusion through the open rearview window. "Why would it be my fault?" she demands.

I swallow. "The SuperVariant Program… it's all a trap. The people picked are essentially sacrifices to defend the city against Doctor Defect. They all—" My heart is pounding like I've just tried to climb the stairs to a three-story building. "It's the final serum. All the Supers, ever, have been killed. They just kept it a secret."

The words hang in the air between us. Every muscle on her face is frozen. Her mouth is open just enough for her two front teeth to peek through, but she doesn't exhale, like even the act of breathing is now suddenly too much for her. I shouldn't have told her this while she was driving a car. I shouldn't have told her this at all.

"Juniper…" I began warily.

She says nothing. And then the whole car jerks.

"*Juniper*!" I shriek as I lose my balance and roll toward the edge of the truck bed. Oliver lunges for my arm and drags me back to the safety of the corner, squeezing me in between himself and Sanjeet. The view has changed; instead of looking at the mess Penny has made of the forest, I can now see the towering skyscrapers of the city. She's turned the truck around.

"Juniper, stop!" I clamber onto my knees to peer through the back window. Her knuckles are clenched around the steering wheel; her eyes are fire. "Are you crazy? We can't go back there!"

"Yes, we can!" she snaps without looking at me. "I have to fix this."

"We're going to," I plead. "We're going to fix it. But we need a plan. And the Supers need to recover."

"I'm *fine*," Oliver starts to argue, but I kick him. I turn my attention back to Juniper. "I'm serious, Juniper. If we go barreling back there right now without a strategy, we're all going to die. Turn the car around, okay?"

She glares at the road in front of us as the trees whistle by, and I'm already mentally preparing myself for fighting Crenshaw again, giving up hope that she'll listen to me, when she suddenly jerks the wheel to the left, and I go flying sideways again, smashing Oliver's face into the side of the truck.

"Ow," he groans, pushing me off him. "This is happening a lot today."

"Maybe you should drive your own truck then, buddy," I say, relieved that Juniper has actually controlled her fury enough to turn us back around. I nudge Sanjeet out of the way to give myself room to sit back down.

"Well, we can't go into hiding," Penny says fiercely. "Even if we do, he'll just replace us with more Supers. We have to get that serum before he can do that. There's two replacements this month."

"I stole one of the serums!" Sanjeet pipes up helpfully. "It's in the front seat."

"One isn't enough," Juniper says quietly. I can barely hear her over the sound of us speeding along the road. Her voice is numb and hollow, every trace of the fierce determination that had laced it since she first knocked on my door three days ago gone. "There's at least two dozen more completed vials inside the facility, not including the formulas in development. It's pointless."

"But what about Meg's video?" Oliver asks. "Once everyone in the city sees that, he'll have no choice but to stop, right?"

"Right," I agree, "but that might take a while."

"What do you mean? I thought you said you live-streamed it."

"I mean, I did, but that doesn't mean it's gonna instantly

go viral. It's almost midnight on a Tuesday, you know. It might take longer than you want it to for this thing to spread, and by that point, it won't matter if everyone knows Crenshaw is a maniac if he's already killed you," I point out.

"So, what, are we just going to drive around until we come up with a plan?" Oliver asks. "Is anyone going to give me gas money, by the way?"

"Oh!" Sanjeet cries, startling me so badly that I immediately raise my umbrella rod up defensively before I realize that he's made the exclamation out of excitement, not warning. "I know where we can go!"

"If you say your uncle's basement or something…" Penny warns.

"Oh, yeah, that won't work," I agree. "No houses. Nobody's house. Way too obvious."

"No, no! It's someplace they'll never check, trust me!" He leans around me through the window and eagerly gives Juniper some directions. Oliver and I look at each other and shrug.

Instead of following the road into the center of the city, we veer off around the edge and, about ten minutes later, end up in a small neighborhood full of identical one-story houses. I was expecting some kind of bunker, so the Stepford Wives vibe is throwing me off. Other than a few knocked-over fences and some neatly piled debris on the curb, the houses are extraordinarily non-damaged. It must be nice not to have to live in the center of the city, where most of the action usually goes down.

We turn into a cul-de-sac, and Sanjeet directs Juniper toward another cookie-cutter house on the left; one with a cavalcade of cars parked haphazardly around the driveway and on the lawn.

"Okay," Sanjeet says, stuffing his mask in my backpack and snagging Oliver's goggles from the top of his head. "Now…"

"Hey, what are you doing?" squawks Penny. "What part of 'secret identity' do you not get?"

"Yeah, what gives, man?" I agree, looking around nervously. What if someone looks outside the window and sees them?

"Look." Sanjeet jumps out of the car. "Just trust me, okay?"

I'm too tired to argue. Besides, if I can't trust the people in this car, I won't have anyone left. I grab my backpack, which has been getting steadily heavier all day, and step off the truck bed after him.

"Are you going to tell us where we are?" Penny demands as the rest of the Supers pile out of the truck and follow him up the walkway to the front door. "Or are we just all going to walk into a strange house with no information?"

Sanjeet cracks a smile. "Actually, I think it'll be funnier to walk into a strange house with no information."

"Come on, Sanjeet," I say, sneaking another worried glance at Juniper. She's said nearly nothing since I told her the truth about Crenshaw. She stands a few feet away from us, her arms crossed over her chest, staring at the ground. "We've had enough surprises for the day."

"You can handle one more!" He grabs the front doorknob and pushes it open without knocking.

Another SuperVariant Two stands on the other side of it.

THIRTY

I SIGH. I DON'T EVEN CARE ANYMORE. We're so far into the realm of nonsense today, nothing else can faze me.

"Okay," I say, elbowing past the other Supers into the house. "Now what? Clones? Evil twins? Body-swapping? Lay it on me. I—" I get all the way inside and freeze.

I'm met with a frenetic, dimly-lit, cacophony of noise. Loud music is pumping out of a speaker attached to the TV, and what feels like a hundred people are lounging around on every possible surface, drinking out of plastic cups and shouting animated conversation at each other over whatever Top 40 song is playing. Everyone is dressed in something outrageous. Some are in cheap, party store knockoff costumes of popular characters—the kinds of costumes that come labeled with names like Apple Princess and Wizard Student. Some are in normal clothes, with just a pair of animal ears or a prop. And some are—

"Oh, wow." Oliver cringes into himself when a shirtless

teenage boy wearing orange jeans, boots, and hand-painted goggles parades past, chugging something out of a can. "Wow. I hate that."

"Join the club." Penny grimaces as she notices two other kids dressed as sexy versions of One and Two making out in an armchair. Sanjeet goes a shade of red that could rival my hair when he sees where she's looking. A less provocative, very homemade-looking version of One is over in the kitchen, still recognizable in just a purple V-neck, a purple skirt, and a felt mask. With a quick scan, I count at least fifteen people wearing some kind of Super-inspired costume. A guy who could very easily have passed for the real Four if not for his short height and twig-like frame, wearing an absurdly detailed costume that replicates everything from the tiny honeycomb pattern in Oliver's supersuit to the particular way that his hair swooshes back, is slumped over in a corner, glaring at the shirtless Four who'd walked by us earlier. Shirtless Four is now surrounded by a cluster of girls. Exact-Replica Four looks angry that his costume isn't getting more attention.

"Sanjeet," I yell over the wave of noise assaulting my eardrums. "What *is* this?"

He grins broadly and herds everyone else farther into the house. "This girl in my class has a big Halloween party every year."

"It's the *middle of Sep*—"

"Hiding in plain sight." Penny looks around and nods appreciatively. "Not bad, Two."

His whole face glows. "Come on," he announces, starting to push through the crowd. "Let's go blend in."

"Yeah, okay," I mutter, letting him herd us through the crowd. "Me, blending in at a party. That'll look normal." I notice that Oliver hasn't followed us and backtrack to grab him. He's still staring at the shirtless guy in the homemade Four costume, who's dancing with three girls at once.

"This is the weirdest thing that's ever happened to me," he

mutters as I grab his hand and drag him off toward the rest of the group. I let go when I realize that someone else is missing, and turn around in time to see a flash of pale blonde hair disappearing through the front door.

"I'll catch up," I say, pushing Oliver toward the other Supers, then turning to fight my way back through the crowd between us and the door.

A blast of cool night air ruffles my shirt as I make it outside. The sparse street lamps aren't providing much light, but there's only one person out on the street.

"Juniper!" I cry, and the figure stops, but doesn't turn around. I sprint to close the distance between us until we're only ten feet apart. "What are you doing?"

She says nothing. Then—"I don't know." It's less than a whisper. "I just don't want to be here anymore."

I take ten careful steps, and then I'm on her other side, facing her. Her face is blotchy and tear-streaked, her eyes fixed pointedly at the ground. "Juniper, I already told you," I say quietly. "This… this wasn't your fault."

Her reddened eyes snap to mine. "I don't care if you think that," she says. "It is. It is my fault. I'm part of a program that's been—" She chokes, like even thinking about finishing the sentence is too much. "And you know what? I don't want to do this anymore. I'm tired of fighting and planning and running all over this stupid city."

"Juniper—"

"Sam is *gone*!" she screams, and the echo swirls around the cul-de-sac, wrapping us in her words as they mimic each other cruelly for eternity—*gone, gone, gone, gone.*

She sinks to the ground next to Oliver's truck and rests her back against one of the tires. "He's gone," she repeats dully. "I haven't even gotten to take a moment to think about what that means. It was almost like if I could keep myself busy enough, I could never have to feel the pain. Like if I focused on saving the other Supers, it would somehow bring him back. But it won't. And he's gone because of me." Her head tilts back as she stares at the sky, her eyes vacant. "I know you're out here to tell me to come back and help you guys fight Crenshaw, but I can't, okay? I can't do anything right." She takes a deep, rasping breath and huddles into herself, her arms wrapped around her legs. "I've been trying to be strong this whole time. But I'm not. And I don't know what to do."

Another gust of air breezes through, rippling both of our hair. I push my bangs aside and sit down next to her, leaning against the rusted orange metal. "It's okay," I say quietly. "I'm not going to tell you to come back."

Juniper looks up from her knees. "What?"

I stare up at the stars that have managed to peek through the light pollution. "You know," I observe, "I think there's this thing, like if you want to prove that you're strong, you have to never show any emotion. Like if you do, no one will ever take you seriously."

Juniper doesn't say anything.

"But you shouldn't have to," I continue, pulling my knees into my chest. "Being emotional isn't gonna make us think you're weak. And if you want to leave… no one will fault you. If I were you—" I swallow. I don't have to speculate. I was her. My parents died, and I know exactly how I reacted. I didn't fight. I didn't try to fix things. I just let myself be angry. I look back up at the sky. "Well, at least you ran toward your problems, instead of away from them. All I've ever done is shut everyone out. But you… you tried to fix things."

"Don't do that," Juniper mutters. "Don't pull that bit. 'Oh, look at me, I'm such an angsty loner.'"

I start laughing before I can stop myself, the sound puncturing the air. "Is that what I sound like? *Damn* it. I was trying so hard not to be a trope."

A tiny snort of laughter escapes her, but then her face grows stony again. I study the forced lack of emotion on her face. "You know," I say, "For the last three days, you've been running away from how you're feeling. And I just want you to know that if you want to, you can stop."

Juniper's mouth closes and she tilts her head back against the truck again. I wait, the vague, distant hum that always accompanies nighttime in a city underscoring the heavy pause. "I lost someone too, you know," I say suddenly. "My mom. When I was nine. And my dad… he closed everyone out, including me. And I thought—" I swallow. "I thought that was what you were supposed to do, when you lost someone. I thought you were supposed to protect yourself from ever feeling that way again. So I shut everyone out, too. And when he died, most of him was already gone, so it didn't feel like anything."

"So that's what you think I should do?" Juniper asks dully. "Shut all of you out?"

"No." I shake my head. "That's not what I'm saying at all. Look how well that turned out for me."

"You're alive, aren't you? And you have Oliver."

Oliver—the last, the only person I didn't shut out. I haven't thought about why in a while, but now, the memory is flashing in a projector screen inside my head. After my mom died and my dad shut down, I stopped talking to everyone too. And then this kid—this Korean kid in my fourth grade class who I'd never even spoken to before—somehow noticed that no one was making me lunch anymore, and in the midst of an overwhelming swirl of 'are-you-okay's and 'do-you-want-to-talk-about-it's, he walked over to my table and handed me a sandwich and said, "Here." And then he just sat there, not saying anything, while I ate his sandwich. And the next day, he did the same thing. And the next, and the next, until somehow, without even exchanging a word yet, there was a sort of mutual understanding that we'd adopted each other. I had lost one family member, but I replaced her presence with his. And I thought that was all I needed.

And then I realize something else. "If I lost Oliver," I say slowly. "I wouldn't even have anyone else to help me get through it." The thought makes me feel like I'm inside a vacuum, screaming for help. For so many years, I've thought it made sense—if you only care about one person, the statistical odds of losing someone you care about are much lower. But now I'm realizing that by letting him be the only person I care about, I've turned myself into a person who would be a shell in his absence, forever. The thought makes the space the vacuum is occupying in my mind multiply. I don't want to be alone anymore. I don't.

I don't realize that I've said those words out loud until I hear Juniper say, "Me neither."

I look at her.

"Every part of this has been"—she continues, her eyes vacant and numb—"a nightmare. One long, endless nightmare that I keep hoping I'll wake up from, but don't. And I know it's dumb, given the circumstances, and sort of twisted, but..." She looks right at me for the first time in this whole conversation. "I'm sort of glad that out of all of this, at least... at least I got to meet you."

My mouth falls open. *What*? "You're glad you got to meet *me*?" I gape.

"Of course," Juniper says, looking surprised. "You're the bravest, scariest person I've ever met."

I choke back my laughter—not because I don't believe what she's said, but because I was about to say the same thing about her.

Instead I sigh, shaking my head, and climb back to my feet. "I'm glad I met you, too," I say, and I mean it. "And if you don't want to do this anymore, I understand. You've done more than enough. And when this is all over, if you want to like, get together and cry about life," I hold out a hand to help her up, "I'm here for you."

She hesitates, then unfolds herself enough to take my hand and let me pull her to her feet. Something in her face breaks, and before I can do anything to stop it, she's hugging me.

I think she might be the first person I've let touch me since my parents, besides Oliver, but I don't pull away. I can't help it—I've expanded the circle of people I care about without wanting to, without planning it, but this fact doesn't fill me with terror or paranoia, like I always thought it would. In the most paradoxical way possible, it makes me feel more… safe. Protected.

"Okay," I say, patting her back awkwardly. "I'd better get back inside before one of those dorks blows up the house or something. Are you going to be okay?"

"I think I—" she begins, but then freezes. Every muscle in her body tenses, and I unwrap her arms and step back to make sure she's not going into cardiac arrest or something.

"Hey, what's up? What's happening?"

Her eyes are wide. "I'm not going home," she whispers. "I have to stay and fix this."

"Um, we just talked about this," I say. She's freaking me out. "You don't have to fight anymore. You can give yourself time to heal."

"No," she shakes her head. "I can do both. I'm just going to stop pretending that I'm strong enough to get through this without feeling anything. But I have to stay."

"Why?"

"Because," Her eyes snap toward mine, wild and maniacal. "I just came up with a plan."

THIRTY-ONE

"HEY, HAVE YOU SEEN a bunch of people dressed up like the Supers?" I ask somebody inexplicably dressed like a giant sunny-side-up egg once Juniper and I are back inside. He gives me a confused look and gestures to the room behind him, where there are now close to twenty teenagers wearing Super-inspired costumes of varying degrees of crappiness. "Never mind," I mutter, grabbing Juniper and using our elbows to push our way through the crowd. We check three different rooms—all of which are occupied with couples doing things I had no desire to see tonight—until we finally reach a door at the end of the corridor with a piece of notebook paper taped to it, announcing "Parents' Room. Don't Go In or You're Dead." I push the door open.

Penny wheels around with her hands in firing position immediately, and Oliver leaps up from where he's been lounging on the bed's burgundy comforter. "Really?" I say, shutting the door behind me in exasperation. "What if I were someone else?

Come on, guys. The point is to not act suspicious."

"What was going on out there?" Oliver asks as he relaxes back onto the bed. "Everything okay?"

"It's fine. We're fine." I nod at Juniper.

"Good," Penny says, "Because we don't have time for this. We need to figure out our next move. How do we destroy Crenshaw? He's invincible, just like us. Any battle is going to be a stalemate."

"We're not going to destroy Crenshaw." Juniper steps out from behind me. "We have to destroy the serum. All of it."

Everybody gapes at her. The serum. Without the serum, they can't inject anyone else, at least not before we alert the rest of the city about what they're up to. *Duh.* I can't believe all of us have been sitting here thinking that the only possible solution was to punch our way out of the problem.

"So smart." I push Oliver out of the way to give myself room to sit on the bed next to him. "This is why we keep you around."

"Okay," says Oliver, flopping forward onto his stomach. "So what you're saying is that, instead of battling a crazed, ultra-powerful mad scientist, we just have to take out a couple of bottles? I'm down."

"Well…" Juniper scrunches her mouth up. "Kind of. So, the first thing we need to do, obviously, is steal all the active serum from inside the lab. But it's very volatile, so it'll react with anything it comes in contact with. We can't just flush it down the toilet or throw it away."

Something about the words *throw it away* remind me of a different conversation we had about disposed-of serum. I leap off the bed. "Wait, what about that bunker you told me about? The failure graveyard? The one where you store all the experimental serums for new powers?"

Juniper shakes her head. "That won't work. We can't just store the vials in there; Crenshaw could just get them back out."

"No—what? You think my plan is to just put them in storage where anyone can get them?"

"Well I don't—"

"It's underground!" I yell in part-exhilaration, part-frustration. "It's an impenetrable underground bunker! Let's just throw all the serum down there and then *destroy the entire bunker!*"

Juniper blinks. "That could work."

"Yeah?" Penny crosses her arms and leans against the dresser. "How are you gonna destroy an indestructible bunker?"

"Hey, I already supplied the first part of the plan, somebody else can be in charge of bunker destruction," I pout, but Juniper swivels to reach behind me and pokes my backpack. Her face lights up with something like mania. "Still got that grenade?" she asks.

I thought I'd made it abundantly clear that I didn't have any interest in handling explosives today, but yes, I do still have the grenade. "Why?" I ask warily.

"I told you, it's an incredibly powerful design! Don't you see? We can throw it down and blow up all of the serum from the inside, without the risk of hurting ourselves or anyone still in the lab!"

She looks around hopefully, and I realize that she's wearing the same expression I once saw on her face when she was desperate for Crenshaw's approval. "Yeah," I say. "I think it's a solid plan." She beams, and I look around at everyone else. "Anybody got a backup suggestion?"

"I do," says Oliver seriously, but I narrow my eyes when I see the smirk playing around his mouth. "What if I run around the Earth so fast, it rewinds time, and then—"

I shove him off the bed and he rolls to the carpeted floor with a burst of laughter. "Okay, so Juniper and I will drive back to the lab, and—"

"Are you nuts?" Oliver interjects. "While we all do what? Stay here and drink party punch?"

"As a casual reminder, in case you've forgotten," I reply,

"everyone at that lab is trying to kill you."

"They're not all that fond of you, either!"

"Look," Penny interrupts coolly, "not to be rude, but you can't stop us. Besides, you're going to need someone to be a distraction to lure Crenshaw and any of the other program agents away if you want to pull this off. What do you think you're going to do if someone catches you?"

"Yeah," Oliver chimes in. "I can be very distracting."

I look at him, at the haphazard chunks of hair sticking out in every direction from underneath the stupid goggles perched on his forehead. This is insane. Last week, we were eating cake batter and joking about quitting my job. Today, we both almost died, and we're about to voluntarily go back for more.

He might be dressed up like a superhero, but he's still just Oliver. I haven't had enough time to process—to rewrite a decade of memories backing up the idea that he's just a normal guy, nothing more or less than my dependable childhood best friend. I don't want him to go back and take on Crenshaw. I don't want to either, but somebody has to fix this.

"I don't want you to be bait," I mumble sullenly. "I don't want anything bad happening to you."

He shrugs, flashing me a slight grin. "I mean, me neither." I hit him in the stomach halfheartedly. "Look," he continues, "I'm not going to promise you that everything is going to be okay. But I can't just run away from this."

"You could," I remind him. "Literally. You're very fast, apparently."

He rolls his eyes. "Look, it's going to be fine. Or maybe it won't. But we'll be fixing it together, the way we do everything else. You're part of the team now, too. And team members don't leave other team members behind, or let them go into battle alone. I'm with you on this. And we're not going to die today. Isn't that what we always say?" He looks at me expectantly.

I exhale through my nose. "That had better be a promise." His face breaks into a wide grin, and he hugs me. "This is happening a lot today," I grumble over his shoulder, giving Juniper a look. "Almost dying makes you people so emotional."

"Okay." Penny taps her foot impatiently. "Can we go now or what?"

"Right now?" I pull away from Oliver, terror jolting through my nerves. "You want to go right now? You don't want to like, take a nap and wait for morning?"

"I can't in the morning," Sanjeet reminds us. "I have a test."

"Nah, let's do it." Oliver jogs in place, as if trying to demonstrate how much energy he has. "I'm pumped."

"But—" I start to argue, but suddenly, we're interrupted by a massive, room-shaking cry from the party outside. Oh, god. Are they being attacked? What's happening? I run for the door and poke my head out, but quickly realize that the sound is one of annoyance, not terror. The music has stopped.

"Come on!" somebody whines. "You kidding me?"

"Hold on, I can fix it!" shrieks the girl who probably lives here. I'm about to retract my head back into the bedroom, but then a loud voice comes over the speaker system rigged to the ceiling. "Attention, all Lunar City citizens," says a calm, even voice. "This is an official emergency announcement on behalf of the Lunar City Police Department."

Confused voices overlap each other. "What's going on?"

"Is it another crisis?"

"Please be informed that all currently active SuperVariants have been compromised, and are now considered active threats to Lunar City," the voice continues, and my breath catches as I realize that, of course, it's Crenshaw. "Rogue SuperVariants should not, repeat, should not be contacted for help. To report information regarding their whereabouts, utilize the standard LCPD line, extension one. Please be advised that rogue SuperVariants are likely hiding in the guise of their secret identities, which are as follows..."

"Oh, no. No, no, no." I feel all the blood leave my face. "They can't do that. Can they do that?"

"If they have nothing to lose, yes!" Juniper's face is pale, too.

"...Oliver Lee..."

"Ah, shit," Oliver mutters.

"...Penelope Diaz..."

"*Penelope?*" I mouth at Penny.

"What did you think Penny was short for? 'Pennifer?'" she hisses.

". . . and Sanjeet Mishra. As a precaution..." Crenshaw is still talking, but I can't hear anything else he says on account of the fact that all of Sanjeet's classmates are now out in the living room losing their goddamn minds.

"Wait, *Sanjeet*'s a Super?"

"No freaking way!"

"I always thought it was *you*!"

"I thought it was you!"

"Wait, I think he's here!" shrieks a voice above the rest. "I just saw him!"

I turn around. All four of the others are crowded around within a few inches of me, having crept up to listen to the commotion in the hallway, too. They all look extremely stricken.

"Well," I say, clapping my hands together and walking across the room to the window. I unhook the dusty latch and throw it open. "You were right. We should leave now."

THIRTY-TWO

THE LAB LOOKS LIKE SOME KIND of haunted fortress as we pull back up to it in the darkness. We'd taken a longer route to get back, cutting around the main road and looping around through the sparse forest in the back of the building, in case we ran into any search teams out looking for us or an army of agents waiting for us at the front. I'm also hoping that we have the element of surprise on our side; there's no way he's expecting us to willingly come back so soon.

Oliver lurches the truck to a stop near the edge of the forest, Juniper having enthusiastically relinquished control of the wheel for the drive back. Once we've slipped noiselessly out of the car, I crane my neck trying to find Crenshaw's office floor, hidden somewhere up in the dark clouds.

"Okay," I say, the completely illogical paranoia that the agents guarding the facility will be able to hear me from a thousand feet away forcing my voice into a whisper. "Juniper and

Penny, you're with me. Oliver and Sanjeet—" I grin despite the tension, "—break stuff."

"I can't believe this." Oliver shakes his head. "I can't believe you're actually telling us to destroy things. Who *are* you?"

"Let me clarify," I correct myself. "Break stuff *safely*. Don't hurt anyone. Especially, you know, me and Juniper. And don't—"

"Die?" Oliver finishes with a smirk, then pulls his goggles down over his eyes. "Not today."

"Should we say something?" Sanjeet asks, his voice muffled through his suit. "Like, before we go? Does anybody have a good battle cry?"

I blink at him. "We're not doing battle cries. We're just gonna—"

"Oh, yes we are." Oliver's smirk widens. "You said you needed a distraction."

"Oliver, *no*, just—"

"CRENSHAW!" he bellows before I can stop him, and then he's streaking across the field, a ribbon of orange light against the dark landscape. His words float back to me, elongated by the distance. *"WE'VE COME FOR VENGEANCE!"* The sound of shattering glass punctuates the end of his cry as he bursts through a window.

Something inside my stomach twists. I know what he's doing: trying to make this seem like a joke, like he always does. So I won't be afraid. But this all feels so rushed, so impulsive. What if it doesn't work?

But it's too late for that kind of thinking, because the rest of the group is running behind him—slower, obviously, but still running.

"Hurry up, Meg!" I hear Sanjeet yell before he flickers into invisibility. There's a whoosh a few feet in front of the last place I saw him; he's flying up to join Oliver.

"We're all gonna die," I mutter, and run after them.

✖ TAYLOR SIMONDS ✖

ONCE PENNY HAS lifted Juniper and I over the chain-link fence and into the air vent I used to escape the facility earlier today, Juniper starts to lead. We can hear the sound of muffled shouting and the echo of weapons being fired even from so many floors below the action, and I can't tell if it's me shaking in response or the vent. It's probably both. I force myself to remember that it's a *good* thing we can hear the battle Oliver and Sanjeet and Penny have instigated; it's only when the noise stops that I should worry. Because if the noise stops, it means they're not fighting anymore.

It could mean they're not *able* to fight anymore.

Juniper kicks the vent open in a foreign part of the building right as my knees start to give up, and we slip out into the abandoned hallway in front of a large, windowless door with a keypad embedded into the handle. *Please don't set off an alarm*, I think desperately at the keypad as Juniper scans her ID, looking around furtively before pulling me through the door behind her.

The inside is like a walk-in fridge for a better restaurant than Oliver or I could ever afford to eat at. It's all stainless-steel shelves filled with eerie looking concoctions in varying stages of development. A gold orb that bears a striking resemblance to the silver one the van driver used to vaporize a trash can the other day has a sticky note attached to it declaring, *"Do not touch unless you're Mike."* Some of the other shelves are full of tidily organized technological contraptions: a severed robotic head, some metallic cuffs embedded with large, glittering gemstones, a massive assortment of guns in strange shapes and sizes, the various functions of which are unclear just by looking.

The case in the back, which is cemented firmly to the wall, comes into focus as we move closer. It's heavily locked and looks like it's made of what I'm sure is some kind of impenetrable glass. The inside is flooded with an eerie-looking transparent mist, and contains a dozen or so small vials of the familiar blue serum, each carefully labeled. There are lots of vials marked with the number "3.6"—no doubt the SuperVariant Three serum that I turned down the offer to be injected with. Above those are a set of vials marked with "1.5" and "2.5"—for Penny and Sanjeet—and just two labeled "4.5." The lethal strand meant for Oliver.

I shudder and shuffle out of my backpack, holding it out for Juniper. "Load 'em up."

She pulls a lanyard out of her pocket and uses the attached keys to open three separate locks. Next, she codes in a set of numbers too fast for me to keep track of onto the keypad next to the case. When the screen glows green, she presses her ID to it, and a blue light emerges and scans her face. I flatten myself against the wall and hold my breath, like it'll be able to sense that a second person is in the room, but it beeps squeakily and the case clicks open, releasing a burst of chilly mist. I move in next to Juniper, and she hastily begins pushing bottles off the shelves and into the bag.

"Careful," I whisper as they clink loudly against one another. "What if they shatter?"

"They won't. They'd require much more pressure." She swipes the remaining vials into the bag and glances at the variety of weapons lining the shelves on either side of her. "Should we—"

"*No.*" I shake my head fervently. "We don't have time. We have to *go.*"

"But—" I clamp a hand over her mouth and swivel in terror. The door rattles. "*Shit,*" I whisper and flatten myself against the wall. Juniper has exactly enough time to shut the door to the case behind her before the room floods with light from the hallway and a figure appears in the doorframe.

I peer through the space in between the objects occupying

the shelving unit I'm hiding behind, and breathe a sigh of relief when I realize that it isn't Crenshaw. The guy standing there looks slightly older than me, but younger than Juniper, and has excessively curly hair and a large nose. He must be some kind of intern.

"Mike?" Juniper still looks tense. "What are you doing here?"

Mike of the "Do not touch unless you're Mike" sticky note, I'm assuming. He confirms this by reaching out and taking the gold orb off the shelf, sticking the note to his shirt pocket. "I know, I know," he says hastily, looking guilty. "We're supposed to leave threats to the agents, but I was here working on a personal project, and I just thought I could help…" He appears to notice where Juniper is standing for the first time. "What are *you* doing in here?"

"Oh," Juniper waves a hand dismissively. "Just making sure all the serums are accounted for. Wouldn't want the rogue Supers getting in and tampering with the vials, you know." She tries to sound casual, but I know her well enough to recognize that she sounds really, really suspicious. I hope Mike the Intern isn't smart enough to recognize that she's lying, but the fact that he was smart enough to get this job in the first place isn't giving me a lot of hope.

Miraculously, he nods, yawns, and takes a few more steps into the walk-in storage closet. I practically invert my stomach trying to suck it in. "Yeah, good idea. Hey, pass me that stun gun too, would you? Might be helpful, right? I could knock one out long enough to drain his powers."

My insides contort with fury. *I'll knock you out long enough to—*

Juniper reluctantly moves toward the shelf Mike is pointing to, but I gasp a silent warning as I realize her mistake half a second too late. By moving away from the case, she's now leaving its empty contents wide open for Mike to notice.

He might not have been able to recognize when she was

lying, but he's definitely going to be observant enough to notice that an entire case of highly valuable scientific property is missing.

Even in the dim light, it only takes a moment for him to realize what's going on. "The serum!" he shouts shrilly, pointing a finger. "It's gone! You—" His eyes widen with understanding. "You're working with them?"

"Mike," Juniper says firmly. "It's not what you think. Just listen; Crenshaw is—"

He shakes his head and reaches for his wrist under his sweater, where he's no doubt wearing one of the magic high-tech watches that everyone else who works for this stupid company seems to have. *Dammit.*

I forget about staying hidden and reach for the closest thing I can find—a large, gray, cylindrical something—and prep to throw it as hard as I can. But before I can take two steps, there's a faint whistle and Mike drops like a sack of rice, unconscious. I snap my head toward Juniper, who's holding the stun gun he had asked for straight in front of her, looking both horrified and mildly surprised.

"I—I didn't mean…" she says. "I just didn't want him to…"

"Whoa." I pat her on the shoulder appreciatively, using my elbow to point the gun back toward the floor. "Nice. Let's trade, okay?" I hand her the backpack of serum, then ease the gun out of her hands and push it back onto the shelf. "Yep. There we go. Okay. We should probably run for our lives now, yeah?"

And *then* the alarms go off.

THIRTY-THREE

ADRENALINE IS APPARENTLY a powerful thing when it comes to my ability to perform basic exercise, because I sprint down the hallway faster than I've ever sprinted and make it through the emergency exit leading to the storage bunker first, the flashing red lights and siren wail of the alarms pealing behind me. I really should start packing earplugs. I'm going to be deaf by the end of this week.

I'm all ready to start hitting people with my umbrella, but nobody stops us as we flee the building. Juniper clutches my backpack of stolen serum as I kick open the door that'll take us outside, but there's nothing there either. I suddenly realize that the now-faint sirens are the only sound I can hear, and the notable absence of typical battle noises fills me with even more dread.

"Why can't we hear them fighting anymore?" I ask, scanning the upper floors frantically. There's an uncountable number of holes in the walls of the building; something that looks like a filing cabinet is teetering through a window ten stories up like a ship's plank. "They must have defeated everyone, right? That's why the fighting stopped?"

"I don't know." Juniper's nails dig into the backpack. "I'm sure that's it. I'm sure they're fine."

I don't believe her.

But right as I'm descending into full-on panic mode, there's a flash of light to my left, and I look toward the forest just in time to see a massive tree, at least fifty feet tall, rise out of the ground like a rocket taking off and go careening back down with an earsplitting crash. Leaves explode into the sky.

"Found 'em," I state, overcome with an unpleasant tidal wave of both relief and concern. "Crenshaw. If they're still fighting, it means Crenshaw is still too powerful for them to handle. I have to—" I'm about to start running, but Juniper grabs the back of my shirt. "And where do you think you're going?"

"Uh, to help them?"

"They're Supers! They can take care of themselves! We have a job to do, too, remember?" She holds up my backpack.

I look toward the woods longingly, but let Juniper steer me toward the cylinder emerging from the ground. She slams her ID against the faint green screen on the side, and it lights up with a request for a security clearance code. After she codes in about a billion numbers again, the panel covering the top of the bunker slits in two and slides open. I lean over and peer through the opening, but I see nothing. No storage boxes or cabinets or light or *anything*. All I can see is another circular metal panel with a hole in it about an inch in diameter.

"Are you sure this is right?" I ask. "How are we supposed to get the backpack through that?"

As I finish speaking, a thin device that looks like an upside-down claw emerges from the smaller hole, nearly stabbing me in the face. "What is *that*?" I shriek, and clamber away from it.

Juniper rushes to unzip my backpack and fishes out a vial. "Crap," she whispers.

"What crap? No crap. We don't have time for crap."

"I think…" She reaches for the claw. The ground shakes, and she almost drops the vial she's holding into the opening, but she manages to get it into the center of the machine. The metal fingers clamp around it and instantly retreat back into the ground, the door swiftly closing behind it.

"One at a *time*?" My voice is so shrill, it practically pierces my own eardrums. "We have to put them in *one at a time*?"

"I didn't know! My supervisors are the ones who handle vial storage, not me!" Juniper snaps, wrenching the backpack open and scrabbling to sort out the vials from the mass of other junk I have in there. "It'll be fine! It'll just take a little longer!"

"We don't *have* a little longer!"

A glowing blue rectangle appears at the bottom of the metal panel, and Juniper slams her hand into it. The claw reappears with a sharp jolt. She snatches the nearest vial and crams it in. "Get all the others ready to go, okay? We're gonna assembly-line this. It'll be fine."

A massive *crash* resounds from somewhere in the forest. They're so dead. We're so dead. Everybody is just *dead*.

I reach into the bag, but my hand connects with something cold and angular and not at all vial-like. "Why do I have so much junk in here?" I mutter, pulling my fingers back and tilting the bag toward the light. But it's not my stuff. Mixed in with all the vials is an assortment of clunky metallic objects—some of them cuffs, some of them orbs, some cubes. "What—what the heck is all this?" I squawk, aiming the opening of the bag at Juniper. "Did you steal a bunch of weapons out of the closet when I wasn't looking? I specifically said no!"

Juniper flushes. "We might need something! I didn't want us to be defenseless!"

"Fine, but isn't this a little overboard?" I peer back into the bag and give it a shake, shuffling around everything inside. Something long and silver glints menacingly from within the jumble of stolen property. "Wait a second, is that—" I gingerly pull it out by its back end and dangle it in front of Juniper. "Is this the death serum syringe Crenshaw was going to use on Oliver?"

"Ah, I forgot I put that in there," Juniper admits, grabbing it from me and putting it on the rim of the cylinder. "Sanjeet had just left it lying around in the front seat; it didn't seem safe."

"And you thought this was better?"

She ignores me and grabs a vial out of the backpack herself, placing it in the claw. The entire cylinder comes into brilliant focus for a few seconds as a bright flash comes from the woods. Oliver. If he can still run, he must be doing okay. But the flash of light is followed by a low, guttural scream, and I tense up again. I can't tell who it's coming from or what the tone is; is it a scream of pain or of rage? I instinctively grab my umbrella from the ground and manage to take two steps toward the trees before Juniper grabs my arm again.

"Meg, we talked about this!"

"Come on!" I gesture toward the bunker with one arm. "This is not a two-person job! You don't need someone to hand you the vials! Let me go help them."

"Meg, listen to me." Juniper puts both hands on my shoulders to make me look at her. "Trust me. I know from experience, okay? You won't be able to help. You'll just be another person they have to worry about protecting."

I want to argue, but she's right. I know she's right. "I hate just sitting here," I whisper.

"You're not just sitting here; you're helping me get rid of this serum! They're going to be fine! Okay?" She pulls me back toward the opening. The claw is back and ready, and she jams another vial into it.

"Can we at least try to put in more than one at a time?" I beg.

"That's not how the machine works." She pushes the blue button again. "Look at it; it can only hold one."

"*Who designed this*?" I shout.

As if to punctuate my outburst, an enormous cluster of trees on the edge of the woods suddenly all falls at once, like a gigantic assortment of bowling pins.

"Duck!" I yell, pulling Juniper down behind the cylinder next to me. A wave of leaves and dirt washes over our heads as the trees crash into the ground. As it settles, I chance a peek over the top of the cylinder. All three of the Supers are entangled in the thick, knotted branches, but they only lie there for a moment before everyone's limbs start moving at once, and they all burst from the foliage. They streak onto solid ground, less than fifty feet away from us, and stand in a back-to-back triangle, covering every potential source of attack. I hold my breath, watching the forest for some indication that Crenshaw is coming. And then he's there, materializing in the middle of their circle.

I bellow a warning that's consumed by the loud, constant clanging of the alarm, and then Crenshaw lifts Oliver by the neck and throws him as hard as he can into the side of the truck. He bounces off with a crunch that reverberates throughout my own bones, but rolls into a front flip and lands on his feet.

He's invincible, I repeat to myself over and over, forcing myself to stay hidden. *He's fine, he's fine, he's invincible.*

Besides, Penny is already retaliating. She throws her hand out and lifts Crenshaw into the air, but as she slams him back down, he extends his arm and does the same thing to her. They attack each other mid-air, up and down, like they're on some kind of twisted see-saw. As he hits the ground the third time, his head suddenly whips to the side like he's been punched, and his legs go out from under him. *Nice one, Sanjeet*, I think, handing Juniper another vial. She snakes her arm up over the opening and plants it in the claw, keeping the rest of her body hidden next to me.

✖ COLLATERAL DAMAGE ✖

I know I should probably pull my head back down, but I can't stop watching. Besides, Crenshaw isn't paying attention to me. He scowls up around him—Sanjeet's invisibility still seems to be the one power that he can't figure out how to defend himself from—and goes invisible himself.

"Again?" Oliver glowers, swiveling around himself for any sign of Crenshaw's movement. "Show yourself, you coward!"

God, Oliver, stop insulting him. I cover my eyes, knowing what's coming, but peek through my fingers to see Crenshaw reappear behind Oliver and telekinetically backhand him toward Penny, who, thank god, uses her own telekinesis to slow him in time to put him back safely on the ground.

"Stop throwing me!" Oliver shouts, zipping back over to Crenshaw in the blink of an eye, then bouncing around him like a marble in a pinball machine, too fast for Crenshaw to react to. "Pick a new tactic!"

I hand Juniper another vial, but I'm suddenly distracted. Something doesn't make sense. Why does Crenshaw keep becoming visible before using his telekinesis or super strength? Why doesn't he just remain invisible while destroying everyone? I remember how he held me and Penny immobile earlier, but released us the moment before he used his super-strength to break Oliver's legs. Suddenly, everything clicks.

"He can't use more than one," I gasp.

Juniper looks at me like I'm speaking in tongues. "What?"

I grab her arm and shake it, nearly making her drop the vial she's clutching. "The powers! Crenshaw's powers!" I screech as quietly as I can. "He has all four, but he can't access all of them at once! He can only use one at a time!"

Her eyes grow big as saucers. "You're a genius."

"I know I'm a genius!" I'm trying to victory dance and stay hidden at the same time, but I'm not sure it's working. I cut the dance short as Juniper straightens up, completely exposing her location. "Wait, what are you doing?" I grab her hand and try to pull her back down.

276

"It's fine," she whispers, not looking at me. "Stay here! Finish the vials!" And she starts running toward the battle.

"Juniper!" I hiss, but she doesn't turn around. I put another vial in the claw, watching her anxiously. *What the hell is she doing?*

"Hey!" she calls to the Supers as she runs. Penny and Sanjeet are grappling with Crenshaw in mid-air. Oliver runs up the side of the building and launches himself off a window, rocketing toward Crenshaw, who dodges at the last second. Sanjeet catches him as he soars past and quickly flies him back down to the ground. Oliver immediately takes off running toward the building to, presumably, do the same thing all over again, like some kind of idiotic wind-up toy. Juniper makes it to just beneath them, cups her hands, and cries up into the air, "Meg figured out his weakness! He can only use one power at a time!"

"What?" Oliver shouts back, pausing mid-run and hanging off a windowsill four stories up. "Seriously?"

Crenshaw looks murderous, and I know that I'm right. While Sanjeet and Penny are distracted by Juniper, he extends his hands toward each of them and throws them toward the ground. Grass explodes up around them as they collide with the dirt. Oliver switches directions and races back down the building toward them to help, but as soon as he's within range, Crenshaw holds out his hand toward the patch of earth where they're all clustered together and forms a fist, freezing them all in place. I can't breathe. I want to run over there too, but I know it'll be useless. All I can do is push that stupid blue button again, recalling the claw to put another vial away underground. Crenshaw floats down toward Juniper as gracefully as if he were sitting on a cloud, but she doesn't run away. Why isn't she running away?

"You're involved in this too?" he says, landing about ten feet away from her. Now that everything has stopped moving, I can finally hear his quiet, even voice. Everything seems frozen, even sound. "Miss Jensen, now is not the time to have a moral crisis. You're a scientist. This is your job."

"Science and morality aren't mutually exclusive," Juniper says. "You don't get to use it to play with other people's lives."

"You have a promising career ahead of you." Crenshaw ignores her, taking a step forward. "I know you don't want to do anything to get in the way of that."

"You don't know anything about me." She shakes her head. "You killed Sam. How could you think I would ever ignore that?"

"That's just not true," Crenshaw sighs. He's even closer to her now. Again, why isn't she running? Is she trying to have some kind of brave, heroic, defiant moment against her old boss? It's a level of petty that I would usually get behind, but I'm really concerned that it's going to be the death of her. "You're a brilliant scientist, with an incredible amount of potential," he continues. "Whatever these insubordinates have told you, it simply isn't true. All I want is to protect this city. I know that's what you want, too."

"Not the way you do." She shakes her head again, standing her ground.

He exhales in frustrated impatience. He's less than a foot away from her now, towering over her condescendingly. "I won't repeat myself, Miss Jensen. You're out of your depth. Go home, and forget all this."

She says nothing, and I have a moment of anxiousness as I put another vial into the claw. She's not considering it, is she? After everything?

I shouldn't have worried.

"This is for Sam," she hisses, the words angry and controlled enough to float back to where I'm crouching, and then she plunges something into his neck.

I leap to my feet to get a better view, forgetting all about hiding and storing the serum. I look down at the rim around the cylinder, and my suspicions are confirmed. The syringe full of death serum is gone.

Crenshaw staggers to his knees.

I can feel my jaw drop. I can't believe it. She actually did it.

The Supers, released from his telekinetic hold, break free into mobility, looking confused and wary. They must not be close enough to see what she's done.

Juniper scrambles backward as her former boss falls, but he doesn't pass out or drop dead or spontaneously erupt into a flurry of evil moths, like I was hoping for. Crenshaw wrenches the needle from his neck, looks at it like he's inspecting a bug, and crushes it into dust. In a flash, he straightens back up and extends his hand back toward the cluster of Supers without looking. They freeze in place again, having spent too long in bewilderment to move away from one another or him.

"Juniper, look out!" I scream, but it's too late. He grabs her by the throat with his free hand and shoots into the sky. She kicks her legs, but even without access to his super-strength, he's still stronger than her.

"You foolish girl," he laughs. Oh, no. He's using the word "foolish" unironically. He really has gone full bad-guy. "A good theory, but…" He squeezes tighter. "…my strain is the same formula as Doctor Defect's. That serum won't work on me."

Of course, it won't. Heaven forbid this be the end of it so we can all go home.

"Hey, genius!" I grab a vial at random and hold it straight up in the air, tucking the backpack under my arm. I don't know what I'm doing; I don't know what my plan is; I just know that I need to get his attention away from destroying Juniper. "If you're so all-powerful, you probably don't need these anymore, right?"

His head snaps toward mine. I don't know if he heard what I said, but he can definitely see the glint of the vial off the reflection of light from the keypad screen. I feel myself flood with relief at knowing that my diversion has worked, then terror as I realize that, dammit, now I'm the target.

Shit. I didn't think this through. I just wanted him to put her down, but now he's definitely going to come for me. The claw isn't back yet, and there are all these other serums I have to get rid of, too. I plunge my hand into my backpack, frantically throwing aside all of my old safety equipment in an attempt to find something of use. The weapons Juniper stole from the lab are all foreign objects to me; just a mass of functionless metallic shapes that I don't know how to use.

But then I see the cuff.

A cuff with a silver orb perched on top of it, with the power to twist a trash can into a pretzel.

I snatch it out and swing my backpack over my shoulder.

Without looking at her, Crenshaw drops Juniper, but in his distraction, he's unintentionally released the Supers. Penny reaches out a hand to slow her as she falls, and Sanjeet catches her, carefully putting her right side up back on the ground. There's a blur, and Oliver is in front of me.

"Don't worry," he says, putting his arm out like a shield. "He's not getting through me."

But I know it's useless. Crenshaw's too much of a control freak; he's not going to let me destroy all his serum even if he *does* have the resources to make more. I mean, formulating an arsenal of genetic-enhancement technology is probably expensive. And time-consuming. As if to prove my point, he slams back into the ground with enough force to lower the patch he's standing on by a few inches, then telekinetically wraps Penny, Sanjeet, and Juniper into an impenetrable bubble that he begins to crush into the ground. All three of them scream as the earth opens up around them, sucking them in.

"The serum!" he shouts at me. "Drop it!"

I clutch it tight in my hand and point the silver cuff at the thick, metal panel protecting the rest of the storage bunker. "I'm sorry, Oliver," I whisper. "I have to break my promise."

"What?" he turns around and grows pale as he sees what I'm focusing on. "No. No, Meg, wait—"

As if reacting to my thoughts, a silver beam of light bursts from the front of the cuff, colliding with the panel guarding the entrance to the storage facility. I drop it and hold the serum as high as I can above my head. "Come and get it!" I yell, and as the metal panel creaks and groans, twisting into itself enough to create a gaping mouth of a hole, I jump into the bunker.

THIRTY-FOUR

I DON'T KNOW HOW LONG I was expecting to fall. The seemingly endless darkness I saw in the tunnel from above ground definitely made me prepare myself for more of an Alice-in-Wonderland-type fall, but it only lasts a few seconds before I collide with the ground.

I let out a pained groan as my knees buckle against the hard stone. I'm not expecting to make it out of here, but if I do, I'm going to be replacing all future meals with straight painkillers.

I stagger up one leg at a time, like a newborn giraffe. The air down here is cold and stale, likely from not having circulated properly in the last twelve years. I can already feel my breathing getting shallow from the limited oxygen. In almost every direction, it's about as dark as it feels when you look at the back of your eyelids. The only light I can see is coming from a faint red glow to my left, which I'm really hoping leads to wherever the rest of the failure graveyard is. I start limping toward it.

✖ COLLATERAL DAMAGE ✖

There's a whizzing sound as something whirs toward me, and I manage to duck just as the claw rockets back toward the entryway, finally doing its damn job. There's a faint hiss as it slices through the air like a throwing knife, then a series of loud clangs as it collides with the broken door, over and over. The noise mingles with something else—a scuffling, shouting, chaotic sound, probably caused by the people above ground all fighting to get in after me.

This is crazy. This is crazy. Oh my god, this is stupid. Why did I do this?

But it's too late to change my mind. Even if I wanted to, I have no idea how to get back up. I'm probably already decaying from the inside out from all the radiation down here, anyway.

The red glow finally turns into a solid light panel fixed to the ceiling of the bunker, which illuminates a large room walled in on three sides by glass compartments filled with vials of serum. Behind that layer is another layer of glass compartments, then another, then another, too many for me to count. It's like when you put a mirror across from another mirror, and both mirrors reflect each other forever—that's what the failure graveyard looks like. Reflections of identical glass bottles on identical glass shelves, forever. Jesus, how many failed attempts did they have? Aren't these people supposed to be smart?

Every bottle is labeled with the same tiny placard as the SuperVariant serum vials, but instead of numbers, they all have words: force field; aptitude-based; unsuccessful. Projection; aptitude-based; unsuccessful. Teleportation; aptitude-based; unsuccessful.

I struggle out of my backpack and am about to take the vials out one a time, but then I remember I don't have to do that anymore. I find an empty compartment near the bottom of the wall opposite me, under "Shape-shifting; aptitude-based; unsuccessful," and stuff the entire thing in, only pausing to pull out my umbrella and the grenade. I look at the tiny sphere, small enough to fit inside my palm. When I was above ground, with Oliver, making the decision to die for him and everybody else was the obvious choice. But now, there's nothing here but the sound of my desperate heartbeat, pulsing like a drum at an execution. I finally have a moment to realize that I'm terrified.

Soft footsteps echo behind me. *Crenshaw.* At least he took the bait and followed me down here. I don't know if invincibility applies to being exploded, but it can't feel good, right?

I extend my umbrella with one hand and position it over my chest. Like that'll even help. It's a force of habit at this point. I position the small pin jutting out of the side of the bomb under my thumb. "Don't move," I warn him, hoping I don't sound as afraid as I feel, "or I'll do it."

"No, you won't," he says calmly, stepping out of the shadows. "It'll kill you."

"Yeah, I sort of resigned myself when I jumped down here." I scowl, readjusting my umbrella handle.

His pale eyes twinkle as he regards me. "Okay, I'm listening," he says in a partly defeated, partly amused tone. "What is it you want?"

Somewhere deep behind the hollow terror threatening my cognitive abilities, my brain rattles in confused recognition. "What? What do I *want*?"

"Of course." He adjusts his glasses. "You clearly want to negotiate, so what do you want?"

I can't help myself. I choke out a disbelieving snort of laughter. "You're kidding, right? This isn't a negotiation, Crenshaw. Do you know what I want?" My arm is screaming at me in exhausted protest from holding the grenade up, but I keep it there anyway. "I want a nap. And a coffee. I'm running on pure adrenaline, and it's not fun. And I want to live as far away from you and the rest of this place as humanly possible."

He smiles broadly as he hears my last sentence, like he's found my weakness. "That can be arranged, you know," he says, a little too eagerly. "I can get you and your friends far away from here. I can fake their deaths, say they died in a made-up crisis. I can relocate you all, and no one will ever have to know. You will all get your lives back. This city will remain safe and protected. Just step away from the serum."

Something pounds deep in my head, a searing thrum that rattles my skull and blurs my vision. He has to be able to hear it, even standing fifteen feet away from me. But I'm not afraid anymore. I'm angry. "You didn't let me finish." My knuckles whiten as they press around the grenade. "More than any of the other things, I want you to stop using your ridiculous, twisted logic to excuse killing people. I want you to leave my friends alone, but I also want you to stop turning other people into weapons that you eliminate when you're afraid their power threatens your own. I want you to stop making serum, forever. I want you to fix this city's problems without resorting to trite science-fiction tropes. Did you even think about all the other people you hurt by doing this?" I take a deep breath, glaring at him in defiance. "Did you ever think about all the citizens that were murdered in your attempts to continue this stupid cycle? Or did you think we didn't matter? Because we do. We all do."

Crenshaw's face reverts from the expression of calculated sincerity back to the superior glower that I've become used to as he focuses on my fingers. "Without the Supers, there would be anarchy," he hisses. "You think the crime is bad now? Just you wait. You will be responsible for the ruin of this city."

I look at him. He believes it. He did this because he actually believed it was the best way to fix things.

Twelve years. This has been going on for twelve years. Four people, every two years, chosen like pigs for a slaughter, to be sacrificed for some intangible "good." And countless more deaths on the side, lost in the chaos and written off as necessary casualties that don't matter, so long as the bad guys lose at the end of the day. The bad guys—what did that phrase even mean? What was it based on; who killed more people? Who caused more destruction?

The battle between good and evil—Supers and criminals—was always just a game. A deceptive game we've all been trapped in for the last decade, with Crenshaw controlling the board. It has to end.

I look right into Crenshaw's cold eyes. "This city is already ruined," I say. And before I can give myself time to change my mind, I press down on the pin, spin, and throw the grenade.

THIRTY-FIVE

BEING BLOWN UP, *evidently, was sort of like being sucked into a vacuum. Like being sucked into yourself over and over again, unraveled, turned inside out. The burning sensation was to be expected, given the circumstances, but it was less like being able to feel the flesh melting from your bones and more like being wrapped in a blanket that had been toasting in an oven for ten years. Unpleasant, but not extraordinarily painful.*

The ringing, though—that was unpleasant. The world's loudest gong, amplified three thousand times. Inside your head, your ears, your bones; everywhere, inescapable. That was definitely going on the list as the most annoying part of all of this. The existence of the ringing, though—that was the tipoff. That was the indication that something had gone wrong. Dead people didn't hear ringing, right?

Oliver opened his eyes, and was met with six identically worried expressions. No, wait—three. The other two members of his team, plus Juniper Jensen. Their multiple heads swayed back and forth in

Oliver's foggy vision as he tried to will the clanging in his head to calm down enough to let him focus. Finally, his eyes adjusted enough to bring the number of heads back down to the correct count—three—and he realized he was lying on the ashy ground, with everyone bending over him in concern.

"Oh, thank God," One—no Penny, it was so hard to reprogram his brain to address them by their citizen names now—said as he groaned, all the aches in his body suddenly announcing themselves. "Scare us to death, why don't you?"

"What happened?" he muttered. Speaking was an effort, to say the least. "The last thing I saw was—" Everything came into sharp focus then, and his eyes widened. The bunker. Crenshaw had jumped in after Meg and blocked the gate from the inside, so no one could get in after him. He, Oliver, had run to where the serum was stored above ground and tried to tunnel through to get to her. There was an explosion... Meg. Where was Meg?

The thought was like electricity, zapping his exhausted limbs into motion. He pushed himself up on his elbows, startling the others.

"Okay, big hero." Penny put a hand out, trying to push him back down. "You haven't fully healed yet. You need to rest."

"But I was almost through. I thought I could save her—" His blood was ice.

The edges of Sanjeet's body were fuzzy, like he was half-considering going invisible to avoid being part of Oliver's pain. "I'm really sorry, Four," he said. "She was like your family, wasn't she?"

Sorry. Sorry. The word was a trigger. For the last two years, everything in Oliver's life had felt like it was moving at lightning speed, even when he wasn't running, but now his world became slow-motion. He felt like he was sixteen again, screeching to a stop in front of his parents' demolished office building, which had been consumed by an inferno caused by Doctor Defect. *Sorry, kid. Sorry, there was nothing we could do. Sorry, they didn't make it out.*

It was happening again.

"No," he gasped, and pushed himself the rest of the way up, ignoring the protests from both Penny and his aching limbs. "No."

"It wouldn't have worked anyway, Oliver. The bunker walls were too thick for you; you don't have that kind of power." Juniper's eyes were brimming with tears. Why was she crying? Something inside him twitched furiously—a subconscious desire to feel anger instead of despair. She'd only known Meg a few days. This was his loss to feel, not hers.

"It should have been me!" Oliver spat, staggering over the uneven ground. He couldn't get his legs to work at super-speed; the world was still spinning too much. He could hear the other three trying to keep pace behind him, still trying to explain what had happened, but he didn't care about the details. He should have been the one to jump down there. At least he would have had a good chance of surviving an explosion like that. This wasn't supposed to happen to her.

He reached the edge of the crater and stopped. The grenade had carved out a wreck of a pit twenty feet deep and eighty feet wide; a horrible maze of crushed, twisted metal walls, broken shards of glass, and ash. A dense cloud of smoke, glowing faintly blue in the light of the nearby facility, hovered ominously over the wreckage. Juniper was right; that grenade was insanely powerful. He took two steps back, preparing to jump, but something swooped in and caught him under the arms, gently flying him down to the bottom of the pit. Oliver waited until the instant his feet hit the rocky ground to wrench himself out of the arms that had aided him, not even turning to see whether it had been Sanjeet or Penny. "Meg!" he bellowed hoarsely, choking on the dusty fog, "Meg!"

It was hopeless to think she'd answer. That she'd suddenly appear with a smirk, sitting on the edge of the pit, feet dangling, calling out something like, "Whatcha doing in that hole, Lee? Looking for a better house?"

Oliver's vision blurred; whether from smoke or tears, he didn't know. He brushed angrily at his face with the palm of his hand. "Meg!"

"Over here!"

Oliver spun, his breath catching in his throat, angry at himself for thinking that the female voice that had called to him was hers. Juniper's high, clear shout was nothing like Meg's. "Here!" she cried out again, and Oliver raced toward the spot near the north edge of the pit where the other three were huddled.

He saw the umbrella first. Was it the umbrella? Or was it just a jagged shard of metal sticking out of the ground, marking her location like a tombstone? He elbowed through Juniper and the other Supers and fell to his knees, pushing the debris out of the way.

Her hair wasn't red anymore. It was black with soot. A quarter of it was gone, burned away completely in a horrible chunk above her right ear. Her skin was like a mass of wrinkled coals pressed together, blackened completely except for where it was punctuated with bits of glass and bloody gashes, on her stomach and forearms. He was afraid that if he touched her, she would crumble to dust, but he did it anyway—pulled her to him and hovered over her like a shield, the sandpaper-grit of her skin harsh against his fingers.

This couldn't be happening. Maybe if he closed his eyes and never opened them again, he could pretend this had never happened, that they were still back in her apartment watching bad movies and eating food and laughing at all their problems until they seemed small and easy.

He'd only wanted to be a Super to keep her safe. Okay, that wasn't completely true, but it was the only reason that actually mattered. Maybe if he hadn't been one, Meg wouldn't have had to fight so hard to save him. Then she wouldn't be…

"I wish it were me," he whispered. "It should have been me."

He became aware that the other three were probably still there, staring at him, but realized that he didn't care. They could do whatever they wanted. He had no plans to move, maybe ever.

He pulled away for just a moment, just to get a breath of less smoky air, and was embarrassed to find that Meg's skin was shiny with his own tears. He pressed an orange-clad thumb to her cheekbone to sweep them away, then froze, eyes wide.

The area around her eyes was perfectly clear, apart from her usual abundance of freckles. The patch of uncharred skin outlined a flawless semblance of the masks he and the others always wore. And as he watched, the edges expanded, stretching outward, beginning to turn the rest of the blackened skin on her face clean and rosy.

"What—" he gasped, looking up at Juniper for answers. She was the scientist; she had to know what was going on. But her mouth was open; she was just as lost as he was.

He quickly looked back at Meg, terrified that his distraught mind had made the whole thing up, had created this illusion as one final torment that would be taken away from him as soon as he looked again. But as he watched in shock and confusion, the ash practically melted from Meg's body, the blood seeping back into the gashes in her arms and stomach, the cracks in her skin closing themselves with not even a seamline as proof they were there. Still, she didn't move, and he wondered if whatever magic had just occurred had only worked enough to allow Meg to look like herself again in death, rather than a doll made of coal. It seemed almost cruel to give him this kind of hope, only to stop short of letting her actually come back to him.

He pressed his ear to her heart, desperate for any kind of flicker, but there was nothing.

"Come on, Meg," he whispered. "Don't leave me. You promised, remember? Not today."

He pushed her hair, the only part of her that remained blackened and dirty, away from her face, listening desperately for anything—a breath, a heartbeat, a movement. But she remained still and lifeless. He sunk back into his heels, all hope gone, and felt a hand reach for his shoulder from behind him.

And then she shuddered and gasped for air.

Juniper screamed, Penny swore, and Sanjeet gripped Oliver's shoulder so tightly in shock that he would have broken it in half had he had a different set of powers. Oliver, however, suddenly found himself without the ability to move or speak. It wasn't possible. It couldn't be real.

Even when Meg's eyes snapped open and stared at his in bewilderment, he remained frozen, gazing down at her in unmasked disbelief. "Meg?" he finally whispered, his heart pounding against his rib cage the way it did when he ran up the side of a skyscraper.

She blinked. "So," she said calmly. "Did we win?"

THIRTY-SIX

THE FIRST THING I NOTICE is that everything feels fizzy. Yeah, *fizzy*, like the sensation you get when you eat a bunch of Pop Rocks and your tongue feels like someone's going at it with a tiny drill, but all over my body. Everything, every inch of my skin, feels like it's fizzing slightly. It's not painful, but it's not the sensation I was expecting post-explosion.

The second thing I notice is that everyone is staring at me like I'm a zombie, and Oliver is really, *really* close to my face. He lets go of me immediately, but his expression of undisguised shock doesn't go away. "Meg?" he repeats. "I don't understand. How are you—"

"How am I what?" I say impatiently. "Why do you all look like somebody died—" I push myself up to my elbows and gasp. Oh my god. No wonder everyone's freaking out so much. I'm a mess. By all accounts, I should be dead. The skin has practically been burned from my legs, and I'm covered with blood and scratches from the waist down, although my arms and exposed stomach look fine—better than they've ever looked, honestly. I gag as I notice a particularly large shard of glass sticking out of my thigh. Why is only half of my body a wreck?

"What happened?" I manage to choke out. "How did you get me out?"

"We didn't." Juniper lowers her hand from her mouth in order to speak. Her eyes are taking up at least half her face. "We didn't get you out. You—"

"No way." I shake my head. "Somebody had to. Otherwise I'd be—" I look down again and scream, cutting off my own sentence. My skin. My *skin*. It's healing itself, becoming normal again. The blackened, charred portions of my legs are melting back into regular old flesh, and even the gash around the shard of glass is closing. I pull it out gingerly, and the gash seals itself neatly the rest of the way. Apart from the rip in my pants, there's no indication it was ever there.

"What—" I say hoarsely, then clear my throat. "What's happening to me?" I narrow my eyes toward Oliver. "Are you healing me with the power of friendship, or something? What is this?"

He doesn't say anything. Before I can react, he's lunged forward, wrapping me in the tightest hug I've ever experienced. "I thought you were gone," he whispers in my ear. "I don't understand. You were gone."

The anguish in his voice makes me forget my confusion. Who cares why I'm not dead? We're all alive. The serum is gone. That's all that matters. I hug him back as hard as I can, and suddenly the other three have collapsed to the ground and joined in as well, smothering both of us in a cocoon of warmth. I laugh into whoever's arm is squeezed tightly against my face.

"Wow, I love you guys," Sanjeet says, his voice muffled. "Nobody scare me like that again, okay? I can't take this kind of stress."

"I still don't understand, though," Juniper interrupts, the

first to pull away. Penny and Sanjeet sit back on their heels too, but Oliver keeps his arm looped around my shoulders, like he's afraid I'll die again if he lets go. "How could you have—" But then her already wide eyes get even bigger. They dart frantically around, searching the air around me like the answer is written there somewhere. "Oh no," she whispers.

"Wait, what's 'oh no'?" I ask nervously as the last burn mark on my leg disappears. "Don't say 'oh no.' We need positive right now."

She shakes her head, looking horrified. "I think—"

But suddenly, there's a loud roar of shifting metal from somewhere behind me, drowning out her theory, and Oliver releases me so we can all turn and look. *What now?* The roar becomes a resonance of grating screeches that sends shivers through my skin, and something bursts through a mountain of rubble, sending jagged chunks of crumbling metal flying in every direction. The shadow of a tall, bald figure suddenly stumbles into view through the dense smoke surrounding us, then snaps his head toward us. *Crenshaw.* "Oh, no, no," I groan. Of course he's still alive. If I survived the explosion, it only makes sense that he did, too.

"You've destroyed everything!" Crenshaw's howl cuts through the smoke. I can see his hazy outline clenching its fists. The shadow begins to make its way toward us, and Crenshaw's face comes into view. His clothing is in tatters; his face is streaked with scars that haven't finished healing yet; his teeth are gnashed in a manic leer.

He looks just like Doctor Defect.

In a flash, Penny, Sanjeet, and Oliver are standing in front of Juniper and me, poised to fight. I reach for my umbrella, but then remember that it's gone, lost in the explosion.

"All you've done is slow me down," Crenshaw hisses. "I'll reformulate, and then I'll create a new strand of SuperVariants—ones that will actually follow orders." And he stretches his hand out, aiming under Oliver's protective arm at Juniper.

✖ COLLATERAL DAMAGE ✖

I don't think about the fact that I was dead five minutes ago, or the fact that there are three much more capable people standing right next to me who could take on Crenshaw. I don't think at all.

"*No!*" I lunge in front of Juniper, holding my own arms out like it'll somehow protect us, and brace myself for whatever is about to hit me.

But it doesn't come.

I squeeze an eye open and gasp. The five of us are bathed in a soft, glowing purple light, and everyone's faces are an identical mask of shock and bewilderment as they all look at Crenshaw.

He's trapped in a bubble—an iridescent violet bubble, floating a few feet off the ground, which remains solid and unyielding despite his furious efforts to break through. He punches one of the curved walls with all his might, and the bubble ripples softly, but doesn't break.

"What the—?" I trip over my words, staring up at Crenshaw, and let out an involuntary scream. "What's happening? What is this?"

"Oh my *god*." Oliver gapes. "Meg, was that you?"

"No!" Common sense tells me not to move my hands, just in case, but this isn't possible. "I can't… there's no way…"

"Oh, my God." Juniper stands up next to me to get a better look. Her eyes widen in something like awe. "Biogenetic force fields. I can't believe it finally worked."

"What do you mean, bioge—what? What finally worked?" There's a quiet thumping from a few yards away, where Crenshaw is still actively trying to escape imprisonment, but the bubble continues to hold.

"Well…" Juniper swallows. "I did warn you that the serum is hard to destroy."

"*Juniper!*" I shriek. "You said blowing up the bunker would work. You said it would get rid of the serum."

"No, I said it might!" she defends herself. "And technically, it did. All the active SuperVariant serums, including the ones that cause their deaths, have to be taken intravenously, or they won't work. But—"

"But *what*?" I shriek, shaking my hands. Crenshaw's bubble wobbles back and forth, knocking him off his feet. He scowls and kicks the wall, but remains lying down. "Explain this!"

"Well—" She looks guilty. "Based on what's happened to you, I think maybe some of the failed serums might react when they're inhaled as a gas. I'm kind of mad that we didn't think to try that before we wrote them off as failures, actually."

"*What*?" I look in shock at the foggy blue clouds surrounding us, suddenly realizing why they're such an odd color. It's not from the light off the building. It's the serum.

I'm so stupid. I messed up so much. I didn't destroy the formula. I turned it gaseous.

"It means that it enters your body through—"

"I know what it means!" I want to rip my remaining hair out. "So I'm a Super now, too?"

"Looks like it," Juniper says, looking embarrassed. "And that must be how you healed yourself after the explosion."

"Nice!" Sanjeet exclaims, grinning broadly. "You're one of us now!"

I feel like I might pass out. I can't believe this is happening. I can't be a Super. That was the whole point of this, wasn't it? To halt the number of people running around with powers, not increase it. But still—

I look down at my hands. The fingertips are glowing with the same pulsing violet light as the bubble containing Crenshaw, who's still trapped, unable to hurt anyone. It's not a destructive power. It's a protective one. I could actually help people with this.

I didn't want this kind of power, but now that I have it… it feels *good*. I don't mean to conjure up the images, but they come anyway: images of me putting up barriers to protect buildings when the city's under attack, encasing people in bubbles like the one Crenshaw is in just before falling shrapnel hits them, keeping villains trapped until the police arrive to take them away. I could help. Really help.

"Can I pick my own costume?" I ask. "Or is the spandex non-negotiable?"

"Definitely non-negotiable," Oliver responds seriously, and I elbow him without taking my hands away from Crenshaw.

"Come on," Juniper says. "We should probably get him to the police."

Penny nods and begins to levitate me out of the pit, while Sanjeet gives Juniper a lift and Oliver runs up the side.

"Wait a second," I say to Juniper once we're all at the top and walking toward Oliver's truck. "You breathed in the smoke, too. Shouldn't you also have powers?"

She frowns. "I'm sure I do, but it might take a bit to figure out what they are. The experimental serums were aptitude-based, see, so they're meant to improve the characteristics of whoever is exposed to them. X-ray vision for the perceptive; manifestation for the creative—you know, stuff like that."

"So I'm not getting *all* of the thousands of genetic enhancements you had stored down there? Just the one?"

"I think so." Juniper nods. "I think you could breathe in as much of the gas as you wanted, but your body will only react to the chemicals that were designed to enhance your natural abilities. Defensive protection—" She motions to the Crenshaw-bubble. "—is clearly one of your natural abilities."

"Wait," Sanjeet interrupts, jerking a thumb back toward the hole we just climbed out of. "What are we going to do about the rest of the serum-cloud, then?"

"Well, we're so far out of town that it shouldn't affect anyone else," Juniper replies. "The police—the *real* police, not those awful SuperVariant agents—should be here soon, and we'll make sure they block the area off. After a few days of exposure, it should become less potent. As long as no one else breathes in large amounts of it beforehand…" She trails off as she turns to look back at the pit, then gasps. I follow suit and nearly let go of Crenshaw.

An impossibly huge mushroom cloud of blue gas has just erupted from the smoldering flames at the other end of the pit. As we watch, a gust of wind pushes the entire thing over the trees, where it begins to float languidly toward Lunar City.

"No. Oh, no…" Oliver moans, and races back to the edge of the pit. The rest of us chase after him, coming to a halt right before the ground drops off.

"What do we do?" I cry. "How do we stop it?" I can see Crenshaw out of the corner of my eye, laughing without restraint as he kneels on the floor of the bubble, his crooked smile wide and his eyes gleeful.

Penny launches into the air and aims her palms at the cloud, but the tree on the other side of it shakes loose a huge clump of leaves instead, clearly having been the recipient of whatever she was trying to direct at the cloud. "Okay," she says in a calm voice that doesn't quite disguise the anxiety underneath as she touches back down to the ground. "So, fun fact, I can't control gas."

"Maybe no one will breathe for a few days," Sanjeet whispers.

"Everyone's going to have powers." Juniper looks ill. "The entire city is going to be Super."

My stomach twists as I look out at the dim cityscape, at the thousands of sleeping citizens that are going to wake up tomorrow with superpowers. Good people and bad people alike. Teenagers, grandparents, babies. Carly. Sanjeet's uncle. Government officials, fast-food joint employees, every student at Saint Charles's Academy. Everyone. All of them.

"Well," I say. "That's it. I'm really moving."

EPILOGUE

THERE'S A LOUD BANGING on the door, and I forget how to breathe for a second. *Oh, god. They found us.* I knew this was coming, but I'd forgotten to prepare for it.

I walk toward the door like a prisoner headed for the gallows. There's a blur, and Oliver flattens himself against it before I can turn the latch. "Don't open it," he whispers. "Just pretend we're not here."

"Sure, and what if it can see through walls?" I shoulder him out of the way. "I'm not dealing with that. It'll be fine. I'll just explain what happened." Clearly not on board with my stupidity, Oliver blurs away, leaving me to defend myself on my own.

I open the door, a false smile plastered to my face. "Hiiii, there!"

The kid outside is about seven or eight, and is wearing jeans, a black T-shirt advertising his elementary school's PE class, and a red mask that only covers the area around his eyes.

"Trick or treat!" he announces, holding out a pillowcase.

"Well," I say, hoping I can logic my way out of this. "You're not really wearing a costume, so—" I start to close the door, but he sticks out a pudgy hand and stops it.

"Trick or treat," he repeats firmly.

"Listen," I say, crossing my arms. "Here's the thing. We've had a lot going on, and we don't have any candy. So why don't you just—"

The kid narrows his eyes, and a thin beam of pale-blue ice shoots out of them, aiming straight for my forehead. I barely get my force field up in time, but the ice ray connects with it instead of my face and breaks into a hundred pieces, shattering to the floor. "Hey!" I snap, "Powers are not to be used for violence! Citywide mandate! I will *so* report you."

"It's fine, it's fine, I got it!" Oliver races up next to me, holding a bowl of unwrapped hard candy. He holds it down to the kid's level. "Here, take it. Happy Halloween."

The kid looks at it skeptically, but ultimately takes a large fistful, stuffs it in his mouth, and goes skipping back down the hallway.

I slam the door with a sigh of relief. "Whoever chose this apartment for us," I yell into the kitchen, "without checking on how many children live in this building—just know that I hate you. And Juniper, can you be a little faster next time?"

"Oh, I'm sorry!" She emerges from her bedroom with her hands on her hips. "Next time the doorbell rings, I'll answer it, and you can create candy out of molecular components of other objects."

"You're right, you're right, I'm sorry." I wave her away, returning to the couch. "But speaking of, have you worked out a way to molecularly compose our own water yet? The number of baths you and Penny take—" I shake my head with mock disapproval. "—water bill's gonna be real high this month, is all I'm saying."

Juniper rolls her eyes. "I don't know how many times I have

to tell you, but it doesn't work like that."

"Then what good is it?" I sigh dramatically, then glance over at the recliner Penny's collapsed in. "Were you gonna pick a movie, or what?"

"On it." She doesn't move, but telekinetically flips through channels until she lands on one with a substantial amount of fake blood. "Nice," she says appreciatively, and levitates her glass of punch to her mouth.

Sanjeet is in the other recliner, muttering to himself, a mass of disorganized paperwork spread across his lap. "Hey, nerd." I throw a piece of popcorn at him. "No studying on family holidays."

"I'm not studying," he responds, eating the popcorn. "I'm still looking for a way to reverse the effects of the serum."

I sigh. "Forget it, bud. You and Juniper have been looking for a month. This is our life now."

"But you said..."

"I know what I said." I shrug. "But honestly, I'm already getting used to it. Who knew the best way to stop crime was to make everyone so afraid of each other's hidden powers, they wouldn't pick fights to begin with? Besides, now that everyone has powers, you don't have to have all the responsibility anymore. You can actually get to enjoy your life as teenagers for once. This could have ended up a lot worse."

"Don't say that," Oliver says warningly. "Remember what happened last time we said it could always be worse? The universe took it as a challenge."

He's sort of right, but it really could have been way worse. The whole citywide-quarantine thing definitely put a damper on my plans to move, but things are actually way better now than I can remember them being in a long time. Once my video got passed around the city, everybody knew the truth about Crenshaw and the LCPD agents. They went nuts when they found out what those guys had actually been up to this entire time. The lab is now shut down, abandoned on the outskirts of town. The police also did a pretty good job of setting immediate restrictions on power usage, making sure everybody had registered their abilities within a week of the explosion at the lab. It probably won't last forever, but there haven't been too many issues so far. Even Doctor Defect, who still hadn't been recaptured, crept into hiding after his most recent attempt at attacking the city. I guess it's just not as fun when everybody can fight back.

"Well, we're getting pretty good at dealing with challenges," I reply as I grab a handful of popcorn. There's another knock on the door. "It's open!" I call, my mouth full.

The door doesn't budge, but an area in the center of it shimmers, and a four-year-old girl toddles through the wood. "Twick oh tweat!" she lisps. She's dressed like a ladybug.

"Aww," I squeal. "Juniper, give her some candy."

"I'm not in charge of this. I'm not spending the whole evening on door duty; we're taking turns," she says, lowering the bowl and letting the girl fish a few pieces out.

"Thank you!" the kid giggles as she waddles back through the closed door.

"Come on!" I call toward Juniper. "You're missing the movie." She rolls her eyes and comes back to the living room, squeezing herself onto the couch next to me. I settle into the space between her and Oliver, letting the couch cushions start to swallow me. I've barely gotten comfortable, but then the whole building shakes. Everyone looks at one another in various stages of mild concern.

"Is that gonna be a problem?" Oliver asks, looking like he really doesn't want to move.

"You know what?" I flex my fingers in the direction of the window, and outside it, a transparent, shimmering purple wall appears. The building abruptly ceases shaking, and the sounds of the outside world grow faint and distant; the only noise comes from the fake monsters ripping at each other on the screen. I grin, grab a cupcake from the coffee table, and settle back into the couch. "Not today."

THE END

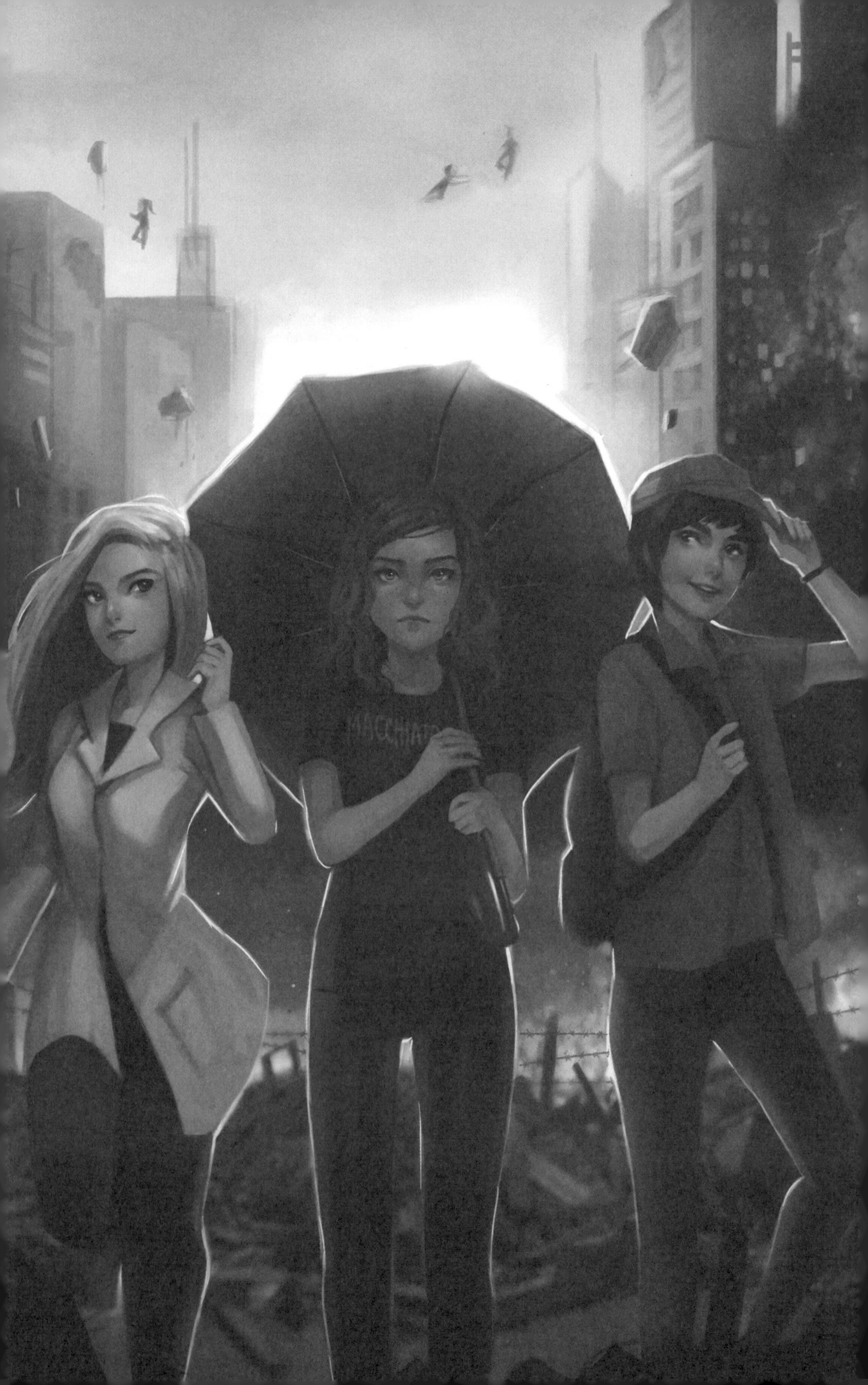

ACKNOWLEDGEMENTS

A book is only ever as much as the people championing it believe it to be, and these are the true superheroes of this story:

Thank you to the entire Parliament House team, especially Shayne Leighton, Chantal Gadoury, Amanda Wright, Celeste Hawkins, and Erica Farner, for taking my weird, sarcastic, mess of a book and embracing it with more passion, love, and creativity than I could ever have dreamed of. You've been the best supporters of my work throughout this entire process and I can't thank you enough for pointing out all the things that didn't make sense, laughing at Meg's humor, fielding my late-night panic emails, and bringing this book to life. I'm so lucky to have such an amazing publishing team on my side, and this book would be nothing without you.

I cringe whenever I think about the earlier drafts of Collateral Damage, and my eternal gratitude and apologies go to the beta-readers and critique partners that waded through them: Sarah Mills, Justin Velazquez, Harrison Beeson, Ciara Bagnasco, and Sarah Richardson.

I promise that you'll never have to receive another WAIT READ THIS VERSION IT'S BETTER email from me (although if post-publication edits were a thing, you know I'd find a way).

I am so, so lucky to have such an incredible group of friends whose love and support literally crafted this book together—Carrie Wogaman, who let me talk through the entire first act while stuck in L.A. traffic and made the plot-altering suggestion that one of the Supers be a high school student (and who let me try to replicate her incomparable sarcasm and wit for Meg's personality). Daniel McCook, who read the very, very first ever garbage draft of Collateral Damage and forced me to dive back into it years later, then brought the book to digital life with his stupidly good cinematography skills. David Wright, my personal angel, who has always, always taught me to "follow the path illuminated." Erin Haus and Phillip Blackburn, my best cheerleaders and the book's first audience, thank you for countless show breaks spent in the greenroom listening to dramatic readings of my manuscript, and for your terrifyingly aggressive refusal to never let me give up on myself. Nicole Visco, you magnificent powerhouse—I don't even know where to begin with how wonderful it's been to have a friend as supportive as you by my side. You are the definition of the "bravest, scariest person I've ever met," and I can't thank you enough for being flattered instead of creeped out when I gave Meg your voice. And finally, Mahaillie Griffith, Savry Martinez, Cara Pinto, and Duy Truong, my "found family," for being there for me emotionally every step of the way—from Cara being my partner in book obsession and listening to me rant about plot points, to Savry holding my hand as I sent my first query letter and answering my thousands of questions about what working at a coffee shop is like, to Duy sending me lists of all the famous people who had failed before they were successful when I was feeling down and literally rewriting my query letters for me, to Mahaillie inspiring me to keep going by being the physical embodiment of what you can achieve if you chase your dreams (even from a thousand miles away). I love you all more than can fit on a page.

I have to give Paige LaVoie her own paragraph. My writing soulmate and one of the greatest people in the world, you have brought so much into my life as both a writer and a friend. I can say without a doubt that I would not have finished writing this book at all if I hadn't met you. Thank you for the countless coffee shop writing dates, for introducing me to my The Writer's Atelier family, for laughing at every bit of Meg's sarcasm, for letting me call you screaming from the shower after the 2017 WA retreat when I finally figured out the Crenshaw twist, for allowing me to accidentally name a character after your dog, for writing sprints that consistently turned into vintage shopping breaks, for field trips to outer space and book conventions and Disney World. Thank you for always believing in me, especially when I didn't believe in myself. Anyone would be lucky just to have you as a friend; having you as a writing partner for the insane journey that is publication is almost too good to be true.

Last but obviously not least, thank you to my family—Mom, Dad, and Morgan—for your endless well of support and encouragement. I'm so fortunate to have a family who wholeheartedly urges me to follow my dreams, who always made me feel like being a "real" writer was an inevitability, not a fantasy, and who fill my life with so much adventure and hilarity that inspiration is never hard to find. Thank you especially to Morgan, for being the final one-third of the trinity of real-life people who inspired Meg's personality, and for your misguidedly kind negligence to give me notes on my first draft because you didn't want to hurt my feelings, followed by the influx of the most helpful notes and critiques given out of anybody once you realized that was the point. I love you all so much.

ABOUT THE AUTHOR

Taylor Simonds is an Orlando-based professional manuscript editor with Write My Wrongs Editing. Taylor holds a Bachelor's Degree in Marketing from the University of Central Florida, and previous staff writing credits include CollegeFashion.net and MuggleNet.com. When she's not hunting down grammatical errors or reading comic books and calling it "research," Taylor can be found almost exclusively at Disney World. Yeah, she's THAT kind of Floridian.

A thorough geek, Taylor enjoys cosplaying, watching anime, buying fan art she'll forget to hang up, and camping out for the next Marvel movie. *Collateral Damage* is her debut novel; the product of a dawning realization after years upon years of superhero fandom that although superheroes are cool, living next door to them would be decidedly not so.

Taylor does not have any kids or pets to mention, but she does have some pretty great friends whose house she likes to burst into announced, a lá Kramer. She resides in the peasant-village behind Magic Kingdom with her "To Be Read" pile and a large collection of unused sewing patterns.

www.taylorsimonds.com

MEG STILL NEEDS YOU

Did you enjoy Collateral Damage? Reviews keep books (and Meg) alive . . .

She needs you now, Super Heroes! Help her by leaving your review on either GoodReads or the digital storefront of your choosing.

She thanks you!

THE PARLIAMENT HOUSE
WWW.PARLIAMENTHOUSEPRESS.COM

Want more from our amazing authors? Visit our website for trailers, exclusive blogs, additional content and more!

www.parliamenthousepress.com

Become a Parlor Peep and access secret bonus content…

JOIN US